SPACE
IN HIS
HEART

roxanne st. claire

Space in His Heart

Editor: Anne Victory
Proofreader: Amy Eye
Cover Design: The Killion Group, Inc.
Interior Formatting: Author E.M.S.

ISBN: 978-0615574424

Published in the United States of America

Critical Reviews of
Roxanne St. Claire Novels

Prologue

July 8, 2011
Merritt Island, Florida

N ormally, a cloudy day in July was a blessing in Florida, a reprieve from the relentless sun and oppressive heat. Today, the sheer white film across the summer sky only meant bad news for Jessica Marlowe. She wouldn't see more than a brief glimpse of the shuttle *Atlantis* as it took off for the final mission in space.

Disappointment pressed on her heart, real enough to cause a physical ache. Maybe she should have gone to Kennedy and braved the crowds to sit in the VIP section with those she held dear, just to witness the majesty of a space shuttle launch up close one last time. Maybe it would have been worth the risk.

But common sense had prevailed. No doubt she would've cried, and she was enough of an emotional wreck without something like the final launch to put her over the edge. The ache in her chest pushed harder, like a weight on her solar plexus, a reminder of what was about to happen, how her world was about to change one more time.

Funny how you make plans…and God has a little chuckle at your expense.

Glancing inside the house, she squinted at the muted TV, a picture of *Atlantis* on the launch pad, billows of steam and smoke surrounding four and a half million pounds of rocket power. In the corner, the countdown clock ticked to T-minus four minutes. No one had to tell Jess what that meant: the crew would close and lock their visors now.

Though there certainly was a time when she had no idea what T-minus *anything* meant.

At that thought, she touched her queasy belly. It was the launch, of course. Every takeoff terrified her, ever since the first one she'd seen twelve years earlier. Each time the countdown clock started ticking, she feared for someone's life, for the loss of a dear friend, a respected colleague or…worse.

So she tried only to think about the miracle of how they got up there, stayed up there, learned and lived up there and then came home.

A miracle that happened almost every time. *Almost.*

No surprise, the beach outside her second-story balcony was jammed with tourists and space fans gathered at one of the area's best launch-viewing sites. Her gaze drifted past the crowd to the gunmetal-gray ocean, then north to Kennedy Space Center, a sprawling complex of science and hope, filled with men and women who lived, breathed…and died…for their dream of exploring space.

A roar from the beach crowd pulled her attention back to the TV to check the clock. T-minus thirty seconds. The onboard computers were taking over. More importantly, most every technological glitch had been conquered.

Launch was a go.

The pressure in her stomach suddenly shifted to stabbing pain, sharp enough to make her suck in a shocked breath. Lightheaded, she used the other hand to hold on to the railing.

"Whoa," she whispered, shocked by the intensity of the pain. Gripping the railing for balance, she looked over her shoulder at the countdown clock. Sixteen seconds. They'd fire up the main engine in ten seconds.

All those lives on board...

A wave of dizziness threatened and she closed her eyes, swamped with memories so vivid she swore she could smell the burn of liquid hydrogen, the pungent stink of fuel and fury that hung in the air after a launch.

The crowd began to chant the numbers, loud and slow and perfectly in unison.

The sound reminded her of another launch, on a crystal-clear day full of promise and possibilities, her hands locked with two people she'd barely known then. But they'd shared a bond, a mutual love of their son. He knows what he's doing, his father had said. *Deke can fly anything.*

Ten...nine...

The knife in her belly suddenly slid and cut deeper, making Jess whimper softly. Holy smokes, that hurt.

Eight...seven...

Two stories below, hundreds of people blurred in her vision, the roar of their counting barely getting through the throbbing beat of her pulse in her ears. Another agonizing fist punched low and hard, and her knees nearly buckled.

Six...five...

She backed into the house, momentarily blinded by the pain, grabbing for the metal rim of the sliding glass doors but missing, then stumbling awkwardly to the floor. *Think, Jess, think. Where's the cell phone?*

Four…three…

Beads of sweat stung her forehead as she crawled to the table, slapping her hand over the phone. Shaky hands made dialing the number nearly impossible. She pressed the green button, looked for the last call…

Two… One…

Please answer. Please, please answer.

"There it is!" The screams floated up from the beach, the excitement of witnessing a miracle in every voice.

On the second ring, Jess managed to open her eyes and look up at the clouds just as the fiery plume appeared for a brief few seconds, orange and huge and headed for space.

"God speed, *Atlantis*." She could barely whisper the send-off as she doubled over with searing pain.

"Jess? Are you watching? Can you see it? A flawless launch!"

She opened her mouth but another wave of pain brought only a grunt.

"Wait, I can't hear you…there's so much noise here. Are you watching the launch?"

Her gaze slipped to the TV screen—the shuttle, well past the bridal veil of clouds, hurtling toward orbit, caught by cameras much closer than she.

"Jess? *Jess*? Are you okay? Answer me!"

But she couldn't speak. Her lids heavy, she tried to focus. At the bottom of the television, the familiar NASA insignia burned bright and proud, white and blue, tried and true. That logo…those letters…they'd once meant nothing to her.

Then they changed her life. That symbol even saved someone's life a long time ago.

"Jessie! Answer me!"

She gave in and closed her eyes, the image of that emblem burning her lids and her memory, only able to whisper one word.

"Deke..."

Chapter One

New York City, 1999

An intruder had taken the place that Jessica Marlowe had worked tirelessly for six years to earn. In the coveted spot next to the president of the world's largest public relations agency sat a sunny, phony, conspiring interloper who twirled her hair and shared a laugh with Mr. Anthony Palermo. Only Carla Drake called their boss "Tony." Already. After only two weeks at the agency.

Jeez. It had taken Jessica two years to work up the nerve to call him Tony.

With as much poise and nonchalance as she could muster, Jessica strode to the opposite end of the table and laid her Palm Pilot in front of an empty chair. She wouldn't muscle or flirt her way next to the boss. She could do so much better than that. She settled into the buttery leather, willing herself to be as cool and calm as her rival.

She would outsmart Carla from California. Right here, right now. At this worldwide meeting of the top brains in Ross & Clayton Communications, Jessica Marlowe would remind Tony Palermo who was his best team player, his most creative vice president, and the most logical choice for general manager of the Boston office. She'd hit a home run and leave Carla choking in her dust.

She just had no earthly idea how.

For a moment, she listened to the buzz of hip and conservative Type A's, charged with caffeine and the thrill of being part of the elite think-tank session in the international agency's New York headquarters. An invitation to the forty-ninth floor conference room on the first Monday of the month meant they'd made it to the top, literally and figuratively. Called in from Los Angeles, Seattle, Chicago, Atlanta, and, like Jessica, Boston, they would concentrate on one client's problem and no one would leave until they'd solved it. Hopefully with a plan that would make the agency beaucoup bucks.

It was bad enough the slinky blonde had blown into the Boston office two weeks earlier and been named "the other" vice president, essentially making her Jessica's professional equal. The fact that she'd gotten the coveted invitation to the New York meeting really rankled Jessica's nerves.

It didn't matter. Carla could be sitting next to God himself, but the better idea won in this room.

Suddenly, a low-pitched rumble drowned out the hum of conversation as electronic room darkeners slid across the massive wall of glass and eliminated the breathtaking view of Manhattan. A young man with thinning hair and black-rimmed glasses stood at the far end of the conference table, wearing Armani head to toe and an expectant expression on his angular face. Until this moment, no one in the room knew what the subject of today's think tank would be. He tilted his head toward the screen behind him as four white letters slowly emerged out of an azure background.

NASA. Silently, he clicked to the next slide. Jessica read

the words with a sinking sensation of dread. National Aeronautics and Space Administration.

Oh, great. *Space.*

Jessica shifted in her seat and resisted the urge to rub her temples as she stared at the slide. Why couldn't it be like last month when they came up with a way to get more people on cruise ships in the summer? Or the time she'd masterminded the Free Fry-Day campaign for a fast-food chain?

Jessica looked up just in time to see Carla shoot a cocky smile at the presenter. Had she been in on the space secret?

Burying the thought, Jessica searched her mental files for anything she knew about space travel other than moon landings in the sixties and Clint Eastwood as an astronaut in *his* sixties.

All she could conjure up was the heart-stopping image of a space shuttle blown to bits against a blue Florida sky. She'd watched the *Challenger* disaster in high school. She'd learned everything she knew about Apollo from a Tom Hanks movie. That just about exhausted her expertise on the great beyond.

"Houston," the presenter said quietly. "We have a problem."

The groan that spread around the table shattered the drama of the moment. The speaker introduced himself as Bill Dugan, a vice president in Ross & Clayton's Washington office and the head of the NASA account.

"Our client needs your help. Only the best and brightest of Ross & Clayton can solve this problem." He issued the challenge with a weak smile.

From the corner of her eye, Jessica saw Carla whisper something to Tony, who chuckled in response. Jessica scratched a meaningless note on a pad in front of her.

As though set to music, Bill Dugan began an eloquent

situation analysis, taking twenty minutes to describe a problem he could have summed up in four words.

Nobody cared about space.

That was why Congress was threatening budget cuts and NASA had disappeared from the radar screens of most Americans. Shuttle launches amounted to little more than truckloads of junk to the space station. No one was walking on the moon or traveling to Mars. Space exploration had become a yawner.

The challenge: NASA needed to be relevant to America again.

The moment Bill stopped talking, the room exploded with ideas.

"We need a nationwide grassroots support program," suggested an account supervisor from Chicago.

"Along with a total Internet-based communication plan," added the general manager of R&C Seattle.

"No, no," one of New York's spirited media specialists disagreed. "We have to tie their work into anti-terrorism programs."

Carla Drake's throaty voice cut in. "We need a press conference, from space. Live with open questions from every major network."

The room's tangible momentum shifted to Carla. A rush of adrenaline surged through Jessica's veins, fueling her bone-deep desire to come up with the Big Idea.

How could they make space travel matter again? How could they capture the imagination and hearts of America? What could make America tune into the next shuttle launch and care about the countdown? *What sells?*

And then she knew.

"Why don't we make NASA sexy?" Jessica's challenge silenced the room. She waited until every eye in the room was riveted on her, mostly because she wasn't quite sure what she'd say next. A trickle of perspiration danced between her shoulder blades. She was committed now. "We need to appeal to women."

"Women?" Bill asked.

"Yes, women. Women are proven to communicate with and influence their Congressmen far more often than men do. Women." Jessica leaned back and crossed her arms in a display of way more confidence than her bare bones of an idea merited. "What could be more appealing to women than a brave and handsome adventurer willing to climb on top of a billion tons of explosives and propel himself into outer space just for the good of all mankind? What could be more heroic than a death-defying explorer who risks his life so that we may expand our horizons?"

Blank faces stared back at her.

All but one.

Tony Palermo's dark eyes twinkled and she saw the old familiar smile from her mentor. "Go ahead, Jess. I think you're on to something."

She leaned on her elbows and looked directly at him. "Well, I'm thinking about…astronauts."

Chapter Two

A man's life depended on Deke Stockard's ability to find a crack no wider than a hair. He traced the smooth surface with his fingertip, his eyes closed in concentration. He knew the deadly imperfection could be found. If it was there. He moved his hands in an almost loving caress, tenderly seeking a break or weakness under his touch.

He didn't care that he had found nothing in the painstaking two-and-a-half-hour search because he'd stay in the same spot for two and a half *weeks* if he had to. He adjusted his footing, his body fully immersed in the space shuttle's main engine nozzle. Holding his breath, he stroked the same square inch of metal for the tenth time and barely heard the voice from below.

"Stockard, come on. That media thing is starting and we should be there. Give it up for ten minutes."

Deke released the coolant tube, memorizing its precise location before responding to Major Jeff Clark. Deke would have barked at anybody else for breaking his concentration but didn't have the heart to give his closest friend a hard time.

"What media *thing*?"

"You know damn well what media *thing*. The Public Affairs presentation that Colonel Price invited us to." Jeff stepped closer to the orbiter and peered up to where Deke leaned against the massive tangles of wires and metal. "You find anything yet?"

"Not a thing. But if something's here, I'll catch it."

"We have legions of engineers who are paid to do that," Jeff reminded him.

"Paid to fill out paperwork," Deke mumbled, climbing out of the engine casing. He swung his legs over the metal scaffolding and easily made the two-foot drop to the ground. "You think that was an invitation or an order from Price? I'd really like to skip it."

"No difference when it comes from the Colonel, pal." Jeff's usual smart-ass grin spread slowly as he poked Deke's chest. "He's expecting a full house."

Deke sighed and squinted back at *Endeavour*, studying the scarred and nicked orbiter, its massive cargo bay wide open like a dissected animal. A few other technicians scurried around, looking more at their clipboards than the shuttle in front of them. And now he had to go to a media presentation?

"Sometimes I think the priorities are a little screwed up around here." His gaze stopped at the American flag and NASA insignia emblazoned on its side. "All right, I'll meet you over at Headquarters. I want to talk to Skip for a second."

"No sweat. I'll save you a seat," Jeff promised and turned to leave.

"Don't bother," Deke called back to him. "I'll stay in the back for a quick getaway."

He heard Jeff chuckle, but Deke hadn't meant it as a joke. He looked back up at the giant nozzle of *Endeavour's* main engine. Every instinct told him the insidious hydrogen leak that had nearly destroyed the shuttle *Columbia* during the last launch could occur again on *Endeavour*. This time, the crew might not be so lucky.

He shook his head and walked away. Damn, it could be right in front of him. Literally under his fingertips. The last thing he wanted to do was listen to a bunch of PR blowhards from some big agency tell them to have another press conference in space.

Deke scanned the vast shuttle bay of the Orbiter Processing Facility for the aging figure of Skip Bowker, the man ultimately responsible for the safety of every mission. He figured he'd find him leaning against the glass wall of one of the offices, his signature coffee cup in his hand, looking a little too damn calm considering the next launch was a mere three and a half months away.

But Bowker was missing and Deke knew he didn't have much time to make the ten-minute walk across Kennedy Space Center to the NASA Headquarters building. He knew better than to be late for a Colonel-Price-issued invitation, no matter how foolish the topic might seem. It was odd for the Colonel to insist any of the astronauts and flight crew attend the meeting, but it wasn't worth questioning the order. He liked to rack up points with the Colonel for when he really needed a favor.

Using a side door, he entered the auditorium and bounded up two steps at a time, bypassing the seven or eight rows of stacked seating to lean against the wall in the back. He nodded to a few colleagues but avoided being pulled into a conversation. He wasn't staying long. He'd catch the essence of the meeting, be sure Colonel Price's secretary saw him, and then he could slip back to the Processing Facility for another few hours.

Deke was mentally reviewing the wiring when Stuart Rosen, the head of Public Affairs at Kennedy, started to address the group. With his mind on some vague dates on the engineering log he'd seen that morning, Deke had to force himself to listen to Stuart. Public Affairs was so damn far removed from the real business of flying space shuttles and operating the space station.

Still, he knew that image was everything to Americans and, last time he checked, that's who covered his paycheck. Plus, he liked Stu. He just hated the BS that had nothing to do with what really mattered in the program.

Stuart droned on about a woman vice president from the Boston office of some supersized marketing firm called Ross & Clayton. She'd come to Cape Canaveral to invigorate NASA's image. Deke almost snorted, visualizing the engine he'd just been examining. If *Endeavour* blew up over the Atlantic Ocean, they'd need to invigorate a helluva lot more than their image.

Stuart stepped off the stage and led a light applause for the Madame Vice President named Jessica Marlowe from *Bahston*. Oh, brother. It was bad enough NASA had to *pay* outsiders to do their PR; did they have to clap for it, too? Deke braced against the wall and checked the path to the nearest exit. He'd give her five minutes, seven tops.

From the front row, a young woman rose, set a laptop on a nearby table and then replaced Stuart at center stage. As she turned to the crowd, she flashed a mega-watt smile to get their attention.

She certainly got his. Holy hell, after staring at frayed wires and the inside of a shuttle exhaust all day, this girl was a vacation for the eyes. And he took it.

He drank in every inch from her deep brown hair twisted neatly in something his sister would call an up-do, all the way down to a pair of high heels that might be hell to wear but were pure heaven to watch. In between were a whole lot of nice curves and long legs.

She stood straight and confident, as close to attention as a civilian could manage, clearing her throat before she smiled again. This time, it hit him right in the gut. He couldn't help it. He smiled back even though he knew she probably hadn't noticed him among her rapt audience of nearly thirty people.

He watched her take a deep breath and smooth a stray hair. Cute. She was nervous under all that poise. He crossed his arms and settled back into his spot on the wall. Maybe he'd give her fifteen minutes.

"Ladies and gentlemen. NASA is in trouble." She clicked a button on the laptop and the screen filled with reprints of negative articles from the *New York Times* and the *Washington Post* that appeared fifty times their original size. Brutal headlines, all reinforcing her point that outside of Cape Canaveral and Houston, most of the world didn't give a crap about the space station and thought the whole shuttle program was a waste of precious tax dollars.

"The fact is, very few Americans know that we have a space station up and manned and even fewer could tell you what it does." She let a laser pointer illuminate a particularly nasty quote from a congressman who wanted to slash NASA's budget. "Space isn't important to America right now. It doesn't touch a chord in our hearts. Not the way it used to."

She switched off the damning headlines and the screen backlit her, showing off her feminine silhouette and giving her an unintentional halo. "The goal of public relations is to create support for NASA and ultimately protect and increase the funding it receives. To do that, we need to make space *relevant* to the average American."

Did Stu Rosen just say that she'd be staying at the Cape for a while? Now *that* was relevant. Deke took another lingering glance at the way her skirt hugged her backside. Relevant *and* nice.

"Ross & Clayton is the largest public relations firm in the world. We've spent a great deal of brainpower on the problem and we have a simple plan. It's the oldest and most effective marketing technique in the world." She paused and lit the room with that sexy smile again. "NASA is about to get some sex appeal."

The echo of his unprofessional thoughts jarred Deke out of his musings and he joined in the uncertain, nervous laughter of the audience.

She clicked to a new slide, her magnificent eyes balancing her serious demeanor with a touch of humor. He didn't know her qualifications and doubted she was thirty years old, but she'd obviously studied this sex appeal stuff pretty thoroughly.

"I'm afraid, ladies and gentlemen, that in a space suit, all astronauts look the same." She paused for more laughter. "We propose to give NASA a face. An unforgettable, grab-at-your-heart kind of face."

You got one of those, sweetheart. Her heels clicked in rhythm as she crossed the stage, a sound as completely feminine as she was. "Then we're going to give NASA a personality. Engaging, attractive, and even a little mysterious. A personality that is the polar opposite of the staid, conservative, and stuffy reputation you are..." she said, teasing them with a wink, "*enjoying* right now."

She had them and she must have known it; a glimmer lit her eyes. "We're going to change your image through one individual who will embody a new NASA."

The silence lasted just long enough to be slightly

uncomfortable, and Deke wondered if he'd missed something that she said. He wasn't paying nearly as much attention to her words as the occasional glimpse of cleavage he caught as she reached to her laptop to click on the next slide.

"What is the sexiest thing about space?" she challenged, crossing her arms and damn, just deepening that enticing valley enough to truly distract him. "Astronauts. Daring, handsome, risk-taking, gravity-defying, reach-for-the-stars space cowboys."

Suddenly, the image of a man in a blue flight suit leaning against a Navy F-18 fighter jet filled the screen behind her. Deke tore his gaze from the presenter to the face on the wall.

Familiar black hair that had been smashed by a helmet stuck to a forehead and touched the collar of the suit in the back. A hint of laughter teased the lips of the photo's subject. Recognition numbed his senses as he stared at the screen.

"Move over, George Clooney and make way, Russell Crowe. America's about to fall in love with Commander Deke Stockard." The audible gasp from nearly every person in the room punctuated her sentence and sucked all the air out of his lungs. "From his outstanding biography and obvious affinity for the camera, we're confident that we can make Commander Stockard a household name and, in the process, make America swoon over space once again."

Each word detonated in his head like unexpected grenades.

"And just how the hell do you plan to do that?"

At the sound of his question, her eyes flashed and she peered into the crowd, but she answered without missing a beat. "Although most of the world doesn't know this, it's a far more scientific process than you realize."

"Scientific?" he shot back, aware that heads had turned his way. "You're in a room full of scientists." Scientists having adolescent fantasies about cleavage, but scientists just the same. "You better explain exactly what you have in mind. *Miss.*"

Just as he uttered the condescending final syllable, her gaze landed on him. She raised her chin, giving him a clear shot of her throat as she took a long, hard swallow.

"That's an excellent question. *Commander.*" Her ebony eyes narrowed, as piercing as her laser pointer. "We do it through strategically placed photo ops and a blitz of TV and print coverage that keeps the public wanting more. We set him up on red carpets at movie premieres, side by side with celebrities. Then we make sure it all gets into *Entertainment Weekly* and on E! Television. We get him on Jay Leno. We drop candid photos on the wire services. We seat him in the front row of the seventh game of the NBA playoffs. It's an orchestrated campaign. That's what a great PR firm does."

Who the hell did she think she was, plastering his picture on that screen and making pronouncements about *sex* appeal?

He started down the steps toward her. "We don't go to NBA playoff games or movie premieres. We don't seek celebrity status." He let the disdain drop like bombs with every word and every step. "We are aviators and engineers and explorers. We develop experiments to advance medicine." He paused as he reached the halfway mark, his gaze locked on his pretty target. "We send satellites into orbit to monitor terrorism." He moved closer, purposely letting his voice intensify with each step. "We fix billion-dollar telescopes so scientists can see into the past and the future."

At last, he stood on the same level, a few feet away from

18

her, glad for the advantage of his height since she wore those stilts on her feet. "That's what *we* do." He leaned in closer so she'd inch away. She didn't. "It doesn't involve Jay Leno."

A spark lit her eyes, but he was blind now to her fiery appeal, furious with himself for admiring her physical assets while she was busy announcing that he'd become some sort of NASA poster boy.

They stood face-to-face, the audience no doubt spellbound at the unexpected showdown. He waited for her to back down.

But, son of a bitch, she just crossed her arms and took a step toward him.

"Without tax dollars, Commander Stockard, there will be no experiments, no exploration and no telescopic views into the present or the past." He could hear the tiniest shudder in her voice, but she held her ground and his gaze. "NASA has called in experts to reverse an extremely negative tide of public opinion. This is one tactic that hasn't been tried and one we know can work."

You are sorely mistaken, sweetheart. He was nobody's *tactic.* He finally broke their eye contact and brushed by her to leave the room.

"Count me out, spin doctor."

Oh, boy. Professional purgatory might be worse than she'd feared. Jessica watched the imposing figure disappear, along with about a quart of blood from her head. She turned and offered a tenuous smile to her audience, hoping the perspiration that had started when she got off the plane in this swamp didn't start forming a puddle around her feet.

Stuart Rosen, bless him, immediately closed the meeting

with assurance that the kinks in the program would be worked out. As the room emptied, Jessica took a chance that Stuart was truly the good guy the Washington-based NASA account team had promised when she had accepted this hellacious assignment. *Your idea, your job,* Tony had said.

As if she'd had a choice.

"Stuart," she said, tapping papers into a manila file, "couldn't you have warned the poor man ahead of time that he'd been hand-picked to be the next household heartthrob?"

Humor twinkled in Stuart's warm eyes. "And ruin that classic NASA moment?" At her flabbergasted look, he laughed. "Just kidding. In all seriousness, I thought Colonel Price *had* told him. We'd better go see our fearless leader right now."

She eyed the burly, slightly balding man who would now be her daily client contact. She had only met him a few minutes earlier, when she arrived at Kennedy Space Center for her first meeting to brief NASA's public affairs team on the plan. She'd been uneasy at the sight of so many people at the presentation, but Stuart had assured her this was standard procedure.

"Then you might have warned *me* he'd be lurking up in the cheap seats."

"Didn't your colleagues at the agency let you in on the NASA secret, Jessica?" He smiled and shrugged. "Brilliant engineers. Lousy communicators."

"I don't know about that. Commander Stockard certainly made himself clear." Jessica turned to the image of a larger-than-life astronaut that still burned on the screen.

The blurred photo really didn't do him justice. It didn't capture the intensity of eyes so blue they were downright navy. It certainly didn't reveal his power or the way he could slash a person with a few words. Mesmerized, she had been barely able to breathe, let alone look away from him while he ranted about explorers and telescopes and terrorism.

"If he has the same effect on the women of America," she muttered, "we could actually pull this off."

And that, Jessica reminded herself as she removed his image with a single click of her laptop's mouse, was really the only thing that mattered. Complete success if she had a snowball's chance of preserving everything she'd worked for years to achieve. Her whole world basically hung in the balance, and she wasn't about to let some astronaut with an attitude tip the scales.

A few minutes later, Stuart and Jessica stood in the lobby outside James D. Price's office. She squeezed the leather strap of her briefcase and studied a dramatic oil painting of a space shuttle poised for launch. A metal plate captioned the picture with five words.

Failure is not an option.

No kidding. She simply couldn't go back to Boston a failure. She'd rather take on all of NASA, including the insolent Commander Stockard, than lose her shot at the highest rung of the ladder she'd been climbing. Much as she hated leaving home and the visibility she needed as she vied for the top job in Boston, this was the biggest opportunity she'd ever have to prove herself to management. Nothing—make that no one—would ruin it for her.

Stuart leaned closer and spoke in a hushed tone, "By the way, our boss is retired Air Force, but everyone still calls him Colonel."

She nodded in understanding.

"We don't want to waste his time," Stuart continued. "So please go straight into your agency's backup plan."

"Backup plan?" Jessica squared her shoulders and turned

to face Stuart. She had a cardinal rule in business and it served her well: pick your battles.

This one was worth fighting.

Plus, they had no flipping backup plan.

"I promise you we have a winner here. Commander Stockard is exactly what we need to make this work." Jessica thought about the force of his penetrating gaze, his classically handsome face. "Central Casting couldn't have sent a better guy for the job."

"Jessica, I'm afraid you don't know Deke Stockard. I do, quite well. He's a pretty strong force around here."

She remembered the towering figure descending on her like a trapped jaguar. "I don't doubt that."

"He has the Colonel's ear and his opinions count. He was brought over from the Navy not just for his legendary piloting skills but for his management and engineering capabilities as well. He's got a central role in the safety of every shuttle launch—a position very few astronauts enjoy—and NASA has him on the fast track."

She tilted her head and winked at him. "I have him on a faster track."

Before Stuart could respond, the Colonel's office door flew open and six feet of royal blue burst through it. At the sight of her, Deke Stockard stopped cold, none of the animosity gone yet from his blazing eyes. His gaze stabbed her and he opened his mouth to say something, but a stocky man came up behind him and laid a hand on his shoulder.

"Let me talk to her, Deke. We'll work out some kind of compromise."

Jessica didn't like the sound of *compromise*, but it was better than *backup plan*. She held Deke's gaze, then stepped out of his path as he strode past her with an expression so stony she almost smiled.

No wonder Bill Dugan was so anxious to pass this assignment off to someone else. Who'd want to spend three months trying to turn that beast into America's sweetheart?

"Miss Marlowe, it's a pleasure." Jim Price offered a warm handshake and a gestured invitation into his office.

Greeting him, she noticed that his thick black brows contrasted with a shock of white hair, as though they somehow hadn't gotten the message that this man had passed fifty years of age. His wide shoulders must have looked commanding in an Air Force uniform, although his charcoal business suit still offered an aura of power and control. Jessica had been informed that he used that control, and few words, to his advantage.

"You caused quite a stir around here this afternoon," he commented as he took a seat behind his immaculate oak desk.

"I believe that was my assignment, Colonel."

"Your ideas are not universally popular." He straightened the one pen on his desk. "At least not with certain members of the staff."

Jessica leaned forward, ignoring the increased thumping of her heart as she faced the man who could make or break her game plan. "Colonel Price, I understood that Commander Stockard had been briefed and agreed to this assignment."

She distinctly remembered the conversation with Bill when he'd promised to handle the background work with the client. He'd briefed NASA and told Jessica they were one hundred percent behind the unorthodox plan.

The Colonel nodded. "I discussed it at length with Washington and it was decided that he should hear the plan directly from your agency to fully understand the rationale."

"Perhaps I could talk to him personally, Colonel," she suggested. "I can explain how little will be expected of him.

I'll do all the logistical work on the campaign. That's why I'm here."

That and the fact that Carla Drake had somehow convinced Tony Palermo that since Jessica had thought of the brilliant plan, it was only right that she go to Florida to see it through to success. Leaving all of Jessica's accounts and staff in Carla's hands for three months.

Jessica forced herself back to the conversation with Colonel Price and away from the office politics that nagged her.

"I happen to like the idea, and I think I understand why you've selected Commander Stockard," the Colonel said. "However, our situation has changed slightly. We've made a commitment to get the next shuttle, *Endeavour*, up on time. There are several folks floating around on the International Space Station who are a touch anxious to get home. One of the Russians, in particular."

Jessica noticed the look that passed between Stuart and Jim and wondered just how a homesick Russian could impact her plans with one astronaut on Earth.

"Deke plays a critical role in getting each shuttle ready and his time for non-mission-related work is limited," the Colonel said.

Scheduling problems she could handle. "This won't take a lot of Commander Stockard's time. He just shows up, gets his picture taken, does an interview and he's done." She held her breath, waiting for him to contradict her slight exaggeration.

"Is it possible we could find another astronaut for your project?"

Not a chance. She'd been through the bios. They were all so *ordinary* compared to Stockard. Short or balding or nerdy. Or married.

She chose her words carefully. "Commander Stockard has an amazing biography and he's obviously an articulate spokesperson." She couldn't resist a saucy grin. "And he looks pretty good in a flight suit."

"Sex sells," Colonel Price shot back with a knowing nod.

"We'll keep it dignified, sir. But, yes. It does."

The older man stood and stepped to his window, his arms locked behind him. Jessica stole a glance at Stuart, who shook his head slightly, silently telling her to say nothing and wait for the decision. It didn't matter. She knew no compelling argument would sway this man. All she could do now was wait for a verdict.

Colonel Price turned slowly before he spoke. "You can have him on a very, very limited basis, Miss Marlowe. You must accomplish this campaign with as little of his time as possible. No lengthy media tours and he only travels for emergency situations."

Like an appearance on *Oprah*. "Of course, Colonel."

He tapered his gaze to underscore his point. "If, for any reason, we have to stop the program, you'd better have another tactic at the ready. Is that understood?"

She nodded, imagining all the military underlings who'd flinched in the face of Colonel Price's demands. She wanted to ask why they might have to stop mid-way, but he picked up his phone to make a call, indicating that the meeting was ended.

She stood and thanked him, following Stuart out the door. He shot her a smile both sympathetic and knowing. "About that backup plan…"

"Do you think we'll really need one?" she asked.

"At NASA, we live by them. Everything has a redundant system, in case one fails. You'll get used to it. Anyway, would you care to officially meet your guinea pig now? I can take you to Deke's office."

Jessica slowed her step. She wasn't prepared for another encounter with Mr. We-Are-Explorers-Not-Movie-Stars just yet. "I think I better get to my own office and call the team. They could start working on our 'redundant system' in case mine fails."

But it won't, she thought as she followed Stuart to the Press Facility.

Failure is not an option.

A few minutes later, Jessica stuck a fingernail in the chipped edges of the metal and Formica desk in her new office, briefing Bill Dugan on the Colonel's instructions.

"We've got him for now, but Price made it clear our time is tight and we need to have a backup plan in case he has to stop. Do you have any idea why that might happen?"

"Not a clue."

She could imagine the twisted frown on Bill's thin face as he adjusted his glasses and tried to look as important as he had somehow managed to become. He'd never had much visibility in the agency until recently, and now, because he headed the NASA account in Washington, Jessica reported to him. At least for the next three months.

"What about our Naval aviator hero turned astronaut?" Bill asked. "Have you met him yet?"

She turned away from the open door and lowered her voice. "Yes, I met him at the briefing. He's a little less than enthusiastic."

A response came from the hallway. "That's an understatement." She spun in her chair to see the man in a familiar blue flight suit: tall, dark, and still not smiling.

Chapter Three

Deke heard her slight intake of breath when she realized she'd been caught. He leaned against the doorway, keeping his scowl firmly in place, even though he felt a tug of sympathy when pink stains of embarrassment colored her cheeks.

"Bill, I have a meeting starting. I've got to go." As soon as she hung up, she stood and reached out her hand. "We haven't been formally introduced."

He saw her study his face, appraising her choice, no doubt, for the idiotic campaign she'd cooked up. He steadfastly refused to meet her phony PR smile with one of his own.

Still, he couldn't help noticing how the smile, phony or not, softened her pretty features and revealed straight, white teeth. With a will of its own, his gaze continued down, over the open-neck collar of her blouse and finally stopped at the pink-tipped fingers she extended toward him.

He took her slender hand and nodded. "I wish I could say it's a pleasure." Her hand was damp. And very soft. He considered holding it a moment longer, but she pulled back immediately as though she'd been shocked.

"Colonel Price seems to think we can work out a schedule that will accommodate yours."

"I doubt that," he said, narrowing his eyes in warning. "My schedule just got full. You better start auditioning other talent."

"I have assured Colonel Price that I will take as little of your time as possible, Commander. We don't intend for our campaign to negatively affect your career."

He sincerely doubted if this firecracker gave a damn about anybody's career but her own. "I bet a plum assignment at the Cape could do wonders for yours, though."

She paled, flecks of gold flashing in her dark chocolate eyes. The same color combination as her hair, he noticed. "My career has nothing to do with this, Commander."

He needed to get his mind off her hair and eyes and let her know who was in charge. In one swift move, he stepped into the room and flipped a straight-backed guest chair around before dropping into it, leaning the backrest toward her desk. "I'm willing to bet you're here because you think you could skyrocket with this little stunt."

He saw her attention drop to the lower half of his body, wrapped around the chair, then return to his face. "Skyrocket, Commander? Clever pun." She stayed standing but appeared to get some support by touching her desk.

Good. He was unnerving her. He rocked a little on two legs of the chair. She'd be tough, but he'd faced tougher. None as pretty, but that wouldn't affect him. "How much do you know about the space program, Miss Marlowe?"

She met his gaze, her fingertips splayed on the desk. "You don't need to question my credentials, Commander. I've been thoroughly briefed, but I don't claim to be an expert on space. That's your department. What I do need to know is how the media works and what appeals to the American public." Finally, she rounded the desk and took her chair. "And I assure you, I know that."

He really needed to take her down a notch or two. "But do you know what an orbiter is? Do you know how many shuttle missions there have been? Do you have any idea what experiments are being done on the space station? Do you—"

"I'm a quick study." She cut him off and adjusted her collar as though the heat in the room was stifling her, but unknowingly offered him a tantalizing glimpse of the rise of her breasts. "I'm here to handle the media, to create and promote your image. My job is to get you recognized, publicized, and *adored* by the American public."

He *had* to stop looking at her body and start listening to her words because they were frightening. *Adored by the American public?*

But before he could force his attention back to her face, she cleared her throat.

Good God. He'd been caught ogling her like a teenager. He stood and gently kicked the chair back to its original position. This was no time to start a mating dance. She was here to ruin his life, slow down his progress, and force him into ridiculous PR stunts that he abhorred.

He couldn't let a little cleavage—well, not *exactly* little— make him forget that.

"My schedule is extremely tight," he said, hearing the tension in his own voice. "I'm here this week, but I usually spend several days a week in Houston. You won't get much of my time." He glanced at the hallway, anxious to leave. "You really should find someone else."

"Perhaps you can do some of the work during your flights. Reading and preparing for interviews, for example."

For the first time in several hours, he laughed out loud. She was as clueless as she was cute.

"Why is that so funny?"

"I go in a T-38, that's why."

"Okay." She sighed, holding her hands up in surrender. "What's a T-38?"

"It's a supersonic two-seater jet that I fly over the Gulf of Mexico." He deliberately widened his grin. "I don't get much reading done on those trips."

She opened her mouth to say something, but suddenly brightened. "Oh, is it like a fighter plane?"

He cocked his head and used the same patient voice he'd offer to a child on a tour of the Space Center. "Yes. But T is for Trainer. F is for Fighter. This is a T-38. We don't generally fire any missiles on our way to Texas."

Her eyes sparkled. "Does it have clear NASA logos everywhere?"

"A few." He didn't like the direction she was taking. "Why?"

"It's a great photo op. You in the cockpit of a little fighter-type plane, the NASA emblem blazing, an astronaut taking off to Houston for some space business." She tapped her cheek with one finger. "I could do something with that."

"What the hell would you *do* with that?" He didn't even want to think about the possibilities.

She bit the corner of her lip. "Well, I'm not thinking *Aviation Week* magazine, Commander. I could take it to the wire services, or *Us,* or *People.*" She stopped, a definite glimmer in her eyes. "Maybe even *TheEnquirer.*"

"*The National Enquirer?*"

She smiled slyly and moistened her lower lip where she'd just nibbled it. "That was just payback for the T-38 comment," she said softly.

His heart rate, damn it, actually kicked up. "I'm glad you think this is a parlor game."

Parlor game? He sounded like a damn librarian.

"I don't—"

"You can communicate with me through email or my secretary."

"I'll do that, Commander. And I'll set up media training immediately."

"Media training?" He spun back around, feeling like a marionette yanked back every time he tried to exit the stage. "No. Not necessary. I don't need to be trained."

"Yes, you do." She nodded, a look of determination in her eyes that she probably saved only for difficult clients. *Watch out, sweetheart, I'm going to be the most difficult of all.* "I've trained lots of people who thought they didn't need it. But they did." She stood, reaching across her desk for a handheld device, clicking some buttons. "When are you available? I can do it in one afternoon. All we need to do is make sure you say the right things when you talk."

He tried not to choke. She was *impossible.* "I'm not paid to talk. I'm paid to fly."

"Are you paid to be contrary?"

He grinned. "I do that for free."

She blew out a little breath. "You know, most people can't wait to get their fifteen minutes of fame."

"Then you should find one of them."

"Sorry, Commander." She cast her eyes down at her electronic calendar and pressed a button, her lashes long and dark against a creamy complexion. "There are no other candidates for this job." She glanced up at him. "You're perfect."

He dropped his gaze again, letting it linger over her body with no subtlety this time. "Far from it, I'm afraid."

Three days later, Jessica accepted that heat, humidity, and perspiration were facts of life in the swamp. She sat in an open parking lot, the icy air conditioner of her rented Taurus blowing right in her face. The refrigerated air finally dried the damp tendrils that invariably escaped her clip just from the act of driving to work.

For a moment she closed her eyes and imagined the early November chill as the last of the burnished golden leaves fell on the cobblestones of Beacon Street. No. She refused to be homesick already. No time for it. She had to media train the space cadet today.

She glanced into the rearview mirror to make sure the mascara she'd applied in preparation for her day in the studio hadn't dissolved into black clumps between Cocoa Beach and Cape Canaveral. Her gaze shifted from her reflection to a low-slung silver Corvette pulling into the parking spot behind her, darkened windows eliminating any view of the driver.

Who owned *that* car?

In a moment she had the answer, and she slipped lower into the front seat of the Taurus so Deke Stockard didn't see her. But she couldn't resist using the side view mirror to take a secret study of him, of the aristocratic nose and sensual mouth shadowed by the hint of a dark beard on the square angle of his jaw. His straight black hair was about a halfinch too long for the military, but she wouldn't let him cut it before the first photo op.

As if what she wanted mattered to him.

She tore her gaze away, since she'd get plenty of time to ogle him this afternoon. And if the media training session generated the same kind of heat as he had in her office the other day, she'd better be prepared for more involuntary melting. Suddenly a minivan blocked her view as it slowed down and the driver spoke to Deke before pulling in next to her.

As Jessica climbed out of the car and reached in the back for her briefcase, Stuart got out of the van and came around to greet her.

"Morning, Jess." He held his own briefcase toward the man politely waiting for both of them. "Did you see Deke?"

How could she miss him in his race car? She nodded at both of them. "Good morning, gentlemen."

Stuart closed the car door for her. "You two could commute together, you know. You live on the same street."

Her stomach twisted just a bit as she looked at Deke in surprise. "We do?"

Deke shrugged. "NASA housing."

"Not exactly what I'd call it," she said, directing her attention to Stuart. "I must admit I was pleasantly surprised. I expected a Quonset hut." The blue and white bungalow on Sea Park Road had caught her off guard when she first arrived. Twice the size of her condo with a striking panoramic view of the Banana River and its bobbing boats and swaying palm trees, her temporary home had quickly become one aspect of her new life that she liked.

The three of them fell in step together as Stuart explained the housing arrangements. "Riverfront homes are strictly for VIPs who have long-term assignments at the Cape. But it's great for a sailor like you, Deke."

"I'm taking the boat out tomorrow, as a matter of fact," he said to Stuart. "I've got to get you and Wendy and the boys out there again. I enjoyed that last time."

She stole a sidelong glance at him, noticing that he had abandoned the flight suit today and wore a pair of pressed khaki pants and a black pullover that fit snugly on a wide, solid chest. He certainly didn't strike her as a river rat or someone who entertained seven-year-olds on his boat.

"The twins would love it." Stuart turned to include Jessica on the conversation. "It's fortunate for us that Deke is one of the few astronauts that live here, you know."

"I live here because my non-flying mission time is devoted to pre-flight engineering on the shuttles," he explained with a pointed look to Jessica. "I still spend a lot of time at Johnson like most astronauts."

In other words, *I'm way too busy living in two cities.*

"Convenient for us," she answered brightly. "Since the press flocks to Kennedy for launch coverage. By the way, are you ready for media training this afternoon, Commander?"

He rolled his eyes and then looked at Stuart. "Didn't you warn her I don't train easily?"

Stuart chuckled and put a hand on Jessica's back. "Don't pay any attention to him, Jess. His bark is worse than his bite."

"The only bite she's worried about is a sound bite," Deke remarked as they separated.

Not the *only* one.

In her office, Jessica inched the air conditioner controller down to help eliminate the flush that still burned her skin after the run-in with Deke. Stuart came back with coffee and she tried to forget Deke Stockard's attitude while they discussed the contents of the press kit and she described some of the media strategies she had planned. By the time she left for the NASA TV studio, she had grown even more confident about the campaign.

Once she had a chance to phone her friends at the *LA Times*, *People* and *Newsweek*, not to mention *Entertainment Tonight* and some of the syndicated shows, Deke Stockard and NASA would make a high-impact entry into the consciousness of America. Whether he wanted to or not.

"Son of a bitch," Deke muttered as he stared at Jeff Clark standing in his office doorway. "Who the hell does he think he is?"

"He thinks he's the person who single-handedly landed a man on the moon."

Deke blew out a disgusted breath. "Funny how history changes over a few decades. Skip Bowker was one of hundreds of Apollo engineers."

"Yeah, but he's about the only one left in NASA today, so he gets to change history. Anyway, you need to worry about the present."

Deke stood up and moved around his desk in two easy strides, glowering at his friend. "Skip is not having that meeting without us."

Jeff followed as Deke strode out the door into the hallway of the OPF. "Us? What us? I'm going to Skip's meeting. You'll be playing spin the message with the hottie from Boston."

Deke froze mid-step and slowly turned to Jeff. "That is exactly what I don't want to hear," he said, pointing a single finger in Jeff's face to make a point.

"That she's a hottie?" Jeff asked, an innocent smile threatening.

Deke decided to ignore it. "You're coming to this media training session as my backup. You promised, Jeff."

"Yeah, I will. But we better have somebody be our eyes and ears at Skip's meeting."

"I'm going to talk to him," Deke said. "Is he at the orbiter?"

Jeff shrugged and looked at his watch. "It's lunchtime. Try the pavilion."

Deke strode into the warm November sun and used the five minutes it took to get to the Headquarters pavilion to calm his temper and stay focused on what mattered: Skip Bowker was vague to the point of deception about the inspection process.

He saw the familiar gray head buried in a book, remnants of a brown-bag lunch half-eaten in front of him.

"Hey, Skip." Deke sat down on the bench across from him and waited for the older man to finish chewing and slowly fold a dog-eared corner of his novel.

"Deke," he said with a nod, turning the book face down. "Thought you were off to the TV studio today."

"I may have to change that," Deke said, "if I'm going to miss something important in the meeting this afternoon."

"Nope. Just routine review of inspection logs."

Deke clenched his teeth to keep from lashing out a retort. No matter how old and irrelevant Skip seemed, he still deserved respect. And he still called the shots in Safety & Logistics.

Leaning back, Deke picked an imaginary piece of lint from his khakis and spoke softly. "Nothing's routine these days, Skip. And February thirteenth isn't too far off."

Skip snorted a little. "Don't you hate when they pick those unlucky numbers for launch dates?"

"I'm not superstitious." Deke knew as well as Skip that the date had everything to do with the earth's orbit and timed encounters with the space station and nothing to do with serendipity. "But I am cautious. And concerned."

"You should be a little more like your namesake," Skip said, his grin baring slightly yellowed teeth. "I knew Deke Slayton personally when he was in the Apollo program and a bigger thrill-seeker you never met."

Deke angled his head in acknowledgment. Skip loved the

fact that Deke's parents were such space fans that they'd nicknamed their firstborn son after an Apollo astronaut. But he wasn't here to talk about history.

"I don't find anything about safety control thrilling, I assure you."

Skip waved a thick-fingered hand. "We're in good shape, Deke. Been through that bird fifty times myself. We won't have any trouble meeting that date." When he squinted into the sun, Skip's creases deepened and the bright light emphasized the age spots around his mouth.

He suddenly looked less of a legend who knew the earliest astronauts and more like a weary old man.

A rush of sympathy surprised Deke. "I know if anyone can get that shuttle ready to fly around the world and up to the station, it's you," he said softly.

Skip looked like he might roll his eyes. "Cool the flattery, Stockard. You're the next big thing around here. What do you want? I'm not changing my meeting time."

Sympathy was wasted here. Deke leaned on the concrete tabletop. "I've been living in *Endeavour*'s fuselage, Skip. There's got to be more worn insulation than what we found in there."

"Nope, we got it all. There isn't any more." Skip crunched an empty bag of chips and shoved the remainder of a baloney sandwich into a paper bag. "You're searching for phantom problems."

"I've looked at *Columbia*, too," Deke continued. "I saw evidence of electrical arcing between exposed wires and one metal screw head that'd seen about twenty-two missions. What if one of the backups had failed? That second computer was the only thing that saved that ship."

Skip shook his head. "It wouldn't have exploded."

"But they could have had to land manually, dead stick,

37

without a computer," Deke insisted. "Which could be just as dangerous."

"We can't do anymore wire harness inspections. The space station equipment is nearly packed." Skip winced as he stood up to drop his trash into a nearby container. "You just worry about your own mission on *Atlantis* in May."

Deke watched Skip fight his arthritis as he tried to straighten his back. *Maybe it's time to pack it in, Pops, and let the young blood do your job.*

Standing, he picked up the book Skip had left on the table. "I know you don't want an astronaut anywhere near your domain, but let me just fill you in on a secret. You'll get sick of me when *Atlantis* is in the sling." Deke smiled to cover the edge in his voice. "I'm a real bastard when I have to fly the damn thing."

"You're a real bastard when you don't." The strained smile didn't soften the insult. Maybe Skip's renowned jealousy of astronauts wasn't just NASA folklore. Maybe he really did resent the fact that he never got to go up.

But that didn't explain his vague answers or the holes Deke kept seeing in what logs he could find. Someone was screwing around with the whole inspection process, but he couldn't believe Skip would do that deliberately. Especially since he had to know a little about the drama unfolding on the space station.

"Since I can't be there today, Skip, why don't you forward me the latest logs?"

"Just get what's in the system. It's all there."

Deke remembered the frustration he'd experienced earlier in the day when he'd attempted to do just that. "I tried. Couldn't get in."

"Really?" Skip looked surprised. "Somebody must have deleted your password."

"Imagine that," Deke said dryly.

Skip nudged Deke with his elbow. "Better get goin', Deke. They're waiting for you in hair and makeup."

Before he could respond, Skip lumbered through the doors of the Headquarters building, leaving Deke stuck with muttered curse in his throat and the tattered paperback still in his hand.

He turned it over and looked at the cover. *The Spy Who Came in from the Cold.* Good God. Somebody ought to break the news to Skip that everybody was on the same side now.

Chapter Four

Jessica relished the chill of the studio, rubbing her arms as she watched a skeleton crew set up a camera and lighting just as her subject sauntered in, precisely on time. An entirely new set of goose bumps rose on her skin.

"Hello again, Commander Stockard." She intentionally locked her arms together in front of her but gave him her brightest smile. He nodded and gestured toward a man who'd come in with him.

"Miss Marlowe, this is Major Jeff Clark."

"Have you come along to offer moral support, Major?" Jessica asked as they shook hands in greeting.

He responded with a quick smile that lit his clear blue eyes. "Please, call me Jeff. I'm happy to provide moral support if needed, but it seems I'm being recruited as the B-Team."

An uneasy feeling crept through her. The rat was going to try to arrange his own *redundant system*. She shot a challenging glance to Deke. "We haven't discussed a backup plan."

He spared her a look. "We haven't discussed *any* plan."

"Commander Stockard." She didn't even try to hide her

exasperation. "Please. We really can't succeed without your cooperation."

"You have my cooperation, Miss Marlowe."

"Just Jessica is fine." How did he know it was *Miss*, anyway?

"I'm here, at your service." He indicated the studio with a mocking sweep of his hand. "It seems prudent that we have another astronaut trained to do…this."

"Are you planning to go somewhere, Commander Stockard?"

"At some point, I'll be traveling about a million miles. In my business, there's never any guarantee that I come home from work."

The solemn tone in his voice caught her off guard. She realized that for all the background information she had gleaned from his profile, she really knew very little about this man.

Only the biographical sketch of his thirty-seven years, which she had just drafted into a short article for the press kit. His impressive education included "distinguished graduate" of the U.S. Naval Academy, a master's in aeronautical engineering from MIT, and top of his class at the Navy Test Pilot School. She knew he had been based on an aircraft carrier in the Gulf War and was decorated several times and that he'd been on one mission to Mir, the old Russian space station. Other than that, he remained a mystery.

"I'm sure NASA prefers that you do come home from work, Commander," she finally responded, realizing that she'd been staring a moment longer than necessary. "Of course I'll train you both together. Why don't we start with a mock interview? Major Clark, would you like to be victim number one?"

"Hey, I thought I was backup." He nudged Deke and winked at Jessica. "No, you let Harrison Ford here take center stage."

When Deke settled in a chair across from her and clipped on a mike, Jessica explained she would be interviewing him as though he were on a morning talk show.

"Let me set up a hypothetical situation for you. You've been in the news a lot lately and you've been vocal in your support of the International Space Station, Alpha—"

"I know what it's called."

"And you've been spending quite a bit of time with, oh, Gwyneth Paltrow."

He raised an eyebrow and shot the other astronaut a look.

Jessica signaled the cameraman to roll tape, then leaned back and took on the voice and pose of a talk-show host. "Commander Stockard. You must know there are rumors and whispers running rampant about NASA's next big announcement. Are you planning to marry Gwyneth?"

A shadow of disgust crossed his handsome face. "I thought you wanted to talk about the space station."

Jessica had no idea if he was talking to her or the imaginary interviewer. In either case, she didn't like the answer.

"Might be a long afternoon if you don't play the game, Commander."

"I am playing."

And fighting every inch of the way. Fine. Two could play his game. No more softballs. "Commander Stockard, is it true NASA has cut safety programs to the very core in an effort to save money? Are lives at risk every time we watch a shuttle launch?"

His eyes flickered for a moment, then cut through her. "Risk is a part of our business."

She scratched a note on her pad. "What about the media leaks that something very nearly went wrong in the shuttle *Columbia* during the last launch?"

"It was a hydrogen leak, not a media leak. Ma'am. Miss. Jessica."

"Would you consider an acting career when you've finished being an astronaut?"

"I'm acting like I enjoy this."

"Why aren't you married?"

His lips curled slightly. "Gwyneth's busy schedule."

"Can you give me just one example of how America benefits from the millions of dollars we send into—well, into thin air?"

"Haven't you heard of Velcro?"

She shook her head a little, not wanting to let him see his volleys had scored a point of frustration.

"Okay, Commander. Let's try something else. Medical achievements. I think it's an excellent way for you to highlight the impact NASA has on the world. I read that for every dollar spent on space travel, we receive eight dollars in benefits, such as improved tools and insulated clothing. Can you highlight some of the medical breakthroughs that are a result of space exploration?"

He shifted in his seat. "Maybe you ought to get a doctor to do that. I'm a pilot and an engineer."

"I realize that." She snapped off the microphone attached to her collar and searched his face for a chink in the armor as she leaned forward and lowered her voice. "Listen, I get your drift. You don't want to do this. I don't particularly want to be here any more than you do. But I'd really appreciate it if you'd humor me. The sooner you cooperate, the sooner we can both get back to our real work."

"I thought this *was* your real work."

She offered a sweet, but fake, smile. "As compelling a project as you are, Commander Stockard, I do have other accounts, other clients, and a whole life that I'd like to get back to. Help me succeed and I'll take as little of your time as possible."

He stared at her, and despite the sixty-degree temperature of the studio, a warm rush shot through her.

"Please?" she whispered.

He brought his face closer to hers and she could smell a mix of aftershave and soap. "You're really very tolerable when you let down your guard," he said softly.

She swallowed hard and fought a smile. Genuine this time. "Tolerable? Is that a notch just above or below mediocre?"

He shrugged. "I don't do mediocre."

"Then we have something in common after all, Commander."

He said nothing for what seemed like an eternity, studying her with the faintest spark in his navy-rimmed eyes. Finally, he settled back into the seat. "Okay. Let's just make it fast. Pacemakers, CAT scans, laparoscopic surgery, motorized wheelchairs, hearing aids. We've had a piece of 'em all."

His careless tone teased another hesitant smile out of her and she jotted a random, meaningless note on her pad, trying to still an unwanted thump in her chest.

After a few more minutes of what she feared might be stupid questions, Jessica suggested they rewind the tape and review the interview on the monitor. She tried to explain the technique of answering a different question than the one that's been asked and advised him on how to deflect safety questions.

In response, he crossed and uncrossed his ankles and looked at his watch no less than six times.

"I'm going as fast as I can, Commander. I'm trying to help you because I promise you will not be this comfortable on the *real* set of the *Today* show."

"No, I won't, because I don't intend to do it."

"You'll have to," she insisted. "Don't you follow orders?"

"Let's just make it easy on both of us." He inched closer to her and touched his ear, his voice low and teasing. "If I do show up on the *Today* show, I'll just wear an earpiece and you can whisper in my ear."

Droplets of moisture formed at the nape of her neck as she stared back at him, unable to come up with even a lame response.

"Enough, Deke." Jeff Clark jumped in. "It's my turn. Go sit down and watch a pro."

Deke shot out of the chair and walked off the set.

"So, do you think you can handle that pain in the ass?" Jeff asked in a confidential tone as he dropped into the hot seat for his interview.

"I understand that he doesn't want to do this." She watched Deke leave the studio, oddly disappointed that he wouldn't stay just a few minutes longer. "But, honestly, he has all the right stuff—no pun intended—to capture the attention and attraction of America. I truly believe it will help this country want to embrace the space program along with him. And that's our objective. Making him a sex symbol is merely a strategy to reach that goal."

She heard the poised, professional tone in her voice. But something about that man made her feel anything *but* poised or professional.

He left the set, but Deke wasn't quite ready to leave the studio yet. From the booth behind the darkened glass of the studio wall, he sat in the empty assistant director's chair to observe Jessica Marlowe on three different monitors.

He wasn't the least bit surprised that the camera loved her. And she obviously knew her job, asinine as it was. He took a deep breath and listened to her ask far less intrusive questions of Jeff. She had no intention of using a backup astronaut. He could read her determination a mile away.

Son of a bitch, he just couldn't get his head around this PR business and why Price wanted *him* to do it. His mission at NASA was clear and if it hadn't been, he wouldn't have come over and left the life of a Naval aviator, a life that he loved.

He didn't worry about NASA's image problems. He never cared about image. He cared about flying and exploring and getting the research done right. And he wanted to make sure no lives were lost in the process. He thought of the growing complications up on the space station, something the wide-eyed PR girl knew nothing about. If they didn't figure out what had caused the hydrogen leak, the launch would have to be delayed. And that could be deadly for one man.

Skip's favorite war, the Cold one, would heat up again in a big hurry if the Russians thought the Americans deliberately let a cosmonaut die in space because the engineer-astronaut responsible for getting the shuttle up was out on a media tour. Then they'd have an image problem, all right.

Maybe someone should tell her. But if something leaked, all hell would break loose. They'd have a real media circus on their hands.

No, he couldn't trust her with information that

confidential. No one could know how bad off the cosmonaut was.

His gaze traveled down her body, giving in to the urge he'd fought since he'd seen her in the parking lot this morning. Miss Image-Maker certainly didn't rely exclusively on her impressive gray matter or that little skirt wouldn't shimmy up so far each time she crossed her well-toned thighs. An irrepressible male response annoyed and alerted him.

Shit. He pushed up and left the studio for the OPF, needing to concentrate on some spark-burned wires he'd found near the coolant tubes. The less time spent anywhere near that leggy brunette, the better.

Chapter Five

The Friday afternoon exodus of administrators and managers signaled the end of Jessica's first full week on the assignment. It reminded her that back in Boston the offices of Ross & Clayton were emptying as the staff headed to the conference room for the week-ending ritual known as "Beer Friday." A melancholy wave compelled Jessica to dial her dearest friend and favorite employee.

"Jo Miller," answered a gravelly voice.

Jessica smiled at the familiar sound. "Wish you were here…instead of me."

At her friend's tiny shriek, Jessica pictured Jo running her lacquered nails through spiky blond hair, then unclipping a funky earring to settle in for a chat. "Hey, babe! Ah, we miss you so."

"Thought you'd be at Beer Friday already."

"I'm avoiding it for as long as possible," Jo said. "It's no fun without you." Jessica knew her well enough to believe the sentiment was genuine. "So how's it going, Pygmalion? Have you turned the space cadet into the next media darling?"

"Don't be clearing any wall space for a Silver Anvil yet," Jessica warned, referring to the coveted PR award. "But we have some interest from a couple of the networks and I'm lining up a photo session. The man, however, needs a major attitude adjustment."

"Uh-oh. Captain America meets Wonder Woman. Could get sticky. What's he like?"

Jessica mulled over the right words to describe him. "Intimidating."

"As gorgeous in person as that picture you found on the NASA site?"

"Better," she admitted glumly. "But he needs to be gorgeous for this thing to work, right? He's easy on the eyes but not easy to whip into shape, as I found out in the studio the other day."

"What happened?"

"I didn't exactly dominate with superior media training skills."

"Don't tell me." Jo laughed into the phone. "We had a clash of control freaks."

Jessica smiled. This was why she'd called Jo. Just to laugh at it all. But, even with the open invitation from her best friend, she wasn't quite ready to share the effect Deke Stockard had on her.

"Never mind. How are my favorite clients?"

The silence lasted a beat too long, sending a tug of worry through her.

"Jo, this is me. I can handle it."

"Well, most everyone seems to be fine with Carla Drake as your temporary replacement. She's met with every one of your clients."

Jessica dropped her head back against her chair and closed her eyes. "I expected that. They know I'm gone. Temporarily. Those clients are loyal to me and to the agency. That's okay, really." Jessica knew she was trying to convince herself as much as her trusted employee.

"True. But..." Jo seemed to be searching for the right words, and for some reason, it was far more chilling than her usual quick wit.

"But what?"

"She kind of talked Dash Communications out of the Next Generation plan."

"Are you kidding?" Jessica shot forward, fire in her veins. "That's my whole strategy for next year. They love that idea! All the events, all the media coverage. Is she crazy? That campaign will make the agency a million in revenue."

"She proposed a different approach. Something she did for another cell phone company client in California."

"And they bought it?" Jessica asked. Not possible. Not remotely possible. "I spent weeks creating that campaign and didn't Tony see the numbers? Next Gen was projected to bill over two hundred and fifty thousand in the first half of the year!" Nothing swayed Tony like profits.

"Evidently. Actually, her new idea is, um, pretty sweet on the bottom line. Didn't you get the memo on it?"

"No." Jessica rubbed her temples where a familiar stress headache threatened. "What a lousy way to end the week."

"Do I have to give you my 'there's more to life than work' speech again, Jess? Come on, what fun things are you doing down there this weekend?"

"Work."

Jo's familiar 'tsks' shot across the line. "Guess I better lecture. Listen, even if you don't get the guy on the front page of the *New York Times* or single-handedly arrange for sixty gazillion in new tax dollars for space–which you will–everyone will still love you."

"Don't psychoanalyze my misplaced ambitions, Jo," Jessica said, not completely teasing with the request. "I know your theories. And before you start with the motivational spiel, please keep my poor little almost-eighty-year-old father and his shortcomings as a single parent out of this."

"You just hate me because you know I'm right."

"I could never hate you, Jo," Jessica said, twirling the phone cord and fighting a smile. "But that new blonde who has her eye on my promotion could stand to have a few pins stuck into a Carla doll I'm making."

Jo moaned a little. "Listen to me. Don't give her any ammunition while you're down there. She's waiting for your first misstep. Not that you make professional mistakes, but consider yourself warned."

Jessica thought of the media training session. A disaster, in her opinion. And she hadn't yet managed to schedule a photo session.

"So, are you learning to surf this weekend?"

"Good, clean subject change, Jo." Jessica laughed. "I am going to a party. Stuart Rosen is having a barbecue Saturday night so I can get to know everyone."

Jo chuckled. "A barbecue in November. How absolutely Florida."

"Please. It's hot as July here."

"Don't complain. It snowed last night."

A pang of envy shot through Jessica. The first snow of the year, falling outside her picture window, dancing around the iron gaslights of Beacon Street, covering her world with white fairy dust...and she missed it.

"You just made me so homesick," Jessica said softly.

"Honey, I'm sorry, I forgot how much you love winter. Go do your five-mile run on the beach tomorrow instead of the ice-covered paths of Back Bay. You'll forget about snow. Then, when you go to the November barbeque, wear those amazing white jeans you stop traffic in."

Jessica laughed in response.

"I'm serious," Jo insisted. "And don't forget some high-heeled sandals, which beat snow boots any day. The pink ones we picked out in Saks last summer. I promise you won't be intimidated by anyone."

Jess stretched, inching her chair back to rest on two legs, feeling better just listening to the heartfelt, sisterly advice. "I do love you, Jo. And I know you love those shoes."

"Excuse me. Is this urgent or can I interrupt you for a moment?"

Jessica's eyes popped open and her chair slammed forward on the floor at the sound of Deke's voice, dripping with sarcasm and impatience.

"I gotta go, Jo. Bye." Blood rushed from the base of her neck as she dropped the phone into the cradle and stared at him. "Don't you *ever* knock?"

"The door was open," he said with a dubious glance at her phone. "Was that a reporter?"

"One of my employees," she responded with what she hoped was an appropriate amount of professionalism.

"Interesting management discussion." He held out a folder marked 'P.R.' "I reviewed your press materials and have some comments."

She took the folder eagerly. "Great. What did you think?"

"You want the truth?"

She flipped open the file and saw the first page of her press release, red slashes and handwritten comments along every margin. "Maybe I don't."

"I'm a stickler for accuracy."

She looked up at him, but his intense blue stare forced her attention back to the page, to study the tiny notes in perfectly formed capital letters with diagrams and arrows and asterisks of additional information. A sea of red. A sea of change.

"You tend to write things a little, uh, fluffier than I would," he said. "But I suppose that's your business. Bury the facts in bull—baloney."

She snapped the file shut. He just didn't get it. This was to benefit *his* organization, *his* livelihood. "It's not bull. It's called *positioning*. Careful, planned, strategic—"

He held up his hand to stop her, all softness disappearing from his face. "Go ahead, spin doctor, position whatever you want. Just get it *right*. Do your homework. You've never even *seen* a space shuttle."

She resisted the urge to smirk at him. "No, Commander, not in person. Perhaps I'll arrange a tour at the Visitors' Center tomorrow."

"More propaganda."

"Then take me through *Endeavour*." She dropped the gauntlet with ease, knowing he'd never take it.

"Excuse me?"

She opened the folder again and scanned the red ink. "You're absolutely right. I'd like to see *Endeavour* up close."

He shook his head, his frown deepening. "The OPF is highly restricted. Even if I took you, the orbiter's under intense inspections right now."

"Every minute of every day?" She dropped the papers on top of another pile on her desk. "I'll go in the middle of the night if necessary. I'm willing to do what I have to, Commander."

She saw his jaw clench before he responded. "Fine. Meet me at the East entrance of the OPF tomorrow at six. Sharp."

"I'll be there."

"That's tomorrow *morning*, Miss Marlowe. Six *a.m.*"

She held his challenging gaze. "I know what six means, Commander. Otherwise, I'm sure you would have said *eighteen hundred hours*."

He ignored the comment and turned to leave. "By the way, I have to go to Houston next week."

"Great. I'll line up a photographer to go with you."

He shook his head, a sigh of frustration escaping. "I told you. It's a two-seater that flies about six hundred miles an hour. You can't just pick somebody out of the Yellow Pages to climb on board and take pictures."

"I'm sure NASA has a photographer trained for it."

"No. Not this time. I'm flying with Jeff Clark."

Pick your battles, Jess. She began gathering her papers, then glanced at him. "Fine. We'll just take photos on the ground before you take off."

He took a step back and stared at her. "Good God, woman. Don't you know when to back off?"

She bit her lip and picked up a pencil from her desk. "Not when I need to get something done."

Her fingers tightened around the pencil, almost cracking it. She saw his gaze drop to her hands and slide back up to meet her eyes as she waited.

"I'm leaving Tuesday at dawn from the airstrip at the north end of the Cape. You can have thirty minutes during my pre-flight check. I'll be busy, so shoot around that."

She exhaled. "Great. Thank you."

He stepped into the hall, then glanced back at her with a teasing smirk. "Now you can call your boyfriend back."

The conversation played again in Deke's head, as he eased the Corvette into fourth gear and felt the surge of all four hundred horses take the curve of South Tropical Trail just a touch over the speed limit. Not exactly the thrill of a Tomcat, but almost enough to take his mind off Jessica Marlowe.

Almost.

Why had he agreed to take her to the OPF? Why was he letting her take pictures of him?

He had so much to do for the launch in February and then more work to get ready for his own mission just a few months later. He had no business fooling around with this PR stuff.

And what, he wondered miserably, would his father have to say about this latest stunt? He could just imagine. The thought of Deke as some kind of sex symbol would blind Jack Stockard with tears of laughter. They'd named him after an astronaut, not a movie star.

For his dad, it was always about flying, ever since they went to their first air show. Together, they had ogled the stunt planes and toured the warbirds. They had sat in the cockpits and Jack had pointed out every gauge and explained its function. As they ate hot dogs under the sweeping wings of a B-52, Jack had explained that his eyes alone kept him from realizing his dream of being a Navy pilot. Deke knew his father always felt that life, although it had been very full with love and good health, had cheated him of his ultimate passion.

Deke had inherited his father's keen coordination, superior instinct and sharp engineer's mind. He did not have Jack's deep brown eyes or their flawed sight. With his own blue eyes came perfect vision and a well-honed sense of purpose that had propelled Deke to Annapolis and Naval aviation. Vindicated, Jack soaked up Deke's career with pride and pleasure, and because of it, they shared a deep connection.

His dad would surely wonder why the hell NASA and that PR agency picked him. Well, he knew why. He knew precisely why. All it took was a quick look down the roster to figure it out. Except for him, every one of them—married. With kids, too. NASA required discipline and personal stability to stay with the program. He had both, in spades. He just had his reasons for keeping clear of anything that resembled a lifelong commitment to one woman. So he got stuck doing the publicity gimmicks.

Watching the Friday-afternoon revelers heading toward the Cocoa Beach pier to play with the opposite sex, Deke grabbed his car phone and punched in a number.

"Hello?" Her greeting was breathless, sexy.

"Hey, doll."

"Deke!" The squeal of delight in Caryn Camden's voice was unmistakable. "It's been so long since I've heard from you!"

Only two weeks. *Is that long?* "How are you?"

"Oh, I'm great, Deke. I'm so happy to—well, it's nice to hear from you." He knew the casual tone was added for effect but, for an aspiring actress, her joy was pretty obvious. He should call her more often. Maybe give her more of a chance.

He had been very turned on by her when she cut his hair a few months ago at some walk-in place near the Cape. He had watched her in the mirror as she trimmed his hair and amused him with animated conversation. All the while, he'd admired her shiny blond curls hanging down her back and the way she filled out a tee shirt and tight jeans. They'd dated several times, but lately he'd been too busy to call. He'd definitely give her another chance.

"What are you doing tomorrow? Have I waited too long to get a date with you?" He had a sense that whatever she had planned, she'd rearrange her schedule.

"Oh, Deke. Um. Let me see. Okay," she said, hard-to-get act lasting about two seconds. "Sure. Tomorrow's great."

"Great. I'll pick you up at six. See you then." He clicked off and swerved right, loving the way the Corvette grabbed the curve and leaned into it. Tomorrow morning he'd have to teach Miss Propaganda a few things about a space shuttle and maybe sneak in a few hours on the boat. Then later, perhaps Caryn Camden's baby blue eyes could distract him from everything else.

Chapter Six

Jessica parked her car in front of the Orbiter Processing Facility at five forty-five Saturday morning. She'd given up her run to beat him there and swore under her breath when she saw the silver Corvette parked in a far corner of the deserted lot. The clash of control freaks was off to an early start.

He sat perched on a retaining wall near the entrance marked Hangar Two, dressed in jeans, a white tee shirt pulled over impossibly wide shoulders.

As she walked toward him, she felt him assess her and instinctively straightened her own shoulders and lifted her chin. He would not intimidate Jessica Marlowe. She repeated the refrain until she reached him.

"Good morning, Commander."

He hopped off the wall and held up a badge. "You need one of these to get in." He slid it through a card reader and held the door for her as they entered the cool hangar. She shivered at the sudden drop in temperature and adjusted her eyes to the bright fluorescent light, following him across the expanse of shiny blue linoleum, past darkened offices and conference rooms.

They turned into a vast, open area where the massive

white space shuttle hung from a wide metal band, elevated about ten feet from the ground amidst a sea of silver scaffolding. Jessica stopped mid-step and stared at it, awestruck.

"Oh my God. It's huge." As they got closer, she could see hundreds of tiny white panels that made up the outside skin of the orbiter, the NASA logo and U.S. flag painted in deep shades across the side.

"One hundred and twenty-two feet long and seventy-eight feet from wing tip to wing tip," he told her as they walked toward the three enormous engines in the back. "It can carry a railroad car."

They continued around the body of the shuttle. Before she could ask one question, Deke spewed technical facts at lightning speed, no doubt to confuse her. She tried to follow, but the size and scope of the vehicle left her speechless.

He explained the role of the crew and described what happens to a shuttle as it makes its eight-minute ride into space. He took each step around the orbiter with confidence and familiarity and that uniquely masculine pride men get over machinery. He seemed to forget he didn't want to be there as he explained how the panels heated upon reentry. Every time he gestured with his strong hands, Jessica's attention was pulled away from the shuttle and riveted on him.

"Can I go in it?" she ventured.

He started to shake his head, then shrugged. "Okay, just don't touch anything." He pointed to a metal ladder near the front of the vehicle. "Go through that hatch. I'll be right behind you."

She navigated the five stairs and pulled herself through the hole in the side of the shuttle. He popped in right after her.

"Living quarters," he explained as she looked around the cramped area. "All the space is in the cargo bay."

She turned to study a sea of displays and gauges, buttons and levers.

"That's the glass cockpit." He put his hands on the back of one of the sleek captain's chairs and raised an amused eyebrow toward the screens. "One and a half billion of your tax dollars to replace the technology of the seventies."

"We better keep that tidbit out of the press release."

"Why?" he countered. "This is what makes it safe. This is the reason we only have one blow up in a thousand launches instead of one in four hundred and thirty-eight."

She stepped back and stared at him. "Are you happy with those odds?"

"Those are the odds I live with."

"Why?" The question popped out before she thought about it.

He assessed her with a long glance. "You probably wouldn't understand."

"Try me."

"If someone didn't take the risk, where would we be?"

Her gaze traveled back to the wall of technology and then returned to Deke, a quote and headline forming in her mind. "We should play that up. You became an astronaut to discover new horizons and make your mark on history."

He put a hand on her shoulder, the warmth of it seeping through her thin cotton blouse. "Spare me *and* the American public that misconception. It has nothing to do with making history."

"Then why?"

His sudden grin blinded her. "Because the son of a bitch flies seventeen thousand miles an hour, that's why."

The shrill tone of a cell phone eliminated the need to

respond. She reached into her bag and flipped open the phone, her attention still on him.

Bill Dugan didn't even give her a chance to say hello. "Man, am I glad I found you. We have a huge problem with *Newsweek*. They're going with a deadly story about NASA cost cutting. They have an insider who says money is tight and the result is dangerous. They claim to have an internal memo, but it's not authenticated and their source won't go on the record."

"Who's the reporter?"

"It's Paul Zimmerman. He covers technology and space but also does features."

"Zimmerman? That's good. I worked with him on a cover story recently and gave him some scoop *Time* didn't have." She'd also plied him with expensive Merlot on her last trip to New York and listened to him gripe about his salary. She could handle this reporter. "What's he got?"

"He's got an unnamed source, strictly off the record, and an internal NASA memo that claims it's just a matter of one more launch till we have another *Challenger* on our hands."

Her stomach rolled at the thought as she watched Deke peer into the cockpit. One in four hundred and thirty-eight. One in a thousand. What kind of man gambles with his life?

"Who knows about this, Bill? Colonel Price?"

"The Colonel, a safety engineer named Skip Bowker, and some of the staff are gathering at Headquarters now. We need you to get over there, prep them, and get Zimmerman on the phone. He's agreed to do one more interview before they decide."

"Decide what?" she asked.

"Whether or not to go with the story. Apparently the editors aren't sure of the veracity of the source."

Jessica looked at her watch. "That means we have about

four hours. *Newsweek* goes to bed at eleven on Saturday morning. Any story can be cut before that. Has Colonel Price gone on the record yet?"

"Nope. Zimmerman will talk to him, but he's looking for a different angle since the Colonel has done *Time* and *USA Today* already and talked about the hydrogen leak."

"A different angle?" Jessica studied Deke as he fingered the leather on one of the cockpit seats, surely listening to her end of the conversation. "I have an idea."

He turned at the tone of her mystery in her voice, a shadow darkening his eyes. She moved the receiver from her mouth and narrowed her eyes in a challenge to him. "You like risks, huh? Are you willing to take one now?"

He scowled at her, but she ignored it and spoke into the phone. "Bill, I think it's time we launched our astronaut."

"Stockard? Is he ready?"

"He's ready," she assured them both, trying not to let Deke's blazing expression weaken her resolve. "Who better to vouch for safety than someone who has to fly the shuttle?"

Deke shook his head in definitive denial. In her ear, she heard Bill continuing. "Zimmerman would love an interview with Stockard. Nobody ever gets the astronauts on this kind of stuff. He'll go nuts for those quotes."

Jessica talked to both of them, looking at Deke as she responded. "We don't want quotes. Not if we do our work right."

"What's the use of doing an interview if he doesn't go on the record?" Bill asked.

"Our goal is to kill the story, not help it get published." She searched Deke's face for any sign that he would relent. "No ink is what I'm after," she said into the phone, a plea and a promise in her eyes. "Commander Stockard can convince Paul Zimmerman that there's no story here." Then she'd lay a little groundwork for the puff piece on NASA's hottest property, the news she'd spoon-feed America.

"Please," she said as she snapped the phone shut and explained to him about the memo. "You can really help on this and it would be a good introduction to the media for you."

He crossed his arms. "You're nuts, you know that? Astronauts don't speak on safety. Colonel Price does. I'm not going to sweet-talk some reporter and tell him there's no danger. Who knows where the hell he got his information?"

"That's what I'd like to know." She bit back a sigh of frustration. "Will you at least come to the meeting? You don't have to do the interview. Just help us formulate a response."

"You don't need me to do that." He stepped toward the hatch they'd just climbed through, inches from her. "I guess we're done here."

Jessica put her hand on his arm to stop him. "Bad press at this time could really set our campaign back. It will take even longer to…get rid of me."

He paused and eyed her warily. "I'll go, but I am *not* getting on the phone with the reporter."

"Of course not," she agreed quickly.

Unless you're ordered to. She knew exactly what she had to do and how to do it. This was *her* version of flying seventeen thousand miles an hour and, like it or not, Deke Stockard was about to come along for the ride.

Jessica's entire demeanor changed on their way to the third-floor conference room of the Headquarters building. She'd been mildly enthusiastic about the tour, but sparks practically shot out of her as she hustled ahead of him. He did a mental review of who had the most to gain from the public knowing about the problems on the shuttle but didn't dare slow his step and risk losing pace with this determined fireball.

When they reached the room, a few members of Colonel Price's staff and some public affairs people had already arrived. He took a seat at the far end of the table, leaning back in the chair and silently cursing the fact that he'd never get to sail today.

Jessica flew into meet-and-greet mode, shaking hands and flashing that tantalizing smile at everyone. Skip Bowker was on her like a fly to honey, too.

"So you're the PR person who's going to put Deke on the map." Skip shot a smile down the table to Deke. "Shouldn't be too hard for you, Miss. He's born to be famous. Named after an astronaut."

"I've got that in his bio," she assured Skip as she shook his hand. "And it's an honor to meet you, Mr. Bowker. I've read about your work on Apollo and the shuttle missions."

Skip furrowed his brows and a twinkle lit his eyes. "I may be thinning a bit in the hair department and hitting the big six-five this year, but don't you want *me* to be on the cover of *People*?"

She treated him to one of those wind-chime laughs, then lowered her voice in a conspiratorial whisper. "You help us get through this and I'm sure we can work out some kind of feature on you."

Skip beamed. Oh, brother. The old man was dead meat with this woman.

"I can help you, Jessica." Bowker leaned closer. "This is all a bunch of malarkey, you know. There are no safety issues. Those shuttles run like Swiss watches. Flawlessly. I guarantee it and you don't have to go any further than that, Miss."

Deke listened to Skip's words and clenched his jaw to stay quiet. He'd better be right.

"We're going to need your help to prove that today, Mr. Bowker," Jessica said.

She had no idea what she was getting into. But it wasn't Deke's job to save her ass. Let Colonel Price do it. The sooner she screwed up, the sooner the Colonel would send her packing.

With every person that came into the room, the sense of crisis heightened. Deke acknowledged Stuart and the Colonel with a terse nod. Before he could explain that he was only here to help formulate the safety responses, Jessica took over the meeting and started grilling the Colonel, leaning forward like a racehorse that needed to be held back at the starting gate.

An uninvited pang of pure sexual desire ricocheted through him. Did she have this much passion about *everything*? She wouldn't be around long enough for him to find out. One bad *Newsweek* article and surely the powers that be would yank her from the assignment.

"Colonel Price, I understand you've spoken to this reporter already. Did you allow yourself to be quoted?" she asked.

"It was strictly off the record. But, these guys…" He held his hands out to indicate "who knows?"

"Damage control has to start with the facts." She looked directly into Price's eyes, evidently not the least bit intimidated by his title or position. "Is there any truth that cost-cutting measures are having an impact on safety, Colonel Price? I can't formulate our response until I know."

Colonel Price stared at her thoughtfully. "Costs have

been cut in a number of areas, but none that would compromise safety."

Deke ignored the fingers of concern that squeezed his gut. The words were true enough. Maybe cost cutting had nothing to do with the problems they faced on *Endeavour*. But if a hungry reporter started digging around, the real story might not be that hard to uncover. Very few people in the room even knew there *was* another story. Including Jessica Marlowe.

She turned her attention to Skip Bowker. "You're the heart and soul of safety at the Cape, Mr. Bowker. What do you think?"

"Ditto what the Colonel says, ma'am. Absolutely everything is in order: inspected, re-inspected and triple-checked—"

Colonel Price held his hand up to interrupt. "We're not going to give them confidential technical information, Miss Marlowe. How can we kill the rumor started by this memo and stop this reporter from yellow journalism?"

"We can drown him in key messages about NASA's unparalleled commitment to safety." She took out a legal pad. "Then we'll confuse and overwhelm him with indisputable, quantifiable, and non-confidential facts."

Deke leaned forward, ready to fire facts at her. Too much too soon could confuse and overwhelm the pretty spin doctor instead of the reporter. At least he hoped it would.

They shot figures at her, answering her questions as fast as she could ask them. From the number of times the shuttles were inspected before a launch to the aggregate years of experience of inspection teams. Skip Bowker knew most of it, but he was a little unsure on circuit inspections and rewiring. Deke filled in the holes with rapid-fire statistics and mechanical terms that had to bury her.

She wrote furiously, throwing back questions, forcing them to fine-tune the answers and sending an occasional dirty look in his direction when he went so fast she couldn't keep up. But, he admitted with grudging admiration, that wasn't very often. In fifteen minutes she had filled two long, yellow pages with bullet points.

Colonel Price reached out and spun the pad to read it. "I can get these across in an interview."

"With all due respect, Colonel, the real goal is to kill the story." She closed her eyes for a moment and shot a look at Deke. "I have a rather unorthodox suggestion."

A black ball of anger formed in his gut. He opened his mouth to argue, but she deftly cut him off, addressing the Colonel with her practiced, professional voice.

"Perhaps Commander Stockard could do it. There is no better person on earth to speak about safety than someone who has to take the risk. And it would be an excellent introduction to the reporter for...our positive publicity campaign."

She tapped a pink fingernail on the page and turned back to Deke. "You deliver these sound bites, but weave them into a heartfelt speech about your belief in the program and why you became an astronaut. You can convince this reporter he doesn't have a story." She looked innocently at the Colonel. "Colonel Price, well, sir, you don't have to fly that shuttle. Commander Stockard speaks for the people who do."

Colonel Price nodded slowly, his gaze lifting to Deke. "I think she makes perfect sense."

The brat. The little she-devil brat. There was no way he could contradict Price in front of all these people. "Of course."

"Here." Jessica slid the pad down the table toward him. "Can you read my handwriting?"

Deke clenched his jaw and stared at her. "I don't need your notes, Miss Marlowe."

She paled. Good. At least she *knew* she'd betrayed him. She cleared her throat and pulled a speakerphone closer to her, tapping an open line.

"I need to present the idea to Zimmerman before we put you on the line," she said over the dial tone. "And I need to remind him of something."

Paul Zimmerman answered on the first ring. "Jessica Marlowe. So you're working on NASA now? You didn't mention that when we had dinner last month."

"A new plum assignment, Paul," she said with a pointed look at Deke. "I couldn't turn it down. We have to get you to Kennedy for the next launch."

"Love it. It'll be a big story when it blows up."

She cringed and looked around the table at the frowns and shaking heads. "It won't."

"I've got an inside source who says budgets are cut so deep that faulty wires are the norm, not the exception. Not what the taxpaying public wants to hear, nor the families of those poor astronauts, I'd imagine."

"Sorry. You've got bad information. Why don't you talk to one of the astronauts?"

"Fat chance. They keep those guys locked up tight until they want to parade them in their orange suits before a mission."

Jessica smiled at Colonel Price. "Not always, Paul. I can get you one of their best. A former Naval officer deeply involved in safety prep. He's piloted *Discovery* and is scheduled to command *Atlantis* next May. Commander Deke Stockard. This guy's great. Honest, smart, and completely trustworthy."

Deke shifted uncomfortably at her blatant promotion of

him. The propaganda was one thing. His nagging fear that the reporter might be closer to the truth than any of them wanted to admit was even more disturbing.

"I'd love to talk to him. How quickly can I get him? I have about an hour to finish the story."

"Or kill it," she added deftly. "I'm at Kennedy now, Paul. I can get him in a few minutes." She paused a moment. "Oh, by the way, any awards coming your way for the IBM story?"

"No Pulitzers yet, but a ton of email and letters. It really got noticed and I've had a few juicy assignments because of it." The reporter chuckled. "I owe you on that one, Jess."

A satisfied smile lit her face, making it obvious that she expected a favor in return for whatever she'd given him in the past. "Why don't you hold a minute? I have Commander Stockard available for you." She stabbed the hold button and looked up at Deke. "Ready?"

He stood and moved into the chair next to her, his resentment rolling in waves that he hoped she could feel.

"What's the matter?" she asked. "Everything you're about to say is true, isn't it?"

"True enough." He reached for the hold button and met her challenging gaze. "Let's get this over with."

After her introductions, the reporter attempted some small talk. "You're not taking *Endeavour* up in February, are you, Commander Stockard? You're taking *Atlantis* up in May, I understand."

Deke didn't try to keep the annoyance out of his voice. "Correct. But since I'm involved with the pre-launch preparation for both missions, let me address this so-called memo you have."

"Fine. How have cost cuts affected safety?"

"They haven't." The smartest thing she'd said was to

bury him in facts and Deke began immediately. In ten minutes, he could hear the reporter's keyboard quiet as he either ran out of steam or interest. Even Jessica stopped taking notes.

"All that may be true, Commander," Paul finally said. "But you can't eliminate all risk, can you?"

"You know, Mr. Zimmerman, we all take risks in this business, but not stupid ones," he answered slowly. "I don't want to die and neither do the men and women I fly with. We participate in or review data from nearly thirty inspections that take place on every piece of equipment on a shuttle prior to launch. When we sit on that launch pad with sixty tons of liquid hydrogen under us, we intend to come home."

The clicking of Paul's keys stopped completely. "I appreciate your time, sir. I hope I get the opportunity to speak with you again."

"If it's necessary."

Deke watched Jessica quickly slide the speakerphone closer to her, giving him a warning look. Hey, he played her game. He didn't have to play nice.

"We can get you a pass for the launch, Paul," she offered brightly. "Can we expect a response today from your editorial board on this story?"

"I'll give you a call before eleven and let you know what's happening. Thanks again, Commander Stockard. Jess, thanks for handling the arrangements."

"You bet," she responded. "Here's my cell phone. Call me as soon as you know what the editorial decision is."

While giving him the number, she leaned her elbows on the table and pulled the sides of her hair up, revealing fine bones and creamy skin. As she hit the speakerphone button, her gaze moved to Deke, relief shining in her deep brown eyes.

"See? That wasn't so bad."

Wordlessly, he stood, knowing the daggers he shot at her had to be felt. She dropped her hair and it fell around her face, hiding her expression before turning to Colonel Price and Skip Bowker. "Do either of you have any idea who could have sent something to the media? Any unhappy ex-employees?"

"My guys are clean," Skip responded. "We haven't had any problems, and I don't have a clue who would talk to the media."

"Whatever piece of paper he claims to be looking at is a fraud," Colonel Price added with certainty.

The conversation stopped when Jessica's cell phone rang. As soon as she answered, her face brightened and she gave a thumbs-up to Colonel Price.

Into the phone, she lowered her voice and turned from the group watching her. "What do you think of Stockard? He's the best story on the Cape. Can I call you next week? I have an idea for a feature."

When she snapped her phone shut, Deke started to leave the room, avoiding her smug smile of triumph.

"Commander." He hadn't made it out the door before she called him. He stopped, but didn't turn.

"I just wanted to thank you," she said from behind him.

He spun around with such force that she literally backed up. "I've already had enough of your fluffy little assignment and your bulldozer approach. You have no idea—*none*—what kind of fire you're playing with." He forced his mouth closed before he told her that a man's life depended on getting that shuttle up on February thirteenth. She didn't need to know that.

Colonel Price stepped into the hallway.

"Excellent work, my man." He gripped Deke's shoulder

in congratulations. "And good thinking on your part, Miss Marlowe. I'm happy to have you on our team."

Great. Price was supposed to kick her out, not welcome her aboard.

"I'm sorry I blindsided you," she finally said, a gentle truce in her eyes and voice. She reached out and, for the second time that day, burned his arm with the warmth of her soft fingers.

His gaze dropped to her hand and traveled back to her face. Her lips parted slightly and she attempted a smile. "Couldn't we just try and work together?" she finally asked.

An unfamiliar twist seized his gut. He took a shallow breath and leaned closer to her. "You are naïve and relentless." Her eyes widened in surprise. "In my opinion, sweetheart, that is a dangerous combination."

He turned and followed Colonel Price. He didn't trust himself to stay that close to her for one minute longer.

Chapter Seven

Bill Dugan killed time logging his billable hours and reading email while he waited for Jessica to call him back. Hell. He billed sixty hours this week alone, he noted as he logged out of the TimeSheets program. He ran a hand through his thinning hair and stood to stare at the wintry gray waters of the Potomac outside his office window.

Some adventurous sailors were out, trying to take advantage of a sunny, if chilly, November Saturday. He, of course, was stuck at his desk, racking up time so that Tony Palermo could get even richer when the British conglomerate that owned Ross & Clayton handed out year-end bonuses.

He mentally calculated how much Tony would make this year. Too damn much, that's what. A digital tone on his desk phone interrupted his math. The readout flashed one of the KSC phone numbers. Jessica must have finished with *Newsweek*.

"How'd it go?" he asked without preamble.

"Fine. Perfect. We deflected the story and I planted a feature."

Naturally, he thought with a rueful smile. Did he really

think Jessica Marlowe could possibly fuck up? He smoothly congratulated her.

"What was your strategy?" Bill asked as he uncapped his Montblanc pen. Better take notes so he could give Tony every detail. She rattled on about circuit inspections and something called a PLIC while he scratched notes.

"Whoa. You're getting technical on me, Jess."

She laughed. "It's in the water down here."

"Well, it sounds like you put Zimmerman off for now, but do you think we should worry about a bad seed being planted at *Newsweek*?"

"This reporter totally owes me for IBM. I'm thinking cover story. I've got his headline. *America Falls in Love with Space Again.*" With a start, he realized she was serious. He heard that ring of confidence he'd noticed in think-tank sessions. "Give me a few weeks and Paul Zimmerman will be putty in our hands."

"That a girl," he said, adding a measure of warmth to his own voice so that she wouldn't be insulted by the politically incorrect usage of the "G" word.

He had to be careful. He couldn't actually say what everyone knew. Women owned the PR field, so it really didn't matter what you called them. It was a female's business. Unless, of course, you owned the shop.

"Now you go enjoy that barbeque tonight, Jess. You earned it."

"Did you hear about that?" She sounded surprised. "Nice of Stu, isn't it? He's a good guy."

Stu? Didn't take her long to cozy up to his client.

"Congratulations, again, on the good work. I'll put a memo in your file."

He heard her hesitation. "Sure. Thanks, Bill."

He didn't even put down the receiver after he

disconnected her call, but punched in Tony's home number from memory. A terse voice mail only frustrated him.

Flipping open his PDA, he typed three letters into the digital phone book. Would Carla be at home on a Saturday or the office? The office, he decided, as he dialed it.

He'd promised to keep her informed on Jessica's progress. After all, Jessica would be working for her when this was all over.

It was all quid pro quo in this business.

The cars were lined up for blocks in the neighborhood of Canaveral Groves where Stuart and Wendy Rosen lived with their seven-year-old twins, Adam and Jake. Jessica arrived nearly a half hour late, but knew Stuart would understand. After the *Newsweek* interview, she'd gone into her office to debrief the account team back in Washington and mentally unwind from the roller-coaster ride she had taken that afternoon.

The last part had been the hardest. She didn't like doing NASA's damage control. *They* had to figure out how to make the damn things safe to fly. She had to turn the astronaut into a celebrity and get home.

Which wouldn't be too hard if he could only do to the camera what he did to her with one intense look. Like the one he'd given her in the hall a few hours earlier. What had he called her, naïve and relentless? Oh, and sweetheart. Called her that a lot, she noticed.

Jessica dabbed on a little lip gloss using the rearview mirror for a final check. A bulldozer. An overachiever. She'd been called them all. And when faced with such a tenuous hold on her hard-earned position, she couldn't care less. Ever since a grade-school-aged Jessica realized that bringing home straight A's erased the sadness in her father's eyes, she'd done whatever was necessary to succeed.

She tucked her yellow silk shell deeper into the top of her white jeans and took a deep breath as she started up the walk to Stuart's house. She didn't have to explain her motives to Deke Stockard or anyone else.

"Hey, it's 'No News is Good News' Marlowe!" Stuart waved from his patio and stepped out the door to greet her. "What a day, huh? Come on in and meet Wendy."

A petite woman with short sandy hair and a quick smile arrived a second later. "We're so glad you're here. Even more so after today. Stuart tells me you were masterful."

Jessica held out a bottle of Chardonnay and laughed self-consciously. "I don't know about that. I didn't do the interview." She leaned forward in a half-hug. "I'm delighted to meet you, Wendy. Stuart talks about you incessantly."

"Stuart talks incessantly about everything. That's why I love him." She returned the hug and led Jessica back into the kitchen.

"I appreciate the chance to get to know everyone like this," Jessica said, taking the glass of wine that Wendy offered.

"Always better to see your crew away from the office and meet their better halves," Wendy said, lifting a tray of stuffed mushrooms. "Come outside with me while I feed the hungry mob."

They stepped through a doorway that led to the patio where torch lamps cast a shimmering golden tone on the pool and outside speakers carried Bonnie Raitt's blues through the air. A boisterous group of familiar colleagues gathered poolside.

Too familiar.

Deke Stockard held a longneck in one hand and pointed

the other toward the sky, punctuating a story with the animated gesture. They all broke into laughter and he lowered his arm to rest it casually on the shoulder of a stunning blonde in a tight denim skirt and low-cut crop top.

The girl laughed heartily at whatever Deke had said and gazed up at him with admiration. He responded with a relaxed smile, something Jessica wasn't sure she'd ever seen before. Then he raised the bottle to take a sip of beer just as he caught Jessica staring at him from across the patio. The bottle froze.

"Oh, there's Deke and, um, Caryn." Wendy turned to Jessica, interrupting the dance in her stomach at the sight of him. "She's his girlfriend. Sort of. I guess." She guided Jessica to the group. "Okay, stop all the tall tales from Stockard and Clark and meet our guest of honor, Jessica Marlowe."

"I've already had the pleasure, Wendy," Jeff Clark jumped in. "It's nice to see you again, Jessica. This is my wife, Debbie."

Jessica made her way through the introductions, ending with Deke's sort-of girlfriend. Who was sort of gorgeous.

A giggle lilted in the breathless voice that matched a nearly flawless face. "We've heard all about you. I'm Caryn Camden."

Jessica looked away from Caryn's perfectly made-up blue eyes to Deke's navy ones. He took a sip and swallowed, studying her with the same intensity he had earlier in the afternoon. Jessica's nerve endings tingled with the same response.

Caryn leaned just a little closer to Deke, so Jessica turned to Debbie Clark. "Did your husband tell you he's been media trained, Debbie?"

"He talked about it for two days. I think he secretly wants

to be on the *Today*show. By the way, great work today."
Debbie touched her arm in congratulations.

"It was a team effort." Jessica glanced at Deke.

His smile didn't quite reach his eyes. "Guess it depends on whose team you're on."

"Does your agency represent actors?" Caryn interjected.

Appreciating the distraction, Jessica nodded enthusiastically. "Oh, sure. We have a division in L.A. that handles quite a few big names. Are you an actress?"

"I'd like to be. Right now I'm a hair stylist, but I go on a lot of auditions. I worked for Disney for several years."

Jessica brightened. "Disney used to be a big client of our firm. What department were you in?"

Caryn beamed. "I played Cinderella and Snow White."

Cinderella and Snow White. Dear God, she was a living, breathing fairy-tale princess. "What a—a wonderful experience that must have been."

Caryn laughed and let her head touch Deke's shoulder in a comfortable, intimate gesture. "I think he's heard about it a little too often."

"Not at all. It must be every little girl's dream come true." No condescension. No mocking *her* determination or enthusiasm, Jessica noticed.

Maybe he loved this blond beauty. The thought formed a little black hole in the pit of her stomach. Not because she cared, but because he needed to be seen with movie stars and celebrities, not princess hair stylists.

For the rest of the evening, she avoided Deke and his ravishing date and enjoyed dinner with a group from the Public Affairs department. Afterward, she leaned against a wall in the living room, half watching the college football game and also listening to the conversations around her. Two women seated on the sofa whispered heatedly.

"Well, it doesn't seem to matter what they do this time," a woman Jessica recognized from administration whispered. "Price won't even talk about a delay in this launch."

"Probably has something to do with the funding," the other offered.

"I don't know. Pat D seems to think it's more than that." Jessica knew that Pat D referred to Pat DiMensini, Colonel Price's secretary. "But Safety and Logistics isn't coughing up the inspection logs with their usual speed." As in most companies, the assistants were the best informed.

One of the women glanced in Jessica's direction, smiling awkwardly. Without a word, Jessica decided to find the powder room and slipped down a hallway off the dining room.

Closing the bathroom door behind her, an exhausted sigh escaped. Running a hand through her hair, she wondered again about the reliability of the information she had given to *Newsweek*. Information she had offered with certainty.

She rubbed her temples to ward away the first beat of a headache and decided to thank Stuart and Wendy and say good night. Tugging the door open, her breath caught in her throat as Deke blocked her way.

"Oh! Excuse me."

"I want to talk to you." He put a hand on the wall, effectively blocking her. Swallowing hard, she stopped and stared up at him.

"What is it?"

"Don't you ever pull a stunt like you did today again." His voice was low and menacing. "Is that clear?"

The doorknob of the bathroom pressed into her back. She considered feigning ignorance but knew it would never work.

"Yes." The intensity of his stare caused a shudder of

intimidation to threaten her stability. She refused to give into it. "That's clear, Commander."

"We will agree before I do any interviews and you will not spring surprises on me in public." He paused and she felt his gaze travel over her face and settle on her mouth. "Or private, for that matter."

Every nerve in her body fought the war of needing to escape and wanting to move closer. The scent of him, the sheer masculinity of him, drew her like a magnet.

"No more surprises. I promise." She heard the strain in her voice. "Only if you promise that you'll unload your resentment and help with this assignment."

"I don't have a choice." He moved an inch closer to her. "I just hope you can handle complications as they arise."

Handle complications? She couldn't breathe.

"Can you?"

Heat shot through her at the demand in his voice. "It depends on what kind of complications you mean."

He refused to move, refused to give her a reprieve from his proximity. "The kind you cause. Public relations complications."

"They're my specialty," she said, gently tucking a strand of hair behind her ear, aware that his hand was centimeters from her face. "I'm not worried about complications, Commander. Just follow my suggestions and you'll be very good at PR."

An unexpected and devilish grin slowly broke his serious expression. His knuckles lightly grazed her cheek. "I'm good at everything, sweetheart."

The hallway closed in on her, tight and airless.

She managed to find her voice. "Regardless of the complications, I plan to be successful." She tilted her head up. One inch, one tiny inch, and their lips would touch.

His navy blue eyes flashed like the electrical current that zapped between them. "But you need me to succeed."

She took a single breath. "As soon as I succeed, I'll be out of your life. Think of it that way."

"Excellent motivation," he whispered and dropped his arm, freeing her. "Good night." He kept his gaze steady on her face, then stepped back. "Jessica."

Her senses seared at the sound of her first name on his lips and the touch of their shoulders as she passed.

"Good night. Deke."

As Caryn turned the key of her apartment door, a sinking sensation rolled through Deke and he willed it away. Her inviting look matched the warm hand she'd kept on his thigh all the way home from the party. The door opened and he saw her cat jump off the sofa, making room for them to start a long session of grappling before moving into the bedroom.

"It's pretty late, Caryn," he said, pausing at the door. "I don't want to wake your roommates."

She turned, disappointment making her eyes even wider. "It's okay, Deke. They're asleep."

She reached one hand around his neck then pulled him closer to her mouth. Instinctively, he bent and kissed her, liking the sweet taste and responding immediately to the pressure of her feminine curves against him.

He let the excitement grow for a minute longer, then squeezed his eyes shut. Desire stirred and the release would have been welcome.

"Caryn, you are sexy as hell and I know you're not teasing me," he whispered into the blond silk over her ear.

She cooed and moved her hips into a painful sweet spot.

Her intentions were clear and it wouldn't be the first time he'd taken what she'd offered. But the looks he got all night from her were clear and she'd gone past just giving her body. Caryn really wanted to give him her heart.

And he just wasn't the one to take it.

He eased out of her tangled arms and hair and planted a platonic kiss on her forehead. "I've got to hit the OPF early again tomorrow," he whispered. "I better not get too attached to how good this feels."

To her credit, she didn't push. Just ran a finger over his lips and requested that he call her.

Ten minutes later, his Corvette slowed as it passed the blue and white house on Sea Park Road where Jessica lived. It was pitch-black inside. He studied the darkened windows and thought of how she'd sauntered out to the patio in those white pants and clingy yellow top. Long legs and inviting curves. Her hair shining in the party light and her eyes glistening when she caught his gaze. Until he cornered her in the hall.

He couldn't stay away from her. As much as he had wanted to ditch the party, he'd gone anyway. As much as he had wanted to avoid her all night, he'd sought her out. Good God, she was trouble.

His body betrayed him with a sudden response at the memory of how close they had stood. How easy it would have been to follow the powerful instincts that rocked him during their little debate in the hallway.

He threw the 'vette into second gear before his musings got too graphic. He shifted in his seat and let the house disappear into the rearview mirror. With a wry smile, he realized that just the fantasy of kissing her had more impact on him than Caryn's very real and impassioned demands.

Chapter Eight

Jessica made her early morning appointment at the North airstrip of Cape Canaveral with a few minutes to spare. She parked next to a beat-up Jeep loaded down with lighting equipment and various cameras, knowing it must belong to the photographer she'd hired from Orlando, Ron Cooper. Stuart had recommended a NASA photographer, but she wanted somebody who worked with celebrities. These weren't going to be traditional NASA headshots. She wanted an artist who could find that perfect angle that made his subject look a cut above the common man.

Ron looked up to the sky after they'd introduced themselves. "We better do this fast. The light's perfect."

"Have you met the Commander?" Jessica asked, glancing at the plane across the airstrip with one man already in the back of the open cockpit and several others milling about or working on the plane.

"Not the friendliest guy in the world, is he?" Ron screwed up his face in mild distaste.

Jessica shrugged. "He's not crazy about the Top Gun role, but I'll talk to him. Your job is to make him look earth-shatteringly sexy. I'll see you over there."

She flipped her leather bag over her shoulder and started toward the plane. Leaning back on its landing gear, the T-38 looked like a slick white cat up on its hind legs, ready to pounce.

Standing next to it in a dark blue NASA flight suit, Deke called to one of the crewmembers on the other side of the tanker. "Hey, Jack, have you checked the harnesses?"

As Jessica approached, he knelt on the ground and pulled hard at a pin near the landing gear with a slight grunt. He never looked at her.

"Let's make this fast, okay?" He yanked at the metal bars between the tires and the plane. "I don't like to be late." He still hadn't turned to her, but she knew when she was being addressed.

"And good morning to you, Commander Stockard." She reached his side and he slowly stood to his full height and looked down at her, the sapphire flight suit deepening the color of his eyes. Jeez. How did he manage it at six in the morning? The earth-shatteringly sexy part wasn't going to be much of a challenge for the photographer.

"You said I have thirty minutes," she said when he couldn't even be bothered with a greeting. "I'm taking it."

He ran his hand through his thick hair and squinted at her. "What exactly do you need me to do?"

"Just do what you're doing. We'll get some candids. Then I'm going to have you pose."

"Pose?" he barked the word. "I'm trying to get a supersonic jet in the air without mishap. I don't have time to pose."

Jeff Clark looked out from the rear cockpit and gave a quick wave. "Hey, Jessica. Don't let him scare you. He's a bear before a flight."

"Oh, nerves at work?" she asked.

Deke glared at her. "No. Brains at work." He went back to the landing gear.

Perhaps a softer tack would work with him. "How long will all these other people be here?"

"Everybody but the crew chief will leave—including you and your cameraman—before we fire up the engines and taxi out. Why?"

"Well, we can do the posed shots when they're gone, if you'd feel more comfortable. How does that sound?"

He yanked the bar again, forcefully. "It sounds stupid, like everything about this stunt. I don't care if they're here, just make it fast." He looked over at a few guys comparing notes on a clipboard. "Okay, yeah. We'll wait until they leave."

While Ron set up his equipment, Jessica imagined the stunning photos they'd get as she watched Deke climb in and out of the plane, studying the gauges of the cockpit, talking softly to Jeff, and delivering instructions in a calm voice to the rest of the ground crew.

When Ron started snapping, Deke glanced up from his inspections, but then ignored them as he completed his routine. Finally, he stepped back and gazed up at the sky, apparently judging the conditions.

She took a chance and interrupted his reverie. "Can I ask you a question?"

He looked down her, still squinting. "What?"

"Can you explain what you're doing? I'd like to be able to write accurate photo captions."

He looked intently at her for a minute, then indicated the back of the plane with a tilt of his head. "I'm going to check the intakes and exhaust." He walked around the aircraft and gestured for her to follow, pointing at oversized metal rings that resembled the inside of a vacuum cleaner to Jessica's untrained eye. Ron snapped away.

"Isn't she a beauty?" An unexpected tenderness crept into Deke's tone. "This is one of my favorite planes. I guess because it's a trainer. You always love the one you learn on." *Click.*

He stepped forward under the wing and bent down on one knee. "C'mere," he said, holding out his hand.

When he gently guided her next to him, he patted the side of the plane. "See the way the fuselage is curved?"

The magic of the curve was lost on her, but not the pure pleasure of being tucked under a plane holding his hand. Her heart quickened as she searched for a response better than, "Uh huh." None came.

"This is one of the most elegant machines ever built. This angle is my personal favorite." He placed her hand on the white metal, covering her fingers with his as he glided her palm over the contour, as sensuously as a caress. "Feel that slide?"

She didn't feel anything but heat, friction, and about a hundred hummingbirds take flight in her stomach. "Yes," she lied.

"That's why it flies supersonic so beautifully." He looked down at her, his face inches from hers, the steel of the plane as warm as the palm of his hand. *Click.*

"It's lovely," she finally agreed.

Awareness flickered in his eyes, a quick connection sparking between their barely parted lips.

Then his mask went firmly into game face as he stood up and let go of her, an unexpected chill that she felt down to her toes.

While most of the ground crew packed up and left, Ron continued snapping candids, then Deke grabbed a helmet with an oxygen mask dangling off the side.

"Can we get the modeling gig over with?" He asked,

nothing but impatience in his voice. "I've got an appointment at Johnson in an hour."

Her eyebrows shot up. "You're going to be in Houston in an hour?"

He grinned and pulled on the helmet. "We go real fast."

"I bet you do." She pointed a finger at his head. "Take it off, Deke. No hat hair in your publicity shots."

Rolling his eyes, he yanked the helmet off and shot the photographer a vile look. "Let's move it."

Ron jumped right in, instructing Deke on where to stand, how to hold the helmet, but each instruction was met with a disgusted sigh as Deke crossed and uncrossed his arms, shifting his weight.

Jessica watched from a few feet away. "Come on," she finally urged. "I thought you were good at everything, Stockard."

Deke shot her a threatening look, then surprised her with a hearty laugh. Ron caught the moment and then everyone magically seemed to relax.

Ron captured Deke in dozens of different poses and various states: smiling, serious, helmet in hand, leaning on the plane. Delighted, Jessica stood back with her hands clasped under her chin. He was perfect.

"All set, Commander. That's a wrap." Ron shook his hand, then Deke pulled the blue NASA helmet back on with a determined snap.

"You all finished?" he asked Jessica.

"Yes. Thanks. You were great. I know it was..." She gave him an apologetic smile. "I know it wasn't your idea of fun."

"No." He climbed into the cockpit and winked at her. "But this is."

The Plexiglas canopy slowly lowered and locked into

place over the cockpit and the crew chief climbed up to check it. Jessica backed away, her gaze still on him. She finally turned to the photographer.

"Here, I'll help you." She picked up a few lenses and lights and walked with him across the airstrip. They said goodbye, and as she reached her car, the powerful engines of the T-38 roared to life, piercing the morning silence with a deafening thunder.

Transfixed, she watched the magnificent machine taxi down the narrow airstrip. The ground vibrated, grabbing Jessica at her very core. In an instant, the shimmering white machine leapt into the air. She gasped as its engines lit up the sky and Deke guided his pretty plane over the tree line. Suddenly it twisted in a perfect circular roll and then flew off at nearly the speed of sound. Stunned, she felt her heart do a matching flip.

Inside the cockpit, Jeff Clark was just as stunned.

"What the hell are you doing, Stockard?"

The helmet muffled Deke's chuckle. "Flirting."

Skip Bowker locked the door of his dilapidated Toyota just as the thunder of the T-38 shook the space center. The familiar rumble seized his gut and he nearly dropped his overstuffed briefcase as he whipped around to find the source of his favorite sound.

Right over the northern tree line, he saw Deke invert the plane into a graceful roll. *Showoff.*

He watched the orange glow of the afterburners as Deke righted the T-38 and shot into the cloudless sky. Kick the tires and light the fires. God, he loved that sound.

With an effort, he stuffed some loose papers back into his

open leather case and headed toward the OPF. Sometimes the ache for the old days threatened to literally stop his heart. What days they were. Long days at Johnson, always tackling some new challenge. And long nights with Betsy, lying under the stars in the flight path of the Houston airport. Whispering about planes and machines. He loved that about her. She got it. The only woman he'd ever met who cried at the unmatched beauty of the sound of a fighter jet hitting the afterburners.

He switched the heavy case to his other hand and struggled to find the plastic badge that would let him into the hangar. He didn't want to think about Betsy today. He was very good at compartmentalizing that pain, like the real engineer that he was.

A quick glance of the parking lot told him he had enough time alone to do what needed to be done. While Deke was gone and no one was breathing down his back.

The OPF was silent except for the tiny squeak of his rubber soles on the tile. He didn't turn on any lights and decided to forego coffee until his mission was complete.

Scott Hayes had come up with a damn good idea yesterday. Skip dropped his heavy bag and sat down at his desk in the darkened corner of the massive facility. He powered up his computer and swallowed hard. Christ, he wanted coffee. His desk clock told him he had about ten minutes until the early risers showed up for work.

He tapped in his password and found the file he needed. There was Scott's memo. He read it again, nodding at the logic. A brilliant engineer, that Hayes. One of NASA's finest. He was just so shy, he wouldn't dare propose an idea in front of the whole team. He always preferred to run things by Skip in writing.

In a few seconds, he was into the email program he

needed. His swollen, arthritic fingers slowed him down so that his brain was always five words ahead of his hands.

He finished the note to Scott, thanking him for the good ideas and assuring him that they would be considered carefully before the launch.

Then he went to the shared notes file and called up Scott's eloquent memo again. Really, really genius.

In one keystroke, he deleted it.

Jessica returned to the Press Facility knowing it was time to jump-start her plan and prime the media pumps. She had nurtured contacts with reporters and editors in the biggest media offices around the country, and she called each of them to get publicity for Deke Stockard. Everyone loved the story and her office buzzed with activity as she faxed and pitched and emailed with determination.

As she reviewed notes scratched onto a media list, a knock on her office door tore her attention from the page. The photographer from the morning session greeted her with a satisfied smile as he dropped a dozen eight-by-ten photos on her desk.

A breath caught in her throat and adrenaline shot straight through to her stomach.

Mouthwatering, heroic, irresistible pictures of one delicious astronaut that no red-blooded American female could resist. Call your Congressmen, ladies, and keep the rocket man in a flight suit.

Or better, out of one.

Ron stood still in her doorway, grinning as he watched her reaction.

"For a guy who hated his assignment, he sure looks like

he was having fun." She laughed a little as she selected a daring headshot for closer inspection. "Wow."

At the bottom of the stack lay a shot of Jessica and Deke, kneeling under the wing of the T-38, his hand over hers, looking directly into her eyes. The intimacy of the captured moment punched her in the gut as she remembered his passion for the plane and the warmth of his hand.

"Why did you print this?" She tried to sound annoyed.

"I liked it," Ron shrugged. "It shows a different side of him."

It sure did. A side Jessica...liked.

She set that print aside. But after she picked the photos and wrote captions, Jessica slipped the shot into her briefcase, hers to keep and savor later.

She worked the West Coast media until long past nine and by the time she got home, she forgot about the picture in her briefcase. Drawing a warm bath, Jessica let the water run through her fingers, remembering the thrill of the T-38 rolling off into the sunrise.

He was right about one thing. That was fun.

She bit her lip, amazed how easily she felt the most feminine reaction to him.

For a moment, she closed her eyes and let herself imagine what it would be like to kiss him, then twisted the hot water faucet off with a jerk. R&C had unambiguous rules about relationships with clients. Wouldn't someone like Carla Drake, looking for every opportunity to seize the upper hand and capture a coveted promotion, just *love* to see Jessica break the rules?

After her bath, Jessica sank into a patio chair with a glass of wine and cordless phone. *Please be home, Jo.*

"Hey, I need you." Jessica blurted the confession as soon as her friend answered.

"I can be there tomorrow. What's the matter?"

Exhaustion mixed with the reaction to the dry, potent wine to form an achy lump in her throat.

"Oh, Jo, I don't know. I'm so homesick and lonely and tired. And I heard a rumor today from someone in New York that Carla Drake is making a great impression on Dash Communications."

"Please," Jo chuckled. "The real rumor is that you've hit the jackpot with this guy and the media wants everything on him. You've got nothing to worry about."

"I've got Carla Drake to worry about."

"Get a grip. She's nothing. She's your shadow. She'll never be Jessica Marlowe. It kills her and entertains the rest of us endlessly." Jo's unique brand of pragmatism and love spread as swiftly as the wine, dulling pain and lifting spirits.

"Okay. I feel better already. Tell me what she's doing."

"No," Jo refused. "She's boring. And skinny. And simply not as much fun as you are. Let's talk about your Space Man."

"He's absolutely..." *Infuriating. Gorgeous. Hot. Sexy.* "He's kind of..."

"Yeah?"

"It's just that I..." *Want him in the worst possible way.* "Think he's a little..."

"Okay, I get the point. Is the attraction mutual?"

Jessica laughed, relieved to have it out. "It might be. It shouldn't be, but there're definitely a lot of...sparks."

"Okay. So he turns you on. What's the worst that could happen? You're both free."

"No. Yes. I think he has a girlfriend who is absolutely stunning, and anyway, he's a client."

Jo snorted in response. "Stupid ancient rules."

"Doesn't matter," Jessica continued. "He's not interested. Frankly, he hates me. At least, he hates my assignment."

"Funny how work *always* prevents you from having a relationship."

Long ago, after many late-night conversations at the office, Jessica had admitted to Jo that she simply had abandoned any ideas of creating a family life of her own. She just didn't have the role model. Jo had dismissed that with a wave of her hand.

"Some were born to breed, Jo. I was born to work," Jessica reminded her again, sipping the wine and searching the night sky for familiar constellations.

Her father had told her that. Like her mother, he said, she was Saturday's Child...she works hard for a living. So Jessica emulated the mother she never knew. Then she didn't feel quite as guilty for getting all tangled up in that umbilical cord and ending her mother's life.

"But in this case, he *is* your work." Jo mused.

"He's a daredevil, Jo," Jessica told her. "A guy who flies supersonic and thinks nothing of climbing onto a metal tube filled with liquid hydrogen that will take him a million miles into space. He loves danger and risk and speed."

"He sounds like fun."

"Right. So does parachuting until you pull the string and nothing happens."

Jo sighed. "Well, I guess you're right to be careful with the R&C rules. The air stinks around Carla and I think she'd love nothing more than to see you crash and burn. Even though she acts like a big cheerleader for you."

"What about Tony Palermo?"

"What about him? He adores her."

"I know how good that can be." Jessica remembered the many times the agency president had called from his corner office at the New York headquarters to tell her she'd been singled out for another promotion or a great new client.

She would not give Carla ammunition against her. Deke Stockard wasn't worth abandoning her dreams of success.

"Jo, I just have to get the job done here and get home. No matter how appetizing the astronaut might be."

"Darlin', you've yet to meet a man you thought was more exciting than your job." Jo laughed softly. "So be careful."

"What do you mean?"

"As soon as he figures that out, he'll be so turned on by you, you won't stand a chance against Captain America."

Chapter Nine

Colonel Price leaned back in his plush leather chair and listened to Deke lay out an airtight argument why, after subjecting himself to media training, a photo session, and two interviews, he should be allowed to drop the PR assignment.

The Colonel nodded but it didn't fool Deke. His arguments were falling on deaf ears.

"It seems we really need you in several places at once, Commander. Wouldn't you rather do an interview with Jay Leno than struggle with Skip Bowker over inspections? He's got legions of engineers there and they're right on schedule with mission prep."

Deke called on every ounce of military training not to react, but he felt his jaw tighten. The *Tonight Show*? Two months from the launch?

This *had* to end.

"Colonel, I don't mind a few interviews and a couple of photo sessions, but, really, I'm concerned about *Endeavour*."

Jim stood and clasped his hands behind his back as he studied the flats of Kennedy out his window. Deke followed his gaze to Launch Pad 39B, the empty gantry breaking the horizon as it reached into the eastern skies.

"I realize that," the Colonel agreed. "All the PR in the world won't help if that shuttle is delayed and Micah Petrenko gets any worse."

"How is he?" Deke asked quietly, taking the mention of the cosmonaut's name as permission to open the delicate subject.

"Same. He'll be fine if we get up there by the middle of February and get him the necessary medication. The doctors feel comfortable we have about that much time. Of course, they want him home. The Russians are anxious and, frankly, it's getting ugly. Remember, he's the nephew of a diplomat."

Deke nodded, happy to have his case supported but not pleased for the sick man floating about on the ISS. "I've been close to Skip Bowker for the past few weeks, sir. I think he's troubled and I'm concerned about its impact on launch prep."

"I know that he's been unhappy for a long time. He's an old space cowboy who lost his wife and *Challenger* in the same year. Not sure he ever recovered from it. He may be tired of the game, but he's still at the top of it."

Deke pressed on. "There's no doubt Skip Bowker is the best in the world and he seems certain that *Endeavour* is tight as a drum. But, there was a fuel leak on *Columbia* and no one can pinpoint why it happened or convince me that it won't happen again."

Jim Price had to know the deadly results of a fuel leak coupled with a common computer bug on the redundant system.

"That's why I'd rather be at the Cape than smiling my ass off for Jay Leno," Deke finished.

Colonel Price turned away from the window to look at Deke. "NASA is very pleased with the results of this PR effort. I know it's a bit of a hardship on your schedule, but the results, believe it or not, are already beginning to show. Work with me for just a few more weeks. I've asked Jessica Marlowe to join us so we can prioritize and arrange your schedule."

The Colonel hit his intercom to call his secretary.

Deke pressed his hands together and leaned his chin on his fingertips, misgivings about the inspection suddenly taking a backseat to the fact Jessica was on her way in.

"I like that young lady," Price confided. "Very professional. Very smart. And quite effective at her job."

"Absolutely, sir." One helluva package. "She really knows her stuff." Deke looked out the window. When he heard the staccato click of her high heels on the tile floor, he tightened in anticipation. Over the past few weeks, they'd reached a working truce and managed to avoid each other except for interviews, but she always elicited a definite physical response that he was determined to hide from the Colonel. And from her.

She strode into the office with her usual confidence and grace, a subtle and now-familiar, clean fragrance coming from somewhere in the vicinity of her dark hair. "Thank you for inviting me to join you."

Price lightened up immediately, apparently not completely immune to her charms either.

"Deke and I were just discussing his schedule. You know, *Endeavour* goes up in nine weeks. We're focused on preparing for that mission to ensure it is entirely safe and successful. Deke plays an important role in that area. However, he certainly is playing an equally important role in our efforts to reinvigorate NASA's image."

"Oh, he is, Colonel." That sparkle danced in her eyes like it always did when she got on this subject. "I think we're making good progress toward our objectives of positioning

Commander Stockard as a—a popular celebrity." He knew she wouldn't dare say sex symbol in front of him.

"Does he have to go on Leno?"

"It is a wonderful opportunity, sir. After the success of that photo release and then the interview in *People*, the timing's perfect. The *Tonight Show* reaches millions of wom—viewers. It won't take long."

She flashed a quick look at Deke, none too happy with him, he bet. They'd had this discussion in private several times over the past few weeks and she was probably ticked he'd brought it all the way to Price. She'd no doubt called in a few favors to get him on Leno.

"It takes too long to get to L.A.," he said.

"Can't you fly a T-38 and be there in a couple of hours?"

He leaned back and returned her glare. "The airfare is about a hundred grand of taxpayer money for me to fly a T-38 to L.A. and about seventeen million if something happens to it. How do you handle *that* in the media?"

"We haven't had any negative reaction so far, Deke, and you know it," she replied. It's been overwhelmingly positive. You have a Q quotient—a popularity rating—of twenty-six already. That's really unheard of after only a few weeks of publicity. You're becoming a household name." She turned to Colonel Price. "This can only reflect positively on NASA...and the funding, sir."

Deke didn't even listen to Price simpering in agreement after she pulled out *that* trump card. Damn, he couldn't spend this much time away from Safety and Logistics doing any more of this stuff. Each phase of engineering and safety inspections was crucial and he wanted to personally run the computer programs and touch those wires and peer inside each crevice of that shuttle. He *had* to before it got on the crawler and started its long, slow haul down the three-mile gravel road to the launch pad. Then it would be too late. Another thought nagged at him.

"Are you going to L.A.?" he blurted out to her, realizing too late that he'd interrupted the Colonel.

She raised an eyebrow. "I wasn't planning to. You'll be escorted by one of our people out there. We have clients on the *Tonight Show* as a matter of course. It's very routine."

"Okay. Whatever." He waved his hand in dismissal, wishing he hadn't asked. Wishing, for some infuriating reason, that she'd said yes. Damn, this had to come to an end. Quickly.

Colonel Price had clearly taken sides. "It really makes sense, Deke. Take the T-38 to Edwards and you can be back the next day." The Colonel's phone interrupted him and he picked it up and turned away into another conversation.

"What *is* the problem?" Jessica whispered at him, a sarcastic edge lacing her voice. "Do you really think everyone's going to fall apart without you for a few days?"

He stared at her, unable to stop the smile from creeping across his lips. "Only you, sweetheart." Then he thoroughly enjoyed the flush that spread over her pretty face.

☆\

Deke arrived at the Orbiter Processing Facility at daybreak, knowing he had a few precious hours before the pre-flight check of the T-38 and his solo flight to L.A. for the Leno thing. He hoped to beat Skip Bowker to the facility, although the man was known for his pre-dawn arrivals and late-night departures as launch dates drew near.

There were only a few technicians around as Deke ran his access card through the reader and entered the cold and cavernous Hangar Two. *Endeavour* rested silently in the center of the facility, still raised on its landing gear, the mouth of the cargo bay opened wide in anticipation of the rest of the gear and supplies that would be strapped into place prior to launch.

The hangar was virtually soundless except for the hum of a few machines and Deke's footsteps as he walked back to the technician's offices that lined the north wall. He stuck his head into the only one that was lit and occupied by Mike Biggars, another engineer Deke knew well. "Morning, Mike."

"Hey, Deke. What are you doing here? I was just reading about you in the paper. So cool that you're going to meet Leno!" The wiry young technician held up a section of the local paper with Deke's picture in full color. A resident astronaut appearing on The Tonight Show rated big coverage. At least it did when he had an unrelenting she-wolf as a publicist.

"Listen, I need to get into the Pre-Launch Inspection Check files while I'm here. Whose computer can I use?"

"Scott Hayes won't be in for a while. Right next door." Mike pointed with his thumb to the dark, glass-walled office behind him. Deke nodded thanks, flipped the lights in Scott Hayes's tidy office, and powered up the monitor.

Using his own password, Deke quickly called up the files and logs he needed. Scanning through each of the dozens of sections, all detailing the painstaking inspection process for every component of the shuttle, Deke frowned and leaned toward the screen. There were so many holes. So much of these routine things should have been done by now. All the wiring reports checked out, but what about the forward reaction control systems? It didn't make sense. Some piece of the technical puzzle was missing.

He called up another file and glanced around Hayes's

perfectly ordered desk while he waited for the computer to respond. In a standing file folder, he read the neatly typed labels. One was marked PLUG RECS. Recommendations? He reached for it just as the log he wanted flashed on the screen and stole his attention.

Even more holes in this log. When he looked up into the hangar, he noticed more lights were coming on in the offices. He had to talk to Skip. Switching off Scott's monitor, he went in search of a second cup of coffee and Skip Bowker. He found both on the floor of the hangar, with Skip standing behind one of the massive exhaust systems of the orbiter Endeavour.

"Well, if it isn't Mr. Movie Star." Skip held up his steaming cup in a mock toast. "Guess we'll all have to stay up late tonight, eh?"

Damn, this thing was going to ruin his credibility along with his inspection schedules. "Don't let me cut into your beauty sleep, Skip. God knows you need it." Deke put his hand on the older man's shoulder. "Got a minute? I just went through the PLIC and I couldn't find a couple of things. Can you help me out?"

"What're you looking for, Deke?"

"Forward reaction logs? Coolant tube checks?" The list was longer than that, but he didn't want to attack.

Skip cocked his head and looked askance at Deke. "Not there? Both done, several times. These guys must be getting a little behind on the record keeping, but I know they've been done." They started to walk together into Skip's office. "Listen, Deke, would you sign my copy of the newspaper? My niece out in California is hounding me for something from you." He chuckled as he handed Deke a ballpoint pen. "Don't worry about the inspections, my friend. You got bigger things to do for NASA now."

Deke could feel his blood boil with Bowker's blatant kiss-off. The autograph business riled him even more. But an attitude wouldn't get him what he wanted.

"Yeah, well, my focus is still in this hangar, Skip, and on these inspections. I hate to be such a pain, but you know what's at stake."

Skip shook his head. "The next one's the biggie, man. Your first flight as Commander. The press ought to eat that up."

Deke caught himself before he swore under his breath. "Forward those logs to me by email after they're done? I'll be back tomorrow."

"Sure, Deke. No problem. Now, here, can you sign this right here under your picture?"

Deke grabbed the newspaper and scratched his name with a pen Skip handed him. Without a word, he dropped it on Skip's desk and shot him a warning glare. "Email the logs right away."

He didn't remember the file on Scott Hayes's desk until he'd already finished the T-38 inspection and taxied down the runway. Damn it all. He had to get away from all this distraction. As soon as *Endeavour* went up—safely—he would use his impending command of *Atlantis* as the airtight excuse to get off this assignment. He might miss that girl's sexy smile and snappy wit, but he wouldn't miss what she put him through.

The day of Deke's *Tonight Show* appearance started early for Jessica, who watched the sunrise during a hard morning jog and was at her desk at NASA operations before eight. She checked email and prepared for a mid-morning conference call with the account team, including the L.A. people who were handling Deke. She wasn't surprised when her phone rang before eight thirty, expecting Bill Dugan to check in early.

"Hello, Jessica. It's Carla Drake."

Oh, what a lovely way to start the day. "Hi, Carla. How's it going?"

"Awesome, Jess. And how about you, with a client on the *Tonight Show*! Are you excited?"

For some reason, she hated that Carla knew what was happening on her accounts. Sure, it was probably posted all over the agency email loops, but it still irked her.

"Too busy to be excited, Carla. What's up?"

"I wanted to call and congratulate you."

"Well. Thanks." That couldn't be all. It wasn't possible. "How are things at Dash?" She steeled herself for the ultra-positive spin Carla would surely put on her relationship with Jessica's biggest client.

"Great. Surely you've heard about the new campaign."

"Mmmm." Jessica clicked into her email for distraction.

"Tony thinks it's Silver Anvil material for the agency."

For the agency? Or for the *interim* account manager? "Super, Carla. Can't wait to read the marketing plan. When will I get it?"

"Oh, you have so much on your mind with the space program, Jess. Don't worry about it."

She clicked out of email and switched the phone to her other ear. "I'll be up at Christmas to meet with the client, so do me a favor and send it. I'll want plenty of time to review the program in advance." *Don't cut me out, sister.*

"You won't need to see the client, Jess," Carla said, far too smoothly. "By then your new position will be announced and Dash won't be on your account list anymore."

A slow burn warmed Jessica's stomach. "What new position?"

Carla was silent. Ominously so. "Uh, didn't Tony tell you yet?"

The hair on the back of Jessica's neck tickled with a gust of the political winds Jo had warned her about. "Tell me what?"

"Well, when you get back—unless you've fallen in love with Florida and decide to stay—"

"No. I'll be back at the scheduled time, after the shuttle goes up on February thirteenth."

"You've been named the head of the new Emerging Technologies division."

Jessica squeezed her eyes shut and tried to make sense of the words.

"Congratulations," Carla added.

"What in God's name is Emerging Technologies?"

"The goldmine of accounts I used to run in Silicon Valley when I had my own agency. About five of them have committed to R&C as the foundation of our new high-tech division. Bill Dugan says you've become a technical whiz, so it's a perfect place for your skills."

Anger and denial flooded through her. She was getting Carla's cast-offs. A bunch of bankrupt dot-coms and start-ups with no budgets. She modulated her voice with practiced precision. *Pick your battles.* "I don't think I'll be taking that assignment, Carla."

Carla tsked into the phone. "No? I'm surprised. But, if you'd like me to talk to Tony for you, I will. Since you're so far away."

"Thanks, but I'll handle my own negotiating." She had to get to Tony and make him understand. She had worked too hard to get strangled by the strings this conniving bitch had been pulling behind her back. "I have to go, Carla. I'm in the weeds with work today."

"Oh, sure, Jess," Carla cooed. "I'll be watching your astronaut on TV tonight. I saw the piece in *People*. Yummy." She lowered her voice and laughed. "I hope you're getting a piece of that, honey."

The rush of blood walloped Jessica's head. "Oh, Carla. You do have an active imagination."

"Come on, girlfriend. Give me the details."

Girlfriend? Revulsion rolled through her. "Sorry, no details. Gotta go."

She hung up just as Stuart came in her office, before she had a chance to compose herself.

"Hey—you don't look so good."

She swallowed hard and did her best to wipe the emotion from her face. "I'm fine."

"This message came in for you while you were on the phone." He handed her a pink slip. *Liza Watson. Producer, the* Today*show. Calling about DS appearance. Call back ASAP.*

Jessica let out a little gasp. The *Today*show. In *New York* – it was her ticket to Tony. "Stu-*ey*. You are my guardian angel."

He grinned. "I knew you'd be happy about that one, although Stockard'll balk at the travel. The T-38's are all booked for a couple of weeks. Can they do a satellite feed?"

"No, it's never as good. Our Commander can fly commercial for once. He's not going to miss this interview. No way." She treated Stuart to her brightest smile. "I'll take him there myself."

Within a few hours, she had finalized Deke's appearance on the *Today* show for the following Monday morning. It had been so easy. The producer handed her off to an assistant, probably because the regular anchors had already started long holiday vacations. It wasn't that big of an interview, especially since he'd go on air with a young stand-in anchor, Caroline Hunter. Jessica breathed a sigh of relief. Pure fluff and tons of it. Just what she wanted.

She arranged for them both to fly out Sunday night, giving Deke more time at the Cape. He could come home any time Monday after the interview and she would be on Tony Palermo's calendar for a lunch meeting. Tony needed to see her to remember how much he liked her. No matter how well things were going, this disappearance was professional suicide.

Despite the threatening news from Carla, Jessica hummed an upbeat tune as she drove home, fixed some dinner, and waited for the call from Lydia Davis, the account contact in L.A. who'd escorted Deke to Burbank. She calculated the time difference and knew that the taping would start around eight East Coast time. She wondered what he'd say if she called to wish him luck. Something sarcastic, probably.

Lydia's call came at precisely ten p.m. "I think you'll be happy, Jess. He was damn good."

"Really? Well, he's—"

"He's gorgeous, funny, smart, and sexy. You've got yourself a winner, girl," Lydia cooed.

"He's not mine. He's NASA's. And now, America's."

"Really? The way he talks about you, I figured, well...anyway, you watch the show. You'll be happy. I've gotta go."

A thrill slid through her. She couldn't believe he'd say anything that wasn't derogatory about PR in general and her plans in particular. She mentally replayed Lydia's words right up to eleven thirty-five, when she turned up the volume on the TV facing her bed. She crossed her fingers in front of her chest and whispered, "Come on, Stockard. Amaze me."

Leno seemed particularly sharp during his monologue. Then, he promoed Deke with a teaser, calling him 'the coolest thing in a space suit since Clint Eastwood.' Jeez. Deke would hate that.

He was Jay's second guest after a young actor with three names who'd starred in a movie called *The Sixth Sense*. As Deke sauntered onto the set in a Hollywood black blazer and black collarless shirt, a band of anticipation squeezed her. Here you go, Commander. *You gotta play ball in the big leagues.*

Lydia had understated. Cool, funny, a little self-deprecating and completely in command of the interview, Deke adroitly handled Jay's needling. He was divine. Pride and attraction and anxiety volleyed through her until the end of the seven-and-a-half-minute interview.

Then Jay brought out a breathtaking model from Sweden who was just announced as the cover girl for the *Sports Illustrated* Swimsuit edition. As much as she wanted to switch off the TV, Jessica remained mesmerized, watching the lithe beauty flirt outrageously with Deke.

"Ven you get lonely in outer space, you read the issue, yes?" Her hand rested on his arm and she leaned her lush body closer to him.

"Only the articles, ma'am," he quipped. Jessica imagined the feel of his muscular arm in the model's hands and hated the sensation it caused in her stomach.

But this is what she wanted to have happen. It's perfect. Let it go in the *National Enquirer* that these two started up a steamy affair after the taping of the show—

The jangling phone interrupted her thought. Of course, Bill Dugan or Jo would call to congratulate her. She grabbed the phone on the second ring.

"So, how'd I do?" Deke's voice was low and sexy and Jessica thought she just might drown in the sound of it.

Leaning back into her stack of pillows, pure joy washed over her. "Nice wardrobe choice."

"You expected my Navy uniform?"

She laughed. "I knew better than to counsel you on what to wear. You'd just do the opposite anyway. You were great."

"Leno is funny as hell." He sounded relaxed.

"You knew you'd get the inevitable bathroom in space question."

"You called that one the day you were playing the pretend *Today*show," he said.

It reminded her that she had to ruin the moment by telling him he had to travel again. "Speaking of the *Today*show, you're booked for next Monday."

"What? It better be a satellite feed."

"Listen to the media mogul," she teased. "No, you've got to do it in person, Deke. Please. This will be the last one for a while. It's a stand-in anchor. Piece of cake. Please."

He sighed. "At least it's home. I could see my parents."

His comment erased some of the guilt she had about pushing for the in-person interview for her own selfish reasons but left her a little curious about the family he had there. She started to ask, but something stopped her. She didn't need to know about his perfect family.

"Good. We leave Sunday night."

"*We?*"

She tried to sound noncommittal. "I have some other meetings there, so I thought I'd go to the set with you for moral support."

"I don't need it, sweetheart. But you're always welcome."

The tone in his voice and the endearment, however sarcastic, tantalized her. Oh, how she wanted to continue that train of thought. Not a good idea.

"Well, thanks for calling," she said, hoping it didn't sound as lame to him as it did to her.

"No problem. I figured you were still up critiquing the performance."

"I'm surprised you had time, Deke. I figured you'd be having a late dinner with Helga the swimsuit model."

"That's my next call."

She could only laugh a little in response. "Good night, Deke."

Chapter Ten

Throngs of disheveled families, tense from travel with high-strung youngsters, packed every corner of Orlando International Airport. Jessica dodged a ten-year-old with his face stuck in a handheld video game as she rushed to make the pre-arranged seven o'clock meeting.

As she approached, she saw Deke at the gate, dressed casually in work boots, jeans, and a blue oxford shirt. His attention seemed riveted on the aircraft on the other side of the glass, but he turned just in time to catch her staring at him. Her mind raced to think of a neutral greeting that would hide the impact he always managed to have on her.

"You look confused." He stood and stepped toward her.

Confused. That was one way of describing it. "I'm just trying to figure out if you're going to bite my head off or be a polite military man and take this bag."

"I *am* polite." He reached for the suitcase handle and rolled it to where he sat. "I made friends at the desk so you can sit next to me on the plane."

Every muscle tightened at the thought of being thigh-to-thigh with him for three hours. "I thought we had pre-assigned seats."

"We did, but somehow we weren't together." He smiled

and moved his jacket so she could sit down. "But I rectified that. You'll see when you check in."

She tried to shrug casually. "I figured you'd want to sleep or read or second-guess the pilot."

His slow smile was like a wake-up call to every female cell in her body, not that any of them were sleeping with him around. "You just hate it when I mess with your careful planning, don't you, Jessie?"

The nickname rolled off his lips. A name she'd rarely been called, a name that he made sound…sexy.

Determined not to let him know his effect on her, she reached for her handbag and checked out the line to the desk. Not too long. "At least the flight isn't full. Still, I have to check in."

"So you can escape to an empty seat?" He leaned closer and she caught his scent. Clean and masculine and…heady. "Don't you want to try a one of your simulated interviews to get me ready for the big day tomorrow?"

"No need, Stockard. You're a pro. I'll just fire up my laptop and work. I won't bother you a bit." She walked away and took a place at the back of the line. After a moment, she looked back at him. He grinned lazily. She flashed a controlled smile in return.

Oh boy. It was going to be a long flight.

After the boarding call, they followed the routine of finding their row, storing luggage and getting settled in Twelve C and E. Seat D appeared to be blessedly empty.

He stowed her bag and coat and offered her a choice of the aisle or window before they sat down.

"You'd probably be more comfortable in the aisle, so I'll take the inside." She slipped into the window seat and he settled into the aisle seat.

"To be honest, I'd only be comfortable up there." He

pointed to the front of the plane. "This is not a natural place for me in any aircraft."

"Don't tell me you're scared of flying?"

His laughter rang through the quiet cabin. "No, Jessica. I just like to be in control."

"Mmm. I know the feeling."

"I'm sure you do." He pushed his seat back and tried to stretch in the cramped space. "Are *you* afraid of flying?"

"I don't like it. I know the statistics are in my favor." She looked out the blackened window. "But they do go down."

"Don't worry. There's no weather tonight and that's the real problem in most cases. That and pilot error. This is a 727. It's solid and has a phenomenal safety record. It's pretty simple to fly."

"Can you fly this, too?"

He raised a brow. "I can fly anything with wings."

She turned to the window and studied his reflection in the glass, speckled with beads of condensation. As they taxied down the runway, the hushed, darkened plane and their proximity to one another invited intimacy. She decided to ask him something that she'd wondered about since the day she'd media trained him and he spoke fervently about 'not coming home from work.'

"Are you ever afraid that you are going to die in…in your line of work?"

He didn't answer immediately. "Not if I'm in control and I know everything's been inspected and is functioning properly." He ran his finger along the armrest. "But there's no way to anticipate everything when you're moving at hundreds of miles an hour, avoiding incoming missiles, or landing on a carrier in rough waters. You can only be about ninety-nine percent sure. Never a hundred."

"Have you ever come close?" Jessica didn't try to hide the concern and curiosity in her voice.

He nodded. "I had to bail out of an FA-18 in the Persian Gulf. It was hairy." He waited a beat and looked at the window behind her, then back into her eyes. "I lost a really good buddy that same day."

"I'm sorry." She couldn't fight the natural response to touch his arm across the empty seat.

His deep sigh was from the heart. "He left behind a beautiful wife who was expecting their first child. Now that little guy is, well, however old you are in eighth grade. And he's just as full of it as his dad was." His smile broke the mood and she casually removed her hand. "Anyway, to answer your question, shit happens."

His tone effectively closed the topic, leaving her to wonder if she'd opened a tender wound. When they reached cruising altitude, he paged through a magazine without reading a single article and she pulled out her laptop.

"Don't you ever stop working?" he asked, his chin resting on his knuckles as he watched her.

"Only on special occasions. But I have a very important meeting with the president of the agency tomorrow and I want to prepare my notes. Will I bother you?"

"Not at all. Want to tell me about it so I can offer unsolicited advice?" He leaned over a little to look at the screen. She lowered it out of his view.

"No. Thank you." That she'd left on an assignment only to get squeezed out of her position by the competition was the last thing Deke Stockard needed to know.

"Suit yourself. But I'm really good at—"

"Everything. I know."

He laughed softly. "That's right." He closed his eyes and left her alone for the rest of the flight. She tried to think. To input her arguments to Tony. To prepare for her battle. But she remained acutely aware of the man next to her. Somehow, Deke Stockard managed to invade her every thought.

Jessica slept fitfully in her room at The Plaza following their late-night arrival in the city. By five o'clock, she was up and dressing, sipping coffee from room service and trying to organize her strategy for the day ahead. By six, she was ready to meet him in the lobby, walk to Rockefeller Center and then, after his interview was over, she'd plead her case with Tony Palermo.

As the elevator door opened, she saw Deke leaning against a white marble column near the front desk, reading a copy of *The New York Times*. He wore dark trousers and a coffee-colored sweater over a shirt and tie. He'd hooked his bomber jacket on one finger and had hung it over his shoulder, ready for the brisk temperatures.

At the sound of the elevator opening, he looked up with a gleam in his eye that jabbed straight to her heart. The tiniest moan escaped her lips.

Treating her to a half-grin, he folded the paper as she approached him.

"Morning." His voice was soft, confidential, as though they shared a secret mission.

Jessica reached deep down for every ounce of professional training in her, but her true thoughts just came tumbling out. "You know, I sell a lot of products for a lot of companies, but you certainly have the best packaging."

"Is that what I am? A product?" He groaned.

She turned as he helped her slip into the sleeves of her

coat. "Sorry, but we're positioning the brand, Deke. NASA is the brand and you are their top-selling commodity right now."

He shook his head. "I hate being a commodity."

As they nudged their way through the heavy glass doors, the icy December air stung their faces. Jessica took a deep, invigorating breath. "Oh, this is heavenly. Probably too much for your thin Florida blood. Want to take a cab?"

"You keep forgetting I go into space for a living. It's cold there. I defer to you on the transportation."

"Great. Let's walk. It's only eight or nine blocks."

They started off down the sidewalk, assaulted by the temperature, the pungent aroma of exhaust fumes, and Manhattan's constant din of trucks and traffic. They kept a brisk pace, their breath coming out in soft white puffs, their steps synchronized. When they turned the last corner and were met with the glorious sight of the giant Christmas tree in Rockefeller Center, Jessica's gasp broke their silence.

"Look, Deke!" She couldn't keep the excitement out of her voice. "Isn't it beautiful? I love New York this time of year."

"I used to come here every year with my family at Christmas," he told her as they paused at a steel rail overlooking the world-famous Rockefeller Center skating rink. "My mother insisted we all see the Christmas Show at Radio City and eat goose at Luchow's. It was the official start of Christmas."

She closed her eyes for a moment, imagining what it must have been like to have such unwavering family traditions. "Where do they live?"

"In the house where I grew up, in Westchester. My sister is in L.A. In fact, I saw her after the Leno taping. The senior Stockards will never leave New York, but they have come down for a few weeks in the winter since I've been at the Cape."

She longed to know more about his family, but a noisy and excited crowd gathering outside the studio diverted her attention. "We better get going, Deke."

"Aren't you going to brief me before this interview?"

She buried a pang of guilt for not doing a more thorough job of prepping him. "Just expect more of the same. Like Leno, *People* and the rest."

He didn't respond, his gaze riveted on the gathering mass of tourists. "What the hell—?"

She immediately saw the two homemade, hand-painted signs: "DEKE MAKES ME WEAK!" and "FLY ME TO THE MOON, DEKE STOCKARD!"

With a gleeful giggle, she punched him on the arm. "See? It's working! It's working!"

He muttered a curse and glared at her as they entered the elegant lobby of the NBC offices. "Will you stop gloating?"

But she couldn't keep the smug smile off her face, all the way into the studio and through the introductions to the crew and producers. Her sense of victory stayed while she waited as Deke went through makeup and briefings. Liza Watson, the producer, confirmed that Deke was on after the 7:30 news update.

"I'm surprised it's so early," Jessica said to Liza as she settled in a visitor's chair at the far side of the set. "You guys usually save the fluff for the 8:30 segment."

"This isn't fluff," Liza responded coolly, sending an icy chill up Jessica's spine. "Some Russian's dying up in space. We don't consider that fluff."

Speechless, Jessica stared at the producer. Liza held up a finger to silence her and whispered into her headset.

"Quiet on the set. We're going live in three...two...one."

Chapter Eleven

The interviewer and Deke suddenly seemed a million miles away. Cameras and grips and lights blocked her way, but she could see Deke facing the eager young anchor as the news wrapped and a red light flashed at the studio door. Jessica had no way to warn him.

Some Russian's dying up in space. What in God's name was she talking about? She didn't breathe through the whole introduction and bit her lip in anticipation of the first question.

"Commander Stockard, our sources in Moscow inform us that there is a medical emergency on board the International Space Station at this very moment. We understand that the Russian cosmonaut currently residing there is near death. Can you provide some details on that?"

Jessica's entire body turned to water. How could she have been so blindsided? By selfish opportunism, that's how. She'd been so anxious to get to New York, she hadn't even researched this story, grilled the producer, or called any inside contacts to get a handle on the interview.

She watched for his reaction, noting that not an ounce of color drained from his face. "You're referring to Micah Petrenko. He is most certainly not near death. The International Space Station is well-supplied with medical equipment and life-support systems and the health of those on board is monitored closely on a daily basis by a medical team on earth."

"But he has a blood clot."

"I'm not on his medical team, ma'am."

Good answer, Deke. Don't let her take you down the rabbit hole.

"Even so, he's a bit of a medical guinea pig?"

"The men and women who live on the ISS are not guinea pigs, but scientists challenged to conduct research that ultimately improves our own quality of life on earth."

The interviewer glanced at her notes. *Come on, throw a softball, lady.*

"Are you aware he's the nephew of a Russian diplomat?"

"I've heard that." He had? Nobody had mentioned it to the person doing the PR.

"Many critics of the space station question the need for humans in space. They say zero gravity possibly weakens the bones, the muscles, and as in the case of Cosmonaut Petrenko, the cardiovascular system. Wouldn't it be safer— and cheaper—to have the space station unmanned?"

The muscle in his jaw tightened. "Safer and cheaper, but not nearly as effective."

"Why isn't this poor man being brought home?" She leaned forward, going for drama. "Isn't there some sort of emergency escape vehicle?"

"His condition isn't life threatening."

Jessica recognized the technique of not answering the question, which they'd talked about in media training. Maybe he had been paying attention, after all.

"Why isn't NASA talking about it? It's not like the organization is publicity shy. Certainly you've been making the media rounds lately."

Don't take the bait, Deke.

"A medical situation that isn't life threatening on the space station isn't news." He leaned forward slightly. "Unless you decide to make it news. The ISS is a joint project between America and Russia. We are working closely together to monitor Micah's situation."

The anchor flipped to her next note card. Now comes the fluff, Jessica prayed. "There are reports that the last shuttle launch, *Columbia*, was within seconds of blowing up—like *Challenger*?"

Jessica squeezed her hands into tight balls, sweat stinging under her hair and arms despite the chilly studio. She stood on her toes to see the assistant director noting the time. *Please, let this be over.*

"No, ma'am. *Columbia* was never in any peril. The shuttle commander had to opt for a different orbit because of a fuel leak, but the numerous redundant systems that are in place to anticipate those kinds of situations ensure the safety of—"

"Could it happen again?"

"We're doing everything in our power to make sure it doesn't."

Jessica's nails dug deeper at the skin of her palms with every question and every answer.

"Commander Stockard, what, if not safety, is being cut by NASA in the wake of budget restrictions?"

She looked at a monitor as the camera focused on his face. Just a shadow of discomfort darkened his expression, but he remained calm. "There are literally hundreds of line items in our budget, ma'am. But nothing in terms of training or safety is at stake. In fact, our inspection equipment and personnel have been dramatically increased over the past few years."

"What if this man dies in space? Who is responsible?"

Deke spoke softly, evenly, with no condescension or

malice. "NASA has an extraordinary safety record when you consider what we do, how we do it, and the fact that most of it has never been done before. Is there some risk involved in space exploration? You bet. Calculated risks that come with any exploratory venture that allows us to grow and learn and literally expand our universe. Is there stupidity involved? Only from people who think NASA would carelessly risk the life of any man or woman for any reason."

The assistant director held up a ten-second hand signal and Caroline mercifully wrapped the interview. Jessica finally exhaled. She should have known this was coming. Deke would be furious. And Colonel Price. And, oh God, Tony Palermo. What a day to screw up.

She watched Deke shake the reporter's hand and quietly leave the set. He didn't look around but walked directly back to the dressing area, presumably to calm his temper. She didn't think he'd leave without her, but she momentarily debated if she should try to find him or Liza Watson. She decided on the producer.

"I'd like to have a word with you," Jessica whispered when she found Liza in the crowded control booth, watching the show on sixteen different monitors and whispering hushed directions to the camera crew through her headset.

She glanced at Jessica. "I know, I know. Caro likes to play tough, but he was fine."

Jessica knew she had to tread carefully, but the anger simmered just under the surface. "Why didn't you warn us? We had every right to be more prepared for that."

The producer put her hand over her mouthpiece and frowned at Jessica. "Look, the leak came out of contacts in Russia, not NASA. Anyway, we spoke with someone from your agency yesterday for confirmation or denial."

A chill swept over her. "Who did you speak with?"

"Some woman in Boston who works with you."

Jess stepped aside as Liza brushed by her to get to the set. "Why would you call Boston on this interview? Why not the Cape? Why not NASA PR?"

"One of the other producers heard NASA was now your project. He called your office and was put through to whoever's taken your place in Boston. They were supposed to get in touch with you and tell you. I gotta go."

Jessica squeezed her eyes shut. She had no more fight with the producer.

With his face cleansed of the sticky makeup they had put on him, Deke continued to rub his cheeks and chin with a rough hand towel provided for guests in the dressing area. The room was empty, but he wouldn't have cared if the President of the United States stood next to him. He whipped the damp towel into the porcelain basin and stared at his reflection. "What the goddamn hell is going on? Why didn't she know what I was getting into?"

He took a deep breath and continued to stare but didn't see his reflection. His logical brain was trying to figure out the events, to understand where a leak could have come from and, much more troubling, determine how close these people were to the truth. How sick was Petrenko? What if they didn't get up there in time? Could they be sure *Endeavour* could fly safely?

There'd be hell to pay everywhere for this. Starting with that know-it-all-'it's going to be just like Leno' Jessica Marlowe. She probably let him go on just to bask in the glory of getting her client on the *Today*show. No doubt that was the big time in her business.

No, no. She was too smart for a stunt like that and she had to know that the fallout from this could be fatal to the program. No doubt the phones on Capitol Hill were lit up with angry constituents who would like to kill NASA's budget and start a Save the Cosmonaut campaign.

He flung his jacket over his shoulder and went to find her and figure out what she planned for damage control.

Deke looked around the studio for the tall, lithe figure with shiny hair he'd spent so much time admiring when she wasn't watching. There was no sign of her. She must have slithered out in shame. It wasn't her style, but a quick tour through the open areas of Studio 3B made him begin to doubt that he knew her at all.

Deke left the studio and immediately saw the crowds gathered outside. Pausing to watch them, it occurred to him that he could still save this. He could do the damage control they'd desperately need. But why should he? It wasn't his job to make Americans love and trust NASA.

Aw, hell.

He walked right up to the crowd as they pressed against the roped-off areas reserved for the brief visits from the hosts and special guests. Someone called out his name and he waved in response and witnessed the mob reaction as a buzz of excitement vibrated through the group. The crowd grew around him, everyone shaking his hand and asking for an autograph.

"Way to go, Deke. You gave 'em hell, Commander!" one man exclaimed gruffly and patted him on the back.

"You were fantastic, Deke!" yelled another. He thanked them and signed some autographs, including a quick scribble on one of the "DEKE" signs, whose owner rewarded him with an embarrassed smile. A moment later, the jovial, warm weatherman approached Deke, microphone in hand and cameraman in tow.

"Good morning, Commander. I'm Mark Dobson." His eyes twinkled as he shook Deke's hand. "Nice of you to come out here. I'm about to go to the weather. Can I get you in this shot for one more comment? I promise I'll be cool."

Deke returned his handshake and agreed to one more minute on camera, wondering if he'd lost his mind.

Crouched below the minicam in front of them, a studio crewmember gave the ten-second signal to Mark, then counted down before pointing to the weatherman to indicate he was live.

"What a crowd we have braving the icy cold New York air today!" The cheers of the visitors cut him off. "We are just at the edge of a fairly major storm here in New York and we should see some of the white stuff soon. But folks, who cares? We've got America's favorite astronaut, Deke Stockard, out here with us!" Again the crowd reached a slight frenzy.

"These folks love you, Deke!"

He gave his best "I can't imagine why" smile when he really wanted to ask why the hell anyone would want to be a celebrity. "No, Mark. They love the space program that I'm a part of, not me."

"Are you kidding?" Mark rolled his eyes for the camera. "*I* love you, man!" More cheering. Mark gushed for a few minutes about the heroes of space and how half the breakthroughs in meteorology were a result of NASA inventions and satellite technology. Deke shook some more hands and kissed the windburned, cherry cheek of a baby boy whose mommy thought he would grow up to be an astronaut, too. The camera rolled.

When the excitement died down and it seemed safe to

slip away, Deke backed off from the crowd, then looked beyond it. He touched his chin as his eyes scoped the entire area with the skill of a fighter pilot doing a visual check of the skies and accepted that Jessica was gone.

He turned back toward the skating area to catch a cab on Sixth Avenue. Then he spotted her. She was sitting on a bench across the rink, a white coat wrapped around her against the cold, black boots tapping while her fingers furiously punched numbers on her cell phone. All determination and fury. He watched her hold the phone to her ear and talk, then took the circuitous route around the rink and ended up standing beside her without her ever seeing him coming.

She gasped. "You scared me!" Her eyes were huge, the deep color of ink flecked with gold dust, the thick lashes wet with something he'd never seen on her before. Tears.

Her body shivered in reaction to the icy temperatures, or maybe in response to him. The urge to kiss her hit him so hard, it stunned him.

"Would you like to go inside and get warm?"

Her mouth dropped open in surprise. Clearly, she expected anything but kindness.

☆彡

Jessica had braced herself for Deke's icy attack, prepared for it to sting worse than the frigid air. When she couldn't find him in the studio, she was certain he'd left without her, too disgusted to even bother with a confrontation. But here he stood, with a look so unbelievably tender that the hard and painful lump building in her throat nearly exploded, threatening to ruin her remaining shreds of composure.

It would have been easy to start on the offensive, but she

knew the blame for his ambush lay squarely on her shoulders. "I'm really sorry."

"So you sneak off like a thief, too ashamed to face me?"

"I didn't sneak off." The lump lodged in her throat. "I went to talk to the producer and then couldn't find you." She toyed with the cell phone and looked back at him. "When were you going to tell me about the sick cosmonaut?"

"If you had done your homework on this interview, you would have found out they had that story. Then we could have avoided this altogether."

True enough, she thought. "But if I had known something like this was going on, I might not have pursued the interview."

"And give up a chance to shine? Not Miss '*I'm going to succeed at any cost.*' Never. You'd hang me from a billboard in Times Square if you thought it would help your cause."

The criticism stabbed at her already guilt-laden heart. "I screwed up, Dcke."

He sat on the bench next to her. "Don't they usually warn you about these rumors? I thought you had such a great relationship with all these media types?"

How could she possibly tell him the truth? He would never understand such petty rivalries with so much at stake.

"Someone in the agency knew, but didn't get the message to me."

"I find that hard to believe since I've never seen you when you aren't wired to a cell phone and a PDA."

She reached into her bag and slipped on a pair of black leather gloves over her numb hands. "The account team in Washington is meeting with NASA right now. We're going to issue a joint statement with Russia. It'll die down soon."

"It won't." He turned away from her and watched the

skaters. "I'm not happy that you put me in that situation, but I guess we shouldn't have kept the facts from you."

Damn right. She swallowed the retort. "Tell me the whole story now. Please."

He turned back to her. "Micah Petrenko developed deep vein thrombosis shortly after he arrived at the space station." At her questioning look, he nodded. "That's a blood clot. Right now, it's not serious, but it could be. By mid-February, the supply of anticoagulant medicine on the space station will run out. The doctors feel it's critical to get him out of zero gravity by then."

"So, is he coming home on *Endeavour*?"

Deke shrugged. "If we can get to him in time."

"What could happen if you don't?"

"He could have a stroke or heart attack. A fatal embolism is the most common and serious complication."

"It just confirms what all the critics say about the cost in human and dollar terms of manned space travel," she added.

"You're catching on, Jess." He patted her hands with a bittersweet smile. "Now you see why I hate all this time away from inspections and launch prep. A life literally depends on getting up there on time."

Her cell phone jangled, startling her. When she heard Tony Palermo's secretary's familiar voice, she couldn't fight the urge to pour her story out. "Mimi, don't tell me, Tony's on the line to rap my knuckles. Tell him to cool it. I have plenty to tell him."

Although Deke stepped away to give her privacy, she knew he could hear her end of the conversation. Trying to concentrate on what Mimi was saying and block out the Christmas music guiding the rhythm of the skaters, she put a finger to one ear and looked down self-consciously.

"Well, he can't talk to you now," Mimi informed her.

"Didn't he see the *Today* show?"

"Oh, yes. He saw it." Mimi's thick New York accent dripped with disdain and Jessica's heart sank a little.

"Why can't he talk to me?" The black ball of disappointment numbed her limbs even more than the cold.

"His schedule just booked up completely with some client problems. Including the NASA issue."

"Then he must want me to help with damage control."

"He's working with Bill Dugan."

She was worse than in the doghouse. She was dead. *Emerging Technologies, here I come.*

Deke walked back to the bench when she hung up, studying her face. "I take it this is not your greatest moment at Ross & Clayton."

Once again, his gentle tone got to her. Far worse than his attacks. Surprising her, the burn of tears started swimming in her eyes and suddenly spilled over. She tried to swipe them with her gloves and laughed at her clumsy effort to hide the obvious. "My whole career is about to crumble. And it's not even my own doing."

He sat down close to her and handed her a white handkerchief with the U.S. Navy insignia on the corner. "What drives you so hard, Jessica?"

The combination of tenderness and intensity nearly unraveled her. She dabbed at her eyes and avoided his gaze. "The same thing that drives you, Deke. Motivation to succeed. Really, what else is there?"

He stared at her for a moment, and she couldn't help looking back into his navy blue eyes. "I don't want to succeed for the sake of succeeding," he told her. "I have a job to do and I want to do it well. You seem so focused on the reward and not on the process."

She tried to laugh a little. "You're such an engineer."

"Guilty." He nodded. "And maybe that makes me too analytical. But, I don't think I've ever met a woman like you. Even the female astronauts and pilots I know…they all want something more." He paused and searched her face. "At the risk of sounding horrifically old-fashioned, don't you want to get married, have babies, you know, follow the ticking of the infamous biological clock?"

She folded the white cotton square on her lap. "I love my work. I don't want to give it up."

"Why should you give it up? Lots of women do both. My mom did. She had two jobs—a science teacher and a newspaper columnist. Three if you count raising Melissa and me." He laid his arm on the bench behind her and she thought of how much she wanted him to wrap his arm around her and just…comfort.

"Well, my mother had *one* job," she said, noticing a smudge of mascara on the corner of the handkerchief. "She was a political science professor at Yale. And in those days, tenure didn't come easily to women and babies were considered a liability to your career. There was no nursing lounge in the ladies' room back then. I imagine she wasn't too thrilled when she got pregnant at forty-four."

"Did she tell you that?"

Jessica stared straight ahead. She hated telling this story. "I never knew her. She died in childbirth, having me."

She didn't want to see the pity. The sadness. But she looked at him anyway.

No pity darkened his eyes. "And your father?"

"My father was over fifty when I was born. He's into his eighties now, but still doddering around New Haven, pestering the students and faculty at Yale. We were close, I guess, but the only time he's shown any real pleasure in me is when I emulatemy mother—a workaholic." Jessica sighed and smiled through clenched teeth. "Doesn't take Freud to figure it out, Deke."

"The influence of a father has to be managed," he said. "I learned that in my twenties."

She nodded. Easier said than done, she wanted to add. "As for babies and biological clocks—" She paused and tucked the folded handkerchief in her handbag. "I think you already know the answer to that."

He looked at her questioningly and she smiled before answering, "I might be too 'naïve and relentless' to be a very good mother."

His arm came over her shoulders, heavy and comforting. "But that's exactly why you'd be a great mother."

She let his arm warm her and accepted the truce he was silently offering. "I'm sorry about today. No more interviews. I promise."

He stood and tucked his hands into his jacket pocket. "So, now what? Your meeting's cancelled."

"My flight doesn't leave until four."

"Till then?"

She lifted the cell phone. "Damage control from afar."

"Keep the phone on and come with me. I have a wonderful way to drown your sorrows."

A decidedly unprofessional image flashed in her mind. "Is that so?"

Chapter Twelve

After they left the Plaza with their bags and waited for a cab on Fifth Avenue, Jessica inhaled the smoky, sweet aroma of chestnuts grilling on a street vendor's cart next to them. Amidst the throngs of shoppers striding at a classic New York pace, something soft and cold touched Jessica's cheek.

She threw her head back and looked into the sky, letting the tickle of snow dampen her face and eyes. "Finally! Oh, thank you, God!"

He lifted his hand to the snowflake that lay on her cheek. His touch was a surprise, warm and gentle. His fingers brushed her skin, leaving a burning trail of sensation in their wake.

"You're a snow angel."

"I like winter," she said, softly exhaling and holding his gaze. Deke and snow. Hot and cold.

He finally turned to hail a cab, breaking the spell.

When she heard him tell the cabbie Grand Central Station, she peered at him suspiciously, since he still hadn't said where they were going. "We're taking a train?"

"We are."

"And you're sure you want company on your mysterious mission?"

He grinned and patted her briefcase. "Consider it research."

They entered Grand Central with the rest of the commuting mob and took the escalator down to the train level. He moved with familiarity and ease, his hand resting on her back to guide her. Her feet felt light, her head a little dizzy. How had he managed to transform such a rotten day into something magical?

While he bought train tickets, she checked in with Stuart at Kennedy and the NASA account team in D.C. to hear how they were handling the situation without her.

They'd issued a statement and started fielding calls about the cosmonaut as well as more interview requests for Deke. That surprised her a little, but she told them to put all of those requests on hold and promised to handle them as soon as she got back. No more interviews. She'd figure out some way to get publicity without taking his time. But she didn't tell that to Stuart; nor did she mention that she was off on some secret appointment with Deke.

When they boarded the line that ended in Peekskill, she suspected where that secret appointment might be. "Are we, by any chance, headed to see your parents?"

"Yes, and to lunch, prepared by the best cook I know—my dad."

Of course. He'd told her he wanted to see his parents. "Oh."

He smiled at the mixture of fear and surprise in her voice. "Did you think I'd come all the way to New York and *not* see them? They're expecting me."

"But are they expecting me?" A tiny wave of panic threatened.

"Hand me that cell phone of yours and I'll tell them. Won't matter. He always cooks more than enough." He took the phone and started dialing.

"Your dad is the cook in the family?"

"Mmm-hmm. Mom can't boil water. Dad did all the cooking my whole— Hey, it's me." He directed his words into the phone. "Yeah. That was a bit of a surprise. ... No, we'll tell you about it when we get there. ... I've got someone with me. ... The PR genius behind all this." He laughed a little. "Okay, see you in an hour or so. Bye."

She looked up at him. "Genius? Was that sarcasm?"

He handed her the phone with a wink. "Spin control, Jess. You know all about that."

Tiny flutters took her heart on a thrill ride. She closed her eyes for a moment, reveling in the mildly acrid, metallic odor that permeated the train and the gentle rhythm of the heavy iron wheels as she fell under the spell of Deke Stockard, who not only forgave her for the mistake but seemed bent on making her feel better.

In fact, they never even discussed the morning's debacle, and for the time being, that suited her fine. All through the colorful and storied sections of Harlem, Deke pointed out landmarks and highlighted the forty-five-minute trip with New York history before she got him talking about his family.

"My dad was an IBM lifer but managed to spend his whole career in White Plains, a nearly impossible feat with that company," Deke told her.

"You said your mother's a columnist. What does she write?"

"It's called the 'Women's Corner' and she started writing it for the local White Plains paper when I was a baby. Sort of an information resource for IBM spouses—all wives, in those days—and she still writes it today. Obviously, it's changed, but the column's always been kind of a witty and insightful commentary on things women worry about." He grinned at her. "Like raising high-risk sons."

She laughed softly. "I bet you were a handful."

He leaned close to her ear, his breath tickling the nape of her neck. "I still am."

The screech of the train brakes brought the conversation to an end, but not the pounding of Jessica's pulse. Within a few minutes, they were in a cab driving down an oak-lined street with stone houses and circular drives.

He hadn't even finished paying the cab fare when the front door of the two-story brick colonial flew open and a woman gingerly stepped onto the front porch, the accumulating snow keeping her from running to her son.

"Deke!" The joy at the sight of him lit her lovely face and nearly took Jessica's breath away.

Trim and fit in a creamy sweater and matching wool pants, Valerie Stockard looked very much like an elegant executive wife. When her son reached her, she threw her arms around his powerful body and buried her face in his chest.

"Oh, my darling! I'm so glad to see you! You were wonderful this morning. I was dying of pride!" Pulling back to look at his face, she lovingly touched his cheek.

"Hi, Mom." He showed no embarrassment at his mother's display but turned to introduce Jessica. Only then did he let his mother go. As the two women shook hands, Deke added, "Jess is the one who dreamed up this whole thing. Dad can let her have the hard time instead of me."

Valerie's smile was wide and warm through to her pale blue eyes. "Jessica, it's a pleasure to meet you. I've had so many questions about this special project. How nice to have the opportunity to talk to you in person."

Tentatively, Jessica let Deke usher them all into the front door that Valerie had left wide open. "I'll be happy to give you my side of it, Mrs. Stockard. But it might be a slightly different version than your son's."

"Please call me Val. Don't worry. I've been discerning fact from fiction for many years with Deke." They entered the house to the comfort of a classic center hall, a fire burning in the living room and a giant Christmas tree laden with ornaments right next to it.

An imposing man with a shock of silvery hair and keen brown eyes strode through another doorway toward them. Except for the color of the eyes, she was looking at Deke in thirty years.

"You must be Jack Stockard." She spoke without thinking, admiring the resemblance. Jack welcomed her with friendliness that matched his wife's and then turned to hug Deke.

"Deacon, my boy. Good to see you." *Deacon*? How could she not know that was his name?

The older Stockard pounded his son's back with affection and pulled back to gaze at him with the same love his mother had shown, then turned to Jessica. "So you're the brains behind all this PR malarkey? Well, I gotta tell you, that last stunt was brilliant."

What was he talking about? The *Today*show interview? Was he being sarcastic?

"Oh, yes!" Valerie Stockard piped in. "Mark Dobson was simply fawning over you, Deke. And kissing the baby! It was adorable. Goodness, did you think of that to save the day, Jessica?"

Her sharp intake of breath was her only response and her mouth stayed open, causing Deke's sheepish grin to widen.

"I think Jessica was in with the producer during that part of the show," he said quietly.

"You...kissed...a baby?"

"Why, yes, I did. He was a cute little guy."

"Did...did you go to the outside set, Deke?" And save the

whole morning with one unselfish act? A piece of her melted as he nodded.

"Let's relax in here for a few minutes." Valerie moved them all into the kitchen, apparently unaware of the drama unfolding between her son and their guest. "If you missed it, we have it on tape, Jessica."

Deke allowed Jessica to go into the kitchen before him, and she did so slowly, keeping her gaze on him over her shoulder.

"I'd love to see the tape later," she said, unable to hide her glimmer of admiration.

The aroma of an Italian kitchen, pungent with basil and tomato, surrounded her just like the warmth of the Wedgwood blue and yellow kitchen. Deke followed his dad directly to the six-burner stove and put his arm on the older man's shoulder.

"You love that iron skillet, don't you? I knew you'd use it. I couldn't live without mine."

Were they discussing a pan? Jessica looked to Valerie for some logical explanation as her hostess finished setting the cozy table in the eat-in kitchen. Valerie smiled knowingly.

"Cooking and flying. The rest of the world could come to a standstill and these two would still discuss cooking and flying." She shook her head and gazed at the two men she so obviously loved. "I don't mind. We eat well!"

Jessica picked up the napkins on the counter and began setting them in place. "Your home is lovely."

"Thank you, dear. How long have you lived in Florida?"

"Oh, I don't live there," Jessica explained. "I live in Boston. I'm just on a temporary assignment."

"Oh." Valerie looked vaguely disappointed. "How long will you be at the Cape?"

"The assignment ends in February, when *Endeavour* is launched."

"Jessica's a dyed-in-the-wool New Englander, Mom," Deke said as he approached the table. "Can't find a redeeming feature about the Cape, or Florida, for that matter."

She shook her head to defend herself. "It's not what I'm used to. It's so *warm* all the time."

"You should take her sailing, Deke," his mother said. "She'd love the water."

"Speaking of weather, Deke," Jack chimed in, "I'd check the airport in this storm. You can expect delays."

Deke agreed, leaving Jessica alone with his parents as he went to call the airline. Jack immediately drew her in with a description of the feast that simmered on the stove.

"How did you learn to cook so well?" Jessica asked, accepting a cup of hot tea from Valerie, letting the relaxing comfort of their kitchen and family spread through her like the warm liquid.

"My mother was full Italian, Anna Maria Cipriani," Jack explained. "She moved here and married my father, a stiff and structured German named Claus Stockard, and the result is a very passionate engineer. Me." She could see the influence of the dark and romantic Italian blood in his handsome face as he spoke. "But she never lost her love of cooking and passed it on to me. And I, hopefully, have done the same with Deke."

She tried to imagine her own father cooking and simply couldn't. They'd had a lady who cleaned and left a warm meal for most nights. But Daddy rarely made it home and most often, as she got older, she ate alone while she did her homework. Jessica watched Jack Stockard skillfully handle his beloved skillet.

The house where she grew up in New Haven seemed so far from the tranquility of the Stockards' suburban refuge.

She imagined Deke coming home from school, sharing his successes with interested and loving parents, teasing his little sister and planning his career as a Navy pilot.

"I thought the PR idea was brilliant." Valerie interrupted Jessica's musings. "Giving NASA a face and a personality. And such a good choice!"

Jack groaned from the stove. "He should be flying, not pacifying anchorwomen on the morning talk shows."

Valerie rolled her eyes, and before Jessica could defend her plan, Deke came in. He grabbed one of the maple chairs, turned it around and sat backward like he probably had in this kitchen a thousand times. "We're not going at four, that's for sure."

"Really? Is everything delayed?" Just what she needed— to be gone even longer during a client crisis.

"Our flight is scheduled to take off at eight tonight, but I wouldn't hold out hope for that." He reached out and put a hand on her arm. "There's nothing you can do about it. Relax." Then he grinned at his mother. "What propaganda are you feeding this poor girl, Mom?"

"Propaganda is her business, Deke." Jack added from the stove. Definitely not a fan of the campaign, Jessica decided as she sipped her tea.

Valerie patted her husband on the back. "Just hush up and admire her work. It got him home, didn't it?"

In a few minutes, Jack presented his culinary masterpiece. With the extra time, they lingered over the feast, unable to avoid discussing the topic of the *Today* show interview.

"How serious is the situation?" Jack asked Deke.

"Serious. The guy's going to die if we don't get *Endeavour* up there."

Jessica toyed with a mushroom on her plate, avoiding eye contact with Deke.

"What about the *Soyuz*?" Jack asked. "The Russians still run that, don't they? For emergencies?"

Deke shook his head. "Putting a man with a blood clot in that soup can and dropping him to earth would probably kill him. The X-38, the return vehicle, is on hold...for budget reasons. *Endeavour* is his only safe ride home under these conditions."

"Are there problems with this launch?" Jack asked.

"Might be. A hydrogen leak is nothing to play with. If we don't find it..." His lips formed a thin grimace. "We're still doing inspections."

This time she couldn't help looking at him. She held his gaze and hoped he could read the promise in her eyes. No more interviews.

After lunch, Jessica helped Valerie clear the table while Deke and Jack went to bring in some wood for the fire.

"So, have you been spending a lot of time with Deke?" Valerie's question didn't sound completely casual.

Jessica took the dripping platter Valerie handed her and felt a flush warm her face.

"PR is not his favorite assignment, as you probably know. I've managed to get him to do a few interviews and a photo shoot." She wiped the platter with a dishtowel and decided to nip Valerie's curiosity in the bud. "This is really the most time I've ever spent with him."

Valerie finished the last pot and ran the faucet to clean the sink, then suddenly snapped down the chrome lever and looked at Jessica. "Do you think there are real safety issues with the shuttles? Is it something I should worry about?"

Jessica had forgotten this was Deke's mother. Who could be more pained by the idea of him exploding into space than this dear woman who brought him into the world and nurtured him into manhood? How self-centered to think she was poking around his private life.

"Only if you're Micah Petrenko's mother," Jessica said softly and honestly. "I know NASA does everything imaginable to ensure safety."

Jessica followed Valerie's gaze to the snow-covered lawn beyond her kitchen window. Jack and Deke walked side by side with armloads of wood, leaving a trail of footprints behind them in the newly fallen snow. Valerie turned and smiled.

"I wish he were a pediatrician like his sister."

No. No pediatrician. Jack Stockard had raised his son to be a risk-taker. And try as Deke might to 'manage the influence' of his father, Jack had succeeded.

Chapter Thirteen

All flights were delayed until the next morning, and as much as that irked Deke, the blizzard had its positive side. It gave him the chance to be alone with Jess, to observe her outside of work. He'd never seen her so relaxed. She'd charmed them all, chatting with his dad and reading his mom's old articles. He couldn't ignore the impact she had on him. As the day darkened into a snowy night, he couldn't help but hope his parents still went to bed very early.

When his mother announced that they had to say goodnight, Deke tried to seem appropriately disappointed.

"I'll show Jessica to Melissa's room," he assured them. "And I'll check the flights again before I go to sleep."

Jack promised to take them to the airport early in the morning, and finally, they went to bed.

Jessica leaned on the banister railing and thanked them again for the day. She'd changed into jeans in the downstairs powder room after lunch and the soft pink sweater she wore outlined her feminine figure. *Best not to stare, Stockard.*

"You're not bailing out, are you?" He cocked his head toward the living room. "Let's at least wait till the fire goes out."

She followed him but sat on the floor in front of the coffee table, away from him. "So," she said with a smile. "The baby kissing. I can't imagine how much you didn't want to go outside the studio and face the crowds. Why'd you do it?"

"For love of God, country, and NASA, of course."

She just looked at him like she was waiting for the heap of sarcasm.

"And knowing something had to be done to save your behind, however cute it might be."

A flush darkened her cheeks as she turned toward the fire. He considered how to get her up on the sofa. Or perhaps he'd join her on the floor. Just to see what happened next.

Because something *was* going to happen next.

"So have you had enough snow, Miss December?" he asked.

"You have to admit it feels more like Christmas here than down among the palm trees." Crossing her long legs under the coffee table, she looked out the picture window at the postcard-like image. "Actually, I like to be in it, not just look at it."

That was where he wanted her. In the snow. "Christmas is in the eye of Santa Claus and he gets everywhere. Even Florida." He stood and held his hand to pull her up. "C'mon. Let's go."

She rose slowly, regarding him with caution. "Where are we going?"

"Melissa must have left an old parka around here somewhere—you can't go out in that fancy white thing you wore."

"You want to go out? Now? In the dark?"

He guided her toward the mudroom off the kitchen and flung open the louvered doors of the coat closet. "You scared of the dark, Jess?"

A worn maroon ski jacket that belonged to Melissa hung in the far corner. He took it out and held it toward her with a challenging smile. She said nothing but slipped it on, a light already dancing in her eyes.

He knew that would happen. He'd been around her long enough to know that when something really moved her, she lit up with an inner fire that made her even more beautiful. And, damn, all he wanted to do was stoke those flames.

Outside in the moonlight, she gingerly broke the crispy top layer of snow outside the mudroom door with the laced-up work boots she wore under her jeans.

"Nice boots. You packed for this?"

"I hoped for this. I thought I could steal a few hours to myself in New York, so I brought a change of clothes. It ain't Central Park, but I'm not complaining." She ran a few steps ahead into the foot-high drifts around the cord of wood piled neatly under the back porch. "Hey, I like this, Stockard. Good idea."

He held back, watching her slim legs negotiate the snow and ice. The desire to kiss her hadn't dimmed all day since they'd talked in Rockefeller Center. Hell, since before that, he admitted. But today she had been amazing, handling unexpected crisis, a trip to his family's home, and now the delay because of the snow. Most women would be all aflutter with nerves or complain that they had wasted the day in the suburbs of New York, especially one who cared about her career as much as Jess did.

But she'd just won his parents' hearts without even trying, and his...well, not his heart. But the pheromones were being shot off in both directions.

He slowed his steps as he followed her path, trying to stop himself from rushing her, but a hot ache low in his gut urged him on. He reached down to the snow, scooped a handful, and formed a lightly packed ball.

"Hey, Jess!" As she turned, it caught her on the side of her arm, his intended target. She shrieked in surprise but had a return shot ready in less than two seconds. She was off her mark by a foot.

"A girl's aim, that's for sure." He laughed and threw another, but she was too fast and jumped out of the way, running for cover behind an oak tree, her laughter giving away her hiding place.

"You missed, Top Gun! Don't you do this for a living—lock on targets and stuff?"

He came after her, around the tree, and shot one at her leg. "Watch out, sweetheart, bogie on your tail!"

She knelt down, knowing she was trapped and laughing too hard to get a snowball formed, so she just pathetically splashed him with snow.

"You're dead," he said softly as he knelt in front of her. She leaned back on her heels and searched his face in the moonlight.

"I'm dead."

He reached out his hand and touched just under her jaw, relishing the sensation of her pounding pulse under his thumb. Her lips parted and he heard the quiet intake of her breath in reaction to his touch.

Slowly leaning toward her, he placed his lips on hers, tasting the frosty cold that clung to her. As she responded to his kiss, his tongue gently opened her lips to caress her. Without lifting his mouth, he buried his hands in her hair, pulling her to him as a soft moan escaped her lips.

He moved his hands slowly down the puffy nylon of the ski jacket, far removed from the body he'd been stealthily watching all day. But it was there, just beneath the layers of warm down.

He could sense her hesitation, her hands on his shoulders applying gentle pressure as she returned the kiss. Gently, unwillingly, he parted from her.

She could only manage a whisper. "Why did you do that?"

"Because I wanted to."

She closed her eyes and didn't say anything.

"And I want to again," he whispered, leaning close to her mouth. "And again. And maybe one more time after that." To prove it, he kissed her again.

As their mouths touched, he gently ran his tongue over her icy lips, offering warmth. She sucked in a breath and he pressed harder, touching her teeth. He moved his hands around to the front of the parka and found the zipper at the top. He felt himself grow hard at the heat of her mouth and the anticipation of more. He slid the zipper one inch. Her eyes flashed open.

"I want to warm my hands," he said huskily.

She held her hand on top of his on the zipper and stared at him, the black depths of her eyes shimmering with the reflection of the snow in the moonlight.

"I don't think this is a great idea."

He leaned a few inches away and traced the line of her lower lip with his fingers, wanting to taste it again. "You call the shots, Jessie. Take the risk when you're good and ready."

"I'm not ready."

Under his thumb, he felt her lip quiver. "What are you waiting for?"

"I—I can't."

He wouldn't force the issue, no matter how hot she could make him in the snow. He smiled and stood, taking a deep breath to steady what the close contact and slow kiss had done to his balance and his body. He reached down to pull her up for a second time that night.

"Come on in, sweetheart." He dropped his arm around her shoulder and tucked her close to his warmth, then they headed for the lights of his parents' house.

☆

Jessica shivered, but not from the cold. Aware of nothing but the raw power of Deke behind her as they climbed the stairs to the second floor, both stepping lightly to avoid waking the Stockards, she struggled to keep from quaking. The kiss. The hot, cold, steaming, scary kiss lingered on her lips. Now what?

More. She wanted *more*.

"This is Melissa's room," he said as they reached a door at the end of the long hall circling the entryway. Where was his room? Close enough to…

"This'll be great," she said quickly, quieting her thoughts.

"Mom keeps our rooms exactly as they were when we were in high school. I swear she secretly retreats up here and relives every one of the eighteen years we lived at home."

The comment, no doubt intended for dry humor, struck Jessica's heart. But when he opened the door, the room hit her like a sucker punch. "Oh, my. This is lovely."

Pale lavender carpeting, a down-covered sleigh bed, delicate wall coverings. Museum-quality prints shared wall space with diplomas, awards, and photos of a young girl's every imaginable milestone from dance recitals to prom night.

Drawn to them, Jessica examined each captured moment. A spunky, blue-eyed brunette in a soccer uniform, clutching a ball under one arm. A lovely teenage girl in a pale green dress on the arm of an awkward boy in a tuxedo. And Deke. A loving big brother with his arm around his baby sister as she triumphantly waved her diploma.

"Mom loves to memorialize every minute." He shrugged with a glance at the walls. "And, of course, we were involved in just about everything."

"No need to apologize. You're so lucky." She made no attempt to keep the envy out of her voice. "I always wanted a life like that, but my dad never had the time. I—I didn't even ask."

"Well, surely you went to the prom and graduated from college."

"I did." She turned to him, knowing her eyes were damp and her pain was showing. "But no one recorded it so…so lovingly. And I sure as heck didn't play soccer."

He touched her cheek, not sensually this time. But gently. Maybe the brotherly touch he gave Melissa when she had a down moment. If the fortunate young doctor ever had a down moment.

"Don't be jealous. She was a rotten goalie." Then he kissed her softly on the cheek. "But you would have looked real good in those shorts."

She grinned in spite of her self-pity and punched him lightly on the arm, aching to move back into the kiss. "Go get some sleep, Commander. We're going back, even if you have to fly that plane to Florida tomorrow."

He left her to dream of Melissa's girlhood, but once she climbed into the welcoming bed, she could only remember his mouth and lips tempting her in the snow.

As soon as they parted at the Orlando airport, Deke headed directly for the OPF. He'd hated being away that long. But in the two hours he'd been inside the orbiter, he realized he'd spent nearly every moment thinking about Jessica.

He carefully lifted the fuel cell panel and began fingering the wires behind it. Holding one strand, he stared at the electrical connection for a good three minutes before he realized how utterly destroyed it was. Shaking his head to clear his thoughts, Deke ran his finger over the frayed metal edge and then tore a piece of bright orange tape from the roll next to him to mark it. Jesus.

He didn't know what bothered him more. The fact that someone had missed this one or the fact that while he looked at it, his mind was far, far away. In the snow. In the dark.

He laid the roll of tape in its proper place and scooted out of the orbiter for a cup of coffee. Lack of sleep, too much travel and a certain spin doctor was ruining his concentration.

At the coffee station, Scott Hayes greeted Deke with a quick smile. The guy was quiet, but usually dead-on in his assessments of the entire inspection process.

"Have you been through the wiring behind the fuel cell panel, Scott?"

The engineer frowned and fingered his thin moustache. "I thought that whole section was done already. I'm sure I saw signed-off logs in the PLIC."

Deke studied the black ink of the coffee he'd just poured. This was only going to make his stomach feel worse. He flipped the cup upside down over the sink. "Maybe you did. But I went in there a few minutes ago and found another problem."

"I'll get the electrical team to look at it." Scott shifted

from one foot to the other, looking like he wanted to say something but didn't know how.

Deke leaned against the Formica counter and crossed his arms. "Everything else okay, Hayes?"

"I was sort of wondering what you thought of my idea with the engine plugs."

Damn it, he'd meant to talk to Scott about the plug rec folder he'd seen on his desk. But he was more tangled than those wires these days. "What was it?"

"I ran it by some other folks a while ago, and it got shot down."

Shot down by whom? Had he been briefed and missed it, somehow? Was his brain that fogged by all the PR and this...PR person? "Who saw your ideas?"

"The inspection team," he said. "The idea was...not universally loved."

"And budget's tight." Deke said to ease the obvious hit to Hayes's confidence and his own guilt.

Scott nodded and headed out of the kitchen area. "Yeah. That's what I've been told."

Deke stood and stared at the empty doorway. Had he seen something from Hayes and just forgotten it? Good God, this was a disaster.

He had to do something about it.

He had to do something about *her*.

His logical mind reviewed the options and discarded each, one by one. He couldn't get rid of her. He couldn't avoid her. He couldn't forget her.

He crunched the empty Styrofoam cup and pitched it into the trash. There was only one option left. He had to have her.

"Hey, Jess. It's almost 4:30—don't we have a conference call?" Stuart stopped in Jessica's office door, a stack of files balanced in one hand, his late afternoon coffee in the other.

"Already?" She couldn't believe that only a few hours ago she and Deke had landed at Orlando and headed independently and directly to the Cape.

She had spent the afternoon trying to lose herself in work and forget the magical kiss. But that was impossible, since the man in the snow *was* her work. Jessica had called on every compartmentalizing skill she'd ever learned in management classes. He turned up in every compartment.

The media's lust for bad news was evident on every phone call. They wanted a disaster. Could the shuttle fly in time? Would Micah make it? Were the rumors of hydrogen leaks true?

Guilt knocked at her when she thought of why she'd scheduled the conference call in the first place. She had wanted some colorful, Hollywood-type photo releases out there and had asked the West Coast account people for some ideas to get Deke in front of the paparazzi. But now she understood why he didn't want to take the time to travel or do any more PR stunts. She decided she'd just talk to them and see what they had. Then let it drop.

The excitement in Lydia Davis's voice jumped through the speakerphone as soon as they connected.

"We hit the jackpot for you," Lydia bubbled. *Lost Hero.* The Premiere. In Orlando. At Universal. Is this making sense to you?"

"Isn't that a war movie with some big names in it?" Stuart's face lit up. "I just read about it. The story's loosely based on Scott O'Grady, the Air Force pilot who was shot down in Bosnia and rescued. In fact, Deke and a couple of our astronauts were still flying fighters at the time and were involved in the actual rescue."

"Perfection!" Lydia cooed. "The premiere is right after Christmas at Universal Studios in Orlando. The big name is Marc Sebastian, but guess who plays the feisty and lovely lieutenant he flings with in the movie?"

Jessica could practically hear Lydia bursting with her news as they all waited for her to say a name.

"Sydney Lynn Lancaster. Now I ask you, Jessica Marlowe, who is more perfect to escort the gorgeous Ms. L to the premiere than your former fighter pilot turned astronaut?"

Jessica squeezed her eyes shut. She'd promised. No more interviews. But, it was in Orlando, so he didn't have to travel and it wasn't exactly a hardship to spend one evening with a beautiful movie star.

"Sydney Lynn Lancaster is a media magnet," she agreed with a look at Stuart.

The event specialist in L.A. started spewing details. "Universal will have everyone—E!, *Entertainment Tonight*, *People*, FOX. This is a black-tie night on a grand scale at the new IMAX theater and ballroom at Universal Studios. They're doing all events out there to push the theme park in Orlando. Face it, on Friday night, December thirtieth, you guys are in the hot spot."

Lydia laughed. "What a couple! Stockard and Lancaster will be in every newspaper in America the next day. The tabloids will have them engaged by the middle of January."

"What did Sydney say?" Jessica asked. Maybe the Hollywood hottie would say no and she'd never have to ask Deke to do this.

"We're talking to her people. We've sent Stockard's press kit and some video from the Leno appearance. We'll see if they bite."

After they signed off, Jessica stared at Stuart. "Think he'll go for it?" she asked.

Stuart's face twisted in mock surprise. "Are you kidding? What red-blooded American male would say no? Let's call him."

"No, no." Jessica shook her head emphatically. "Let's wait to see what Sydney Lynn says."

Sydney Lynn was a perfect choice. A steamy, sexy blonde with a drop-dead body and a face the camera adored. Every man was bound to react like Stuart at the thought of a date with her. Every man but the one who hated PR stunts. The phone interrupted her thoughts.

"Hello, gorgeous," Jo Miller rasped in her best fake Streisand accent.

Jessica tucked her feet under her for a chat. "Hey, Jo. Wait till you hear what we just cooked up."

Stuart took his notebook and stood up. "I sense girl talk starting. Think I'll go look up Sydney Lynn's website."

Jessica smiled and waved him out.

"Well, save it for later," Jo told her, her voice suddenly serious. "I have news, Jess. Bad news. You sitting down?"

Jessica tucked the phone into her ear to brace herself for whatever Jo was about to deliver. "Now what?"

"Have you talked to Tony about the Emerging Technologies plan yet?"

Jessica closed her eyes, wanting to forget the whole conversation she'd had with Carla Drake. "He blew me off and I haven't had a chance to call him. I was hoping it would go away."

"It's not going away. Rita just slipped me a copy of a draft org chart that Carla sent down to Tony for review."

The fact that Rita Ross, her loyal secretary, was working

for Carla while she was in Florida cut a jealous edge into Jess. "What did it say?"

"She wants to formally announce your new position as head of Emerging Technologies. And hers as General Manager. She got the promotion, Jess."

A white light popped in her head and the old throbbing in her temples started immediately. "I'll call Tony. And I'll be there in a week, Jo. I'm going to fight her on this. I will not be shuffled off to no-name accounts and stripped of everything I worked for. There's no reason."

"The *Today* show was a reason. Not that he didn't pull it off, but you know she's saying it should never have happened."

"Damn it, Jo!" Jessica fought to control her temper. "*She* knew about the rumor—I told you they called before the interview and she deliberately let me get crucified."

"Just watch your back. She might want you gone altogether. And, puhleeze, don't give into any hormonal urges with the rocket man. She's already suggested no woman could keep her panties on around him. Even St. Jessica."

Snow kisses. "Jo. Really. I'm not stupid."

"I know that, but I have no desire to work in Regurgitating Technologies, so ignore what I said before and be a good girl."

Jessica closed her eyes. "Always."

"Listen, are we on for a Christmas celebration? I have something that is no less than extraordinary for you this year."

Jessica reached for her calendar. "I'll be there all week. I'll need you more than ever, honey. I'm counting the days."

"Good afternoon, Commander Stockard." The attractive receptionist in the lobby of the Press Facility Building smiled brightly as Deke entered the waiting area. "It's always a pleasure to see our newest star in here," she added with a flip of frosted blond hair.

He nodded in response. He sure didn't like being anyone's star, but at least his presence at the press facility required no explanation. Since *he* certainly didn't know why he was there when he had so much to do before leaving for Houston.

He fought a smile. Aw, hell. He knew why.

Because it felt like a lot more than six hours since he last saw Jessica.

His rubber-soled shoes made no noise on the linoleum floor as he approached the corridor of Public Affairs offices. A few feet from her door, he heard the music of her laughter in a one-sided conversation. He slowed his step, taking a moment to savor the sound and not wanting to rudely interrupt again.

Then he heard the endearment. *Honey.*

"Okay, I promise. Absolutely nothing will change this, Jo. We will be together on Friday."

He'd cut in on her conversations with this guy before.

"I'm not worried about what's going to happen to us." He heard the soft note in her voice. "I'll be home for good in February and this will all be behind us. I miss you so much and I know I'll love whatever you got me." She paused again, then laughed. That mysterious, wondrous laugh. "You seem very excited about this gift, Jo. Whatever it is, I'm sure I'll love it. No one in the whole world understands me like you."

What the hell was he thinking? That a girl like Jessica Marlowe wouldn't be involved with someone? Why didn't she just tell him that? It would have saved him a trip across the Space Center. And the hours he had wasted thinking about her, messing up the order in his mind. Without making a sound, he turned and headed back down the hallway. He barely acknowledged the pretty receptionist's goodbye.

Chapter Fourteen

The following week, Jessica sipped a glass of Chardonnay and inhaled the salty ocean air that permeated the Driftwood. Nestled among the cluster of casual bars and restaurants at the end of Cocoa Beach Pier, the place pulsed with NASA and Cape employees who'd planted themselves around long wooden tables laden with draft beer and popcorn.

Along the back wall, the Public Affairs department joined their spouses and dates, toasting their own victory and enjoying a private celebration of the news they had received. But Jessica wasn't celebrating like she should.

On the contrary, the news from L.A. and her impending trip home had both filled her with dread instead of glee.

The day before, she'd had her long-awaited conversation with Tony Palermo and made a little, but not enough, progress. He seemed bewildered by her belief that Carla Drake had been aware of the NASA rumors and was way too defensive of his golden girl. He only agreed to look into the matter and urged Jessica to consider the Emerging Technologies position.

Escaping to Boston at least eliminated the task of telling Deke that Sydney Lynn Lancaster had agreed to have him escort her to the premiere of *Lost Hero*. The media would be out in full force for the premiere and the result would be international coverage for Deke Stockard and NASA.

She absolutely dreaded his response.

"So?" With an unmistakable twinkle in her blue eyes, Wendy Rosen leaned over to Jess to ask the inevitable question. "When are you going to tell Deke the news?"

Stuart's longneck froze mid-sip in anticipation of the answer, but Jessica feigned surprise. "Is it *my* job? Sorry. I'm leaving on Sunday afternoon." Pointing to Stuart, she said, "Your husband may have the pleasure."

"Hey, it's your coup, Jess," Stuart insisted. "You should have the honors."

Shaking her head, Jessica disagreed. "No way. It was the Hollywood contingent. I didn't convince Sydney Lynn to accept the offer. They did." She leaned back in her chair. "You tell him on Monday."

Wendy looked across the bar to the Driftwood entrance, then grinned at her husband. "Or you can both tell him right now."

Jessica's gaze followed Wendy's. A breath caught in her throat as she locked on Deke's deep and intense gaze. Her stomach flipped at the sight of him, but within seconds, she composed herself and shot a glare at Stuart.

"A coincidence?"

"I couldn't wait to share our good news." He smiled and waved at Deke who made his way, along with Debbie and Jeff Clark, to their table.

Jessica let the rush settle before she turned directly to Deke, ready to meet the challenge head on. No one, including Deke Stockard, would know the thumping in her heart was drowning out the pounding repetitive chorus of Cher singing "Believe" in the background.

He had been out of sight in Houston for the past few days, but not off her mind. The peaceful truce they'd reached on the trip to New York had melted into far too many unprofessional fantasies. At her quietest, most secret moments, Jessica admitted to herself that she'd developed a full-blown crush on the man. She had to hide it. From him and from anyone else.

He ran his hand through his hair as he approached with Jeff and Debbie. As always, the sight of him lit a fire in her stomach...and lower. Would kissing him in the sand have the same effect as the snow? Desire warred with her conscience, and deep in her heart, she knew that desire could win.

Deke pulled a chair from the next table, turned it around and leaned on the back, his favorite way to sit. He nodded to Stuart and greeted Wendy...but barely acknowledged Jessica.

"How was Houston, Commander?" Stuart asked after they ordered beers.

"Tense." The look he exchanged with Jeff Clark gave the impression they had just been discussing the very subject. "Not as festive as this group. What's goin' on?" He still didn't look directly at Jessica, but addressed Stuart. "I smell PR trouble."

Jessica's tried to swallow. He wouldn't blast her in front of all these people, would he? It wasn't as though she was asking him to do something painful.

Like the *Today*show interview.

Everyone but Deke looked at her.

She took a deep breath. "As a matter of fact, Commander, we're celebrating your enhanced social life." He finally met her gaze when she spoke, which sent the usual thrill through her until something distant in his look caused a vague, sinking sensation to steal the pleasure. She passed the buck quickly. "Don't make the poor guy sweat, Stu, fill him in on the details."

Deke leaned forward, his arms crossed over the back of the chair, his feet hooked in the bottom. *Didn't he ever get ruffled?* "What's up, Doctor?" he asked Stuart.

"Well, it seems the ever-impressive Ross & Clayton has set you up to be a personal escort to the star of *Lost Hero* in Orlando."

"Personal escort? To whom?" Deke still didn't look at Jessica, but everyone else did, obviously expecting that it was her place to share the news.

"Sydney Lynn Lancaster," Jessica replied. "Have you heard of her?"

Jeff Clark let out a whoop that quieted the whole bar for a moment, and the reaction of nearly a dozen Cape employees resonated through the room. Deke was silent, but then a slow and maddening grin spread across his face as he shook his head in slight disbelief.

"Really." He raised his eyebrows and half-smiled at Jeff. "I guess worse things have happened to me."

She never expected compliance. Silence and the piercing stare of disbelief, maybe, but never easy consent. A ping of jealousy shot through her, the last swallow of wine turning sour in her stomach.

She listened as Stuart explained the premise of the movie and why Deke was the ideal choice for the celebrity date. "They thought about having O'Grady there, but apparently, Universal felt you were a bigger name."

Deke nearly choked on his beer. "What a crock. The guy gets shot down, comes face-to-face with the enemy, and lives on bugs till he's rescued. I flew over twice during the search and wasn't even around the day they found him." He shook his head. "And I get the girl."

"You do have to work, Stockard," Jessica said.

"Work?" His gaze was on the bottle in front of him.

"Yep." She wanted to reach out and grab his face. *Look at me.* "Smile for the cameras, look like you're having fun, and pay undivided attention to the lady."

Jeff laughed and smacked Deke's shoulder. "Tough assignment, buddy. Why do I think you can handle it better than anybody I know?"

The comments and jokes flew and Jessica wondered if anyone realized that he hadn't actually acknowledged her presence yet. Was he punishing her for the added assignment or had he simply forgotten the intimate moment they'd shared in New York?

Jessica leaned toward Wendy and Debbie to get in on their conversation. The subject turned to *Endeavour* and whether or not it would be ready.

"Ready or not," Wendy said, "it'll have to fly."

At the comment, the spark disappeared from Debbie Clark's eyes.

"Don't worry." Wendy laid her hand on Debbie's arm. "At least Jeff isn't on it."

"Someone's husband is, though," Debbie said with a sigh. She glanced at Jessica. "It's hard to live with risk your whole married life. I wouldn't trade Jeff for anything, but I wouldn't mind if he'd picked a career that was a little less stressful on me."

Jessica thought again of Deke's mother and her fears. As if she read Jessica's mind, Debbie continued in a whisper, "I know that's why Deke has never gotten seriously involved with anyone. Jeff told me they talked about it. He wouldn't put anyone through the terror."

A hoot of laughter from Jeff grabbed their attention. He held his hands out in an animated replay of the simulator training that he had just completed with Deke.

"It was hairy, that's for sure," Jeff said. "Took about five years off my life and that was in the sim. Next time, I'm wearin' a diaper!" At Deke's smirk, Jeff playfully punched him. "Hey, even you were white as a ghost on that landing."

"They were training for an emergency landing with no backup computers." Stuart explained to Jessica. "It isn't something we want to experience."

"No one talks much about the landing," Jessica said. "It's always the launch."

"There's your PR for you." Deke rolled his eyes and spoke sarcastically. "The landing's fifty times more dangerous than the launch. And most people don't even know that it's happening, except the few who hear the sonic boom when the orbiter breaks the sound barrier."

Her heart dropped at his condescending tone. When a few people started leaving, she seized the opportunity to escape the deep freeze. Deke got up to talk to some engineers at the bar, and she gathered her purse and said quick good-byes, aware of a threatening sting in her eyes.

She had to get away from him.

Deke stayed at the bar long enough for her to make a slow and dignified exit without even catching his eye. As the Driftwood door closed behind her, she increased her speed to a run, narrowly avoiding the tourists and bar hoppers moving in packs. All around her, the incongruous sound of a recorded version of *Joy to the World* battled to drown out the sound of crashing waves. The twinkling of pathetic white lights hanging on palm tree fronds swam in her watery vision.

Christmas in Cocoa Beach. What a miserable concept.

Standing at the bar, Deke watched Jessica leave without so much as a nod in his direction, a slow burn of desire and regret igniting him. Had he imagined the happiness in her eyes when he walked in? Maybe it was just surprise, but he'd seen a glimmer there. But he wasn't going to explore the possibility. She had a boyfriend and a well-documented preference for another state. Any attention she shot his way had to be some kind of tease. Or part of her tireless, harebrained campaign.

Still, he knew her well enough to know she was hurt when she walked out. But, good God. What did that woman expect from him?

He walked back to the table with a sigh.

The week in Houston had been hell from beginning to end. He'd been in a bad mood when he got there, mostly because his plans for Jessica had been shot down before they were even formed. The *Endeavour* crew was testy and tempers were hot and the whole week culminated with a goddamn emergency landing in the simulator that he and two other pilots nearly blew.

"Hey, Deke, we're going for some Chinese. You up for it?" Jeff asked, breaking his train of thought.

He answered without thinking. "Yeah, sure."

"I think Jess is relieved to be off to Boston this weekend," Stuart commented to Wendy.

"I don't think she's too thrilled with the landscape down here," Wendy said.

Deke took a sip of his beer and set the bottle on the table with a thud. "She makes that pretty obvious." The look on Stuart's face made him realize how cold that sounded, so he added, "I mean, it can't be easy for her to be yanked away from her regular job and her boyfriend and all."

Stuart looked puzzled. "She doesn't have a boyfriend."

"She does," Deke replied. "Some guy named Joe she's always on the phone with."

Stuart shook his head as he finished his beer and started to push back his chair. "No, no. That's Jo Miller. J-O. Works at R&C. I think she's Jessica's best friend. You ready to go?"

As the Clarks and Rosens gathered up their lightweight jackets, Deke didn't move. J-O. *Jo. Jesus, what an idiot I am.*

He flipped some money into the pile on the table and stood up. "You know, it's been a helluva week. I'm gonna pass on dinner."

By the time Jessica arrived home, her eyes stopped stinging and she no longer felt like crying. It wasn't her style to get worked up over a guy, she reminded herself as she unlocked the front door. A couple of men had grabbed her attention in the past few years; one or two even moved her to consider serious relationships. But when they split up, she was relieved, not heartbroken.

They all got in the way of work.

But this one? No, she couldn't remember feeling quite like this in a long, long time. How did that man get such a hold on her? It was all lust.

In the bathroom, she flipped the faucet to burning hot and poured some lavender gel.

Since he had kissed her, she had thought entirely too much about where that kiss could have led. The thought made her legs watery and weak and she felt like laughing out loud at her schoolgirl fantasies.

After lighting a few scented candles in the bath and living

room, Jessica picked an appropriately bluesy Anita Baker CD and filled her tiny home with the jazzy sounds of a woman in love. Getting lost in her ritual of bath, candles, and music, she poured a glass of wine, slipped off her clothes and clipped up her hair. The sound of a passing car engine outside caught her attention momentarily as she walked back into the bathroom in her underwear. Then a car door slammed. Unmistakably. In her driveway.

A tingling fear shot up her spine and weakened her knees. She closed the bathroom door to grab a short silk robe that hung there and waited for the next sound. Anita Baker crooned in the background, but Jessica tried to hear over her.

The doorbell rang. *Rapists and murderers don't ring doorbells.* Slowly, she opened the bathroom door and came around the corner, still unable to see the front door, which was blocked by the entry wall.

"Who is it?"

"Deke."

She stopped mid-step as apprehension melted into something far more shocking to her system.

Turning the corner, she peered through the three glass panels in the front door. Was he drunk? He'd barely touched one beer and she'd left the Driftwood less than an hour earlier.

She inched the door open and searched his face. He studied her and his gaze moved beyond her, taking in the flickering candles and soft music. His attention moved back to her, down the robe that barely covered her.

"I—um—are you alone?"

She bit her lip. "As far as I know." The adrenaline rush left her shaky and she leaned against the doorjamb for balance.

"Could I come in?" He looked unsure, uncertain. She'd never seen him this way.

"No." Maybe it was self-preservation. Hell, maybe she was playing hard to get. But, he would *not* come in this house, she decided. Not tonight. Not after putting her in the freezer all evening. She tightened the silk ties of her robe and leveled him with a hard stare.

"Okay. I understand." He raised his hands in a slight gesture of surrender and his gaze slipped down and right back up again. "I wasn't too friendly tonight."

"No. But I don't expect friendliness from you, Commander Stockard." A surge of satisfaction shot through her at his cringe. "What do you want?"

He took a deep breath. "To ask you to go sailing with me before you leave."

"Sailing?" He was too much. "You don't acknowledge my existence in a bar for an hour and then drop by to ask me to go sailing?"

"I can explain that." He reached across the short space between them and touched her chin, the slightest whisper of flesh against flesh. His eyes closed partially, and Jessica's heart started to feel like chocolate left in the burning Florida sunshine.

"So. Explain." *Then kiss the hell out of me.*

"Tomorrow. I can explain tomorrow. You're not leaving until Sunday, right?" He kept his hand on her chin, the steady, guiding hand of a pilot. He lifted her face a millimeter, closer to him. "I'd really like to show you...what's so special about this little corner of the world." His finger trailed a little lower, maddeningly close to the curve under her chin. "So we can be sure you want to come back."

Be sure of it, Deacon Stockard.

Common sense came floating back to the surface, but she

didn't step away from the bliss of his touch. "I don't know. I...I don't think I should."

"Why not?"

"Aren't you mad at me for the Sydney Lynn event?"

His eyes twinkled. "I'm a reasonable guy. I have time for a date now and then."

His knuckle grazed her collarbone, and then his fingers dropped dangerously close to the thin silk material over her breasts. Anita Baker started her next ballad.

"Is sailing with you a date?"

He raised one eyebrow ever so slightly. "If you want it to be."

She shook her head. "No. No. I can't. I have to pack. I have to—"

"Or it can just be a little tour of the river. Strictly aboveboard." He smiled at his own double entendre. Before she could answer, he slowly removed his hand. She had to fight the urge to grab it and put it back on her skin. "Tomorrow morning. At my dock around nine. No photographers."

She laughed a little. "How'd you know what I was thinking?"

He continued backward, easily navigating the half step down to the walk and keeping his gaze on her. He shook his head a little. To clear it, perhaps.

One more time his eyes traveled deliberately over her body, down her bare legs, and back up to her face. She felt dizzy. She felt needy. She wanted him to run right back here and—

"See you tomorrow, sweetheart."

She closed the door, quaking deep and low, and braced herself against the hard wood for support. What did she just agree to? Anita Baker hit a high note of love and longing and Jessica felt her heart go right along for the ride.

Chapter Fifteen

Deke awoke early to check the forecast. By seven o'clock, he had brewed some strong coffee and spent a quiet moment on the dock observing the skies and discerning the direction and strength of the winds.

Deke Stockard had never second-guessed a decision in his life and he wasn't about to start this morning. In fact, he congratulated himself for salvaging what was left of his miserable week. Today, he didn't want to think about coolant tube inspections or emergency landings. He didn't even want to discuss his required role at some silly movie premiere next week. All he wanted was the simple seduction of the wind in his sails and the company of one extraordinarily appealing woman.

Padding about in nothing but draw-string sweat pants, he took his time preparing their lunch, wondering what Jessica might be thinking about today. She was softening to him, he thought with certainty. He wanted her in the most physical way, but something else had nagged at him since they'd returned from New York. He *liked* her. Her cool demeanor that covered a softie inside, her biting, teasing wit she used as a guard, and most of all, her fiery enthusiasm for life. All in a package he couldn't wait to unwrap.

Two hours later with the boat packed, he stood on the deck, wrapping the lines and making his instinctive last-minute checks. He caught sight of her walking down the river path toward his dock. She wore jeans and a white tee shirt that pressed against her in the slight breeze and clung to her body. With a sweater tied around her shoulders and her hair in a ponytail, she looked like a teenager. He never got tired of looking at her.

"Permission to board?" she asked with a tentative smile as she reached the end of the dock.

He reached out and offered his hand to help her onto the deck. "Welcome aboard my humble vessel. She's small, but sturdy and fast."

He guided her to a spot near the helm and continued the last-minute preparations.

"It's not so small," Jessica commented. "What kind of sailboat is this?"

"A twenty-eight-foot Tanzer sloop."

"*Tailwind*. Nice name. Does it have a special meaning?"

"It's a pilot's most favorable flight condition," he told her. "Have you sailed before?"

"A few times around the Boston Harbor."

"You have the option of handling the jib sheets and cranking the winch when we come about and tack into the wind," he said with a smile. "Or you can just sit there and relax while I do the work."

"I'll give it a shot." Of course, she'd rise to the challenge. "I must admit, Deke, you don't strike me as the sailing type."

"I'm in the Navy, remember?"

"Come on—fast cars, fast planes. It doesn't fit. I imagine you in one of those go-fast boats with deafening engines guys like you can't resist."

What he couldn't resist was...her. "You don't think I'm in touch with my sensitive side?"

She laughed out loud and shook her head. "No, not exactly."

"You underestimate me. But, there is a motor, just in case the wind dies." He dangled a key on a rubber key chain in front of her. "A baby diesel, but it gets us away from the dock."

He twisted the key into the ignition and played with the throttle and pedal until they motored off. When they reached the channel of the Banana River, he killed the engine, raised the mainsail, and cut her straight into the wind. The silence, broken only by the whip of the elegant curve of canvas, engulfed them. He took a deep breath.

He waited for the peace he always felt at this moment. But when he glanced at the woman leaning against a cushion, wind whipping her dark hair around an angel's face, he was far from peaceful. The chill in the water's spray left a whisper of goose bumps on her skin and through her white tee shirt he could see the tantalizing effects of the cool air on her hardened nipples.

No peace, he thought, fighting the maddeningly automatic rush of blood at the sight of her. How long would it take him to entice her to the cabin below?

Curling up on the port-side cushion, Jessica tore her gaze from the amazing sight of Deke working the helm. It wasn't easy. He looked like an ad out of a boating magazine, with jeans pressed against his powerful thighs and the sleeves of his lightweight sweatshirt pushed up just enough to reveal brawny forearms. She rubbed her own arms and forced her attention to the shore.

"You know, if you let your eyes unfocus on the tree line, it almost looks like hills along the river," she commented to him. "God, I miss hills."

"No talk of snow or hills on this sail, please. Remember, the Cape Canaveral Chamber of Commerce is hard at work to showcase our natural beauty. Humor me, okay?"

"For a while," she agreed, studying the pastel Florida homes and boats of every imaginable size and shape tucked in coves of mangroves. "Actually," she said quietly, "it's really lovely here."

"Now you're getting it. All right, coming about. You know what to do with that winch?"

She dove into action with a significant amount of instruction from him and every ounce of strength she could muster, but it felt truly satisfying when the boom flipped to the opposite side of the boat and the contour of the mainsail gracefully reversed itself with a resounding snap in the wind.

As they tacked back and forth, he asked enough questions to get her chatting about her job. When she described the wonderful camaraderie she felt with her colleagues, he smiled sheepishly.

"That would include one Jo Miller, I take it."

"Jo, yes, of course. Have I mentioned her?"

He looked out over the bow and paused before he spoke softly. "I told you I owed you an explanation for last night."

Jessica's heart flipped at the intimate tone and she searched her mind for a possible part Jo could have played in it. "Yes?"

"I overheard you talking to her."

"Oh, I remember." It seemed like a year ago. "You walked into my office on one of my first days here and I hung up on her."

He nodded. "And again, last Monday. I was on my way

to ask if you'd like to go sailing today and I heard you talking to her. I thought you were talking to your boyfriend." At her incredulous look, he laughed. "I don't usually call Jeff Clark 'honey.'"

"You don't understand women."

"Never said I did." He shot her a sly grin. "Coming about. Honey."

They reached the intersection of the Banana and Indian Rivers and anchored in wide-open space away from the boats and water traffic. In a few minutes, he transformed the deck into a dining area with a portable tabletop, then proceeded to fill it with his delicious gourmet lunch.

"Wow. Impressive." Jessica lifted a container of oil-cured black and green olives. "I really could get some mileage out of your culinary skills. Let me think, how about *Space in the Kitchen—The Astronaut's Cookbook?*"

He laughed nervously and raised a doubtful eyebrow. "I never know if you're serious about this stuff or not."

"Definitely serious." She smiled contentedly and leaned back on a cushion. "We could release it with the poster."

He froze, a roasted pepper dangling from his plastic fork. "What poster?"

"I didn't mention the poster?" She shifted on the cushions and tried to look innocent.

"No."

"Oh. I thought I…well, we sold one of those great shots of you and the T-38. We presented it to a poster company and they're reproducing it."

He stared at her.

"You'll get big royalties," she added weakly.

"A poster? Like Farrah Fawcett?"

"You're showing your age, Stockard. But, yeah. You could be up on dorm-room walls all over America."

"Good God. A poster." He shook his head and dropped the pepper on a paper plate. "What the hell is next?"

She took a delicate bite of a calamata olive. "The action figure."

He froze and closed his eyes. In a moment he opened them, and a slow, maddening grin spread across his face.

"Why is this man smiling?" she asked.

"I'm just imagining how you'll pay for this." He leaned over the table, his lips just inches from her face. "You will pay dearly, Jessica Marlowe. I promise you that."

An intoxicating thrill shot through her body with her own mental images of just how delicious his torture could be.

Lulled by the waves, the fresh air and the easy conversation, Jessica lazily watched Deke loosen the jib to take them back up the river.

He studied the western sky with a skeptical expression and glanced back at her, a tinge of regret in his eyes. "I'd like to stay anchored a little longer, but we're going to get the inevitable storm." He twisted a line and shrugged. "At least the wind's behind us, so we won't need to tack."

"Is that good?" she asked.

"It means I can settle into this comfortable seat." He sat down and reached his hands under her arms, gently tugging her back, right against his chest. "With you."

She hissed in a quiet breath as his hands brushed the sides of her breasts and he positioned her into the curve of his body. She stiffened as her backside came in contact with his jeans and his fingers eased her head back on his chest. She'd somehow fallen right into the most incredible place, the valley between his long, powerful legs.

She tried to exhale. "Relax, sweetheart." His lips pressed the top of her head so that all she could do was enjoy the sensations that rolled over her as the wind and his skilled hand on the helm carried them north, while his free hand tunneled and tangled in her hair.

They arrived at his dock at the same time as the rain. "Go on in, you're gonna get soaked," he told her as they motored up to the mooring.

"I don't melt, Deke. I'll help you. I'm sure there's a lot to do." The rain was light, still no more than a fine mist, so she pulled her sweater on and followed his direction after they tied up to the dock. They lowered and stowed the sails and secured the dock lines. Just as they finished, the sky opened to a downpour and the first flash of lightning made him jump onto the dock and reach for her.

"Enough, Gilligan. Time to get inside. I'll get the cooler later."

A loud clap of thunder shook the air. He put his arm around her and they ran toward the house. They reached the covered porch just as a bolt of lightning and simultaneous thunder exploded, and she instinctively grabbed him and gasped.

He squeezed her tighter, then stroked her soaking curls and wet cheeks. She knew he was waiting for her to look up. When she did, their kiss was nearly immediate and completely mutual. As their bodies pressed against each other, they explored each other's mouths hungrily. He steadied her with one arm and wrapped his other hand in her hair.

"Come inside," he whispered.

She knew she had to walk but wasn't sure her legs could carry her. Keeping an arm around her, he flipped a key in the lock of the sliding glass door and guided her into his house.

Once there, he returned to the kiss as they moved, connected, lips and tongues intertwined, toward the sofa in the living room. She couldn't go there. Horizontal would be deadly. But the thrilling burn that started in her stomach and sizzled down her thighs took over all common sense. Fighting it and every force of nature in her being, Jessica pulled back to look at him.

His eyes mirrored the sparks that burst through her. He bent his head down to the curve of her neck and kissed her skin, flicking his tongue over her collarbone, moaning softly and moving his hands lower to her waist, her hips, her backside. He pulled her closer and she almost bit his lip at the pressure of him, hard and straining through his jeans.

Warm fingers crept under her sweater and over her cottony tee shirt, seeking the hard tip of her breast. His thumb circled it, shocking her straight down to the aching, feminine tingle between her legs.

She couldn't stop. Control rolled away with each wave of arousal.

Reeling, dizzy, she pushed herself closer to him, and without breaking their kiss, he tugged her onto the cushiony leather sofa. On top of him, her body magically molded to his as Jessica let a primal force of nature and desire take control of her. Her hips kept rhythm with his as she heard herself moan, amazed that he could do this to her. It was magic. It was a spell. It was the risk he kept warning her about and all she wanted was…Deke.

His breath was hot on her neck, his hands starting to tug her tee shirt up. Her clothes were about to come off. This was it. No turning back. Something jarred her back to reality.

"Deke, please."

He kissed her neck, his lips and tongue dropping further, nearly touching her breasts. "Please what?"

"Please stop."

Working his mouth slowly back up her neck, he teased her with his tongue and then nipped her lips before melting into another kiss, slow and deep and warm. Then she could feel his breath as he finally spoke. "Not the please I was hoping for, sweetheart."

Jess closed her eyes, wanting only to press harder against him and give into the breathtaking urge to touch him everywhere: his handsome face, his powerful chest, the sexy, masculine bulge of his jeans.

"Deke, I can't do this." Her words came in gasping breaths, cut off by the pounding of her heart.

"Yes, you can." He chuckled in her ear. "In fact, you are."

She wanted to argue, wanted to agree, wanted to just shut up and lose herself in his body and his kisses, but she didn't. Somehow, she found the strength to pull away. "No. I can't do this."

"You can't or you won't? Big difference." Slowly, he removed his hands from under her sweater and lifted her to a less threatening angle, allowing her to sit up a bit. He inched his way up to sit next to her.

"I won't." She tried to convey a commitment she wasn't sure she believed.

Lifting a strand of her damp curls, he let his fingers play on her face while the arousal subsided. Still, his breathing stayed heavy and slow, his eyes dark with arousal.

He finally sighed deeply. "I'll be honest with you, Jess. I don't think about a whole lot else when I'm around you lately."

A smile played on her lips. "Yeah. Me too."

"Really?" He widened his eyes in a hopeful, boyish look. "That's encouraging."

"Please don't be encouraged." She had to be honest. "You're a client."

The sound of his heartfelt laughter surprised her. "You can do better than that, spin doctor."

"You may think it's a funny and flimsy excuse, but for a man who practically wears his code of ethics on his sleeve, you ought to understand."

"I do understand," he said softly, still smiling. "But we're alone. No hidden cameras. No audience." He gave her a teasing look. "Although with you, one can never be completely sure."

She glared at him. "Not funny. I do have a very real job with very real rules in Boston." And no future with an astronaut in Florida, she thought silently, knowing the words would sound clingy and silly. She stood and walked to the sliding glass doors to gauge the length of the rainstorm. She needed to go home.

"Anyway," she said, studying the clouds. "I don't take this—this situation as lightly as you probably do."

He was behind her in one second. He spun her around and she saw the fire in his eyes. "You've got me all wrong. I don't do this either unless it feels completely right. This does."

"I don't know what you mean by completely right."

"Come on. We've been starving for this since the minute we saw each other."

She started to shake her head, but he put a finger on her lips.

"Don't you dare deny it. This has been coming from the beginning. Since before I even knew you had me in mind for this PR garbage. Hell, I was undressing you in your first presentation."

"That's just lust," she whispered.

175

"You want love?" he countered, his eyes narrowed in warning.

"Of course not." Lightning flashed in the window, jarring her. "I just don't want to do anything stupid. There are people who would like nothing more than for me to fall into bed with you."

"I know. I'm one of them." He reached up and rubbed his thumb along her cheek. "But not for a price you're not willing to pay."

"My career would be an awfully high price."

"I know all about regulations. I live with them and I respect them. But sometimes..." His finger reached her lips. "You gotta break the rules."

At that moment, Jessica wanted to break every rule she ever followed. A throbbing ache moved from her most feminine core right to her heart.

"I'm sorry, Deke. Risk scares me too much."

He leaned forward to gently kiss her lips. The temptation to open her mouth and take the kiss right back to where they were weakened her down to her toes.

"The rain is slowing," she whispered.

He reached his arms around her back and pulled her close enough to feel his heart. "Don't go home yet."

"I have to. I'll just take the path. I run it every morning."

"I know." He smiled. "I try never to miss you jogging by."

She laughed, surprised at the revelation, relieved that some of the tension had faded, if only for a moment. "I'll see you on December thirtieth. Remember? You have a date with a movie star, poster boy. I'll be there to supervise your every move."

"And drag me in front of every reporter."

"That, too." She pulled back an inch and gave him a dubious look. "You do own a tuxedo, don't you?"

"What, no space suit?"

She exhaled a laugh as he took her face in his hands and kissed her lightly on the lips. "Come on, sweetheart, I'll walk you home."

They said almost nothing, dodging raindrops and low-hanging branches on the way to her house. At her patio, he reached down for one last long, wistful kiss.

"Merry Christmas, Jess," he whispered. "Have fun in Boston."

She didn't respond but tried to remember why on earth she was going back there.

Chapter Sixteen

"**D**o you like it?" Before Jessica could see the woman asking the question, she heard the sultry lilt of her voice and caught a whiff of Carla's ultra-hip unisex perfume. "I got so sick of all that dark stuff. No one has cherry wood anymore."

No, no one at Kennedy Space Center did, that was for sure. Jessica looked around the office that had been vacant when she left. Carla had wasted no time establishing her territory and making sure it had the most commanding view in all of R&C Boston.

With a rueful smile, Jessica envisioned the chipped Formica and dented supply cabinet in the office she'd called home for the last six weeks. "It's beautiful."

Carla's thin face squished into what she must have thought was a girlish, innocent expression. "You're not upset, are you? I mean, it wasn't your office and I just hated to see all this gorgeous space wasted."

"Of course I'm not upset." A little jealous and a lot disgusted, but not upset. "I'm sure you fit everything nicely into the overhead budget for the year."

"As if those ogres in finance would let me spend a dime we didn't have." Carla laughed, pulling Jessica further into the office. "Anyway, we're making oodles on Dash. That account's profits will be sky-high at year-end. At least forty percent over our projections."

Over *Jessica's* projections. The dig wasn't lost. Oh, Miss California was good. She was very, very good.

Carla dropped onto a creamy leather sofa and patted the seat next to her. "Come on, girlfriend. Spill the beans. I want to know absolutely everything about that sex god you've got your hands on in Florida."

Jessica took the seat across from her, setting her Palm Pilot gently on the glass coffee table. "Sorry to ruin your fantasies, but we're barely friends, let alone lovers." That's why she said no to Deke: so she could look Carla in the eye and not lie. "I'm still waiting for a copy of the Dash marketing plan."

Carla's eyes narrowed. "You are not letting that archaic R&C fraternization rule keep you from jumping that man's bones, are you?"

"No, I'm not," Jessica said quietly. "I'm letting my own basic morals guide my actions and the fact that I am not even slightly attracted to a man who also happens to be my client. Does Rita have a copy of the plan in her files?"

Without another word, Carla got up and took a manila file folder off her desk and dropped it on the coffee table. "Well, then, Jess. Never let it be said that you fucked your way to the top."

Jessica picked up the folder and lifted her gaze to meet Carla's. The hazel eyes held a dare and a challenge. "Now, who would say a thing like that, Carla?"

Carla sauntered behind her massive, light-oak desk and pulled out the chair. "I understand you didn't have a chance to talk to Tony while you were in New York."

"No. He got pulled into some damage control." Jessica

casually opened the file and started reading the first page of what appeared to be at least an eighty-page marketing plan. Jeez. Even the introduction was good.

"Uh-huh," Carla said. "The *Today*show situation."

That *you* caused, Jessica almost said. But her mantra played steadily in her head. *Pick your battles. Pick your battles.* She would not fight this one. Her fight was with Tony, not Carla.

"And you were..." Carla cleared her throat. "Not available later that day, as I understand it."

The words of the marketing plan ran together. Was this an accusation? Just how much of her personal life did Carla know? She looked up questioningly. "Me? My cell's on twenty-four seven, Carla. You know that."

"Oh, I know. It's just that Tony said he tried to find you, but you'd already checked out of the Plaza." Carla settled into her desk chair. "I guess he wasn't sure where you were that night."

Could she be any more obvious? "What did he need to tell me?"

"That he's announcing a GM for this office by the end of the year." Carla crossed her arms and leaned back, the mistress of her blond-wood domain. "Hasn't he called you yet? It's been a week."

Jessica held her gaze and refused to take the bait Carla was offering. "It's not the end of the year yet. Perhaps he's waiting to make a final decision."

"Perhaps." Carla nodded.

"Hey, stranger. I heard you were back."

Jessica turned to see her old secretary, Rita Ross, standing in the doorway. "Hi, Rossy. I'm here for the week."

Rita grinned and winked. "Good. We'll catch up. Bill Dugan's on three."

Jessica stood and scooped up the marketing plan. "Great, I'm dying to talk to him."

"Uh...he's holding for Carla, actually."

A slow burn warmed Jessica's neck. "Okay." She grabbed her Palm Pilot and shrugged. "I was just leaving anyway."

Skip Bowker hung up the phone and peered through the glass wall of his office toward the main hangar of the OPF. He watched the impressive figure of Commander Stockard stride by without so much as a glance in his direction. Deke was a very, very busy man these days with his girlfriend gone and his time freed up again.

He'd been in the facility nearly fifteen hours a day and showed no signs of giving up. Man, he would have fit right in with the crew back in the Apollo days. They would have eaten up a guy with that kind of determination and dedication. Not like these whiny twenty-something engineers who drifted in and out at their whim. In the old days, they had a purpose. They had a cause. They had an enemy.

Now they had something called the United Space Alliance and a bunch of contractors who were stepping all over each other to get a dollar. *Cosmonauts*, for Christ's sake, living off American taxes on an American space station. It was enough to make a guy want to throw up.

Jesus. It was so different now.

But it could change back so easily. That's what he'd been trying to tell his friend for the last twenty minutes. Things were not exactly as they looked around here, and if the right people knew about it, the wrong people would get shit-canned in a hurry.

Then they might be able to go back to the way things were. He was counting on his friend to help him. He'd seemed intelligent enough the few times they'd met in the past. A smart and ambitious character who would take the information Skip handed him on a platter and do something with it.

No one should have to die. Unless they're dumb enough to climb in that bird and try to take it up to the space station. Then they'd all have to watch that white cloud of death explode over the Atlantic Ocean one more time.

The image made his gut burn. Betsy and *Challenger*. Nothing had ever been the same since 1986.

If they were smart, they'd just let the Commie kick and turn him into space junk.

If they were smart.

He watched lithe Deke Stockard climb into the hatch of the shuttle, clinging to his precious PLIC logs. Now Deke was smart, or at least he was until he'd gotten completely distracted by a pretty girl.

Skip smiled, thinking of Betsy and her trusting brown eyes. Well, hell. That can happen to a guy. That sure can happen to a guy.

Jessica had just finished fluffing out her one-foot-tall, pre-decorated Bloomingdale's artificial Christmas tree when the front desk guard called to announce that Jo Miller had arrived.

Crossing the hardwood floor in bare feet, she opened the door of her condo with an expectant smile on her face. They hadn't had a moment to chat for the last two days. This visit was Jessica's whole Christmas, having gotten the message loud and clear that Dad wasn't up for company over the holiday. She couldn't wait to settle in for a nice long chat with her best friend.

Jo swept in after they'd hugged in the hallway. "Oh, Jess. You broke out the big-time Christmas decorations." She tapped the tiny tree and threw her red wool coat on a chair. "Just for moi?"

"Shut up. I can't find the mistletoe."

Jo crumpled into her favorite corner of the sofa and kicked off her heels. "That's okay. You left the mistletoe-ee in Florida."

"Oh, please. Not you, too."

Jo smiled slyly. "Hey, this is me. I know the truth. How was the sail?"

Jessica stepped behind the kitchen counter and pulled the cork out of the white wine she'd been chilling. "Dee-vine."

"How divine?" Jo rubbed her feet. "And just pour me water, okay?"

"Water? Tomorrow's Christmas Eve, Jo. And God knows after my meeting with the Grinch this afternoon, I could use a drink."

"We'll get to her in a minute. Exactly how divine?"

Jessica sighed, longing to tell her, but not sure if somehow the magic would evaporate if she committed it to words. "Not over-the-top divine, but close. Why water?"

"I'm thirsty. Is that a crime? How close?"

"Second base. Are you pregnant?"

Jo froze mid-foot massage and flashed a guilty look at Jessica. "Don't ruin the present, hon. I have the little plus sign all wrapped up in a box for you."

A rush of warmth poured over Jessica, and a little mewing sound escaped her lips.

"I need a godmother, too," Jo said quietly.

"Oh my God." Jessica put the bottle down and practically ran across the room to Jo, the lump in her throat nearly choking her. "I'd be honored."

Jo really did have a box with a white plastic case with a pink plus sign wrapped for Jessica and she insisted it be opened with all due ceremony. Jessica held the gift for a long time, treasuring it in precisely the spirit it had been given to her.

"I'm so happy for you, Jo. You're going to be a great mother."

"I'd love company, doll," Jo said as she cut a generous slice of brie and smeared it on a piece of French bread. "Why don't you hook up with the rocket man and we can get fat together?"

Jessica smiled and twirled the plastic in her hand. "Get real, Miller."

"I am real. Marlowe." Jo leaned forward and put a gentle hand on Jessica's arm. "There's more to life than work, honey."

"So I've heard."

"What's stopping you?"

Jessica fluffed a pillow on the floor and laid down, her wine glass precariously balanced on her stomach. She looked at it and smiled. "For one thing, if I get as fat as you will, I won't be able to do this."

Jo didn't laugh. "This guy's different, isn't he?"

Jessica grabbed the glass before it tipped. "Different from Gary? Well, he's not an investment banker who thinks he's a Master of the Universe."

"He *is* a Master of the Universe, for crying out loud. He's an astronaut!" Jo laughed a little. "Gary was just a walking ego that you wisely dumped."

Jessica smiled and crunched up enough to take a sip of

wine. She swallowed and dropped her head back onto the pillow, closing her eyes. "He's the most amazing man I've ever met, Jo."

Jo said nothing.

"He's brilliant and driven and caring and stubborn and talented and funny and sarcastic and sweet and oh, God in heaven, he is hot."

Jo chuckled. "I noticed. He looked particularly good on the *Tonight Show*. Did you pick that black outfit?"

"Mmmm. No. He looks good in everything, though. Did I mention that he's brilliant?"

"At least once."

"Did I say funny?"

"Oh, yeah."

"And sexy." Jessica moaned softly. "He's the sexiest man I've ever met."

"Well, I certainly wouldn't slow down your killer climb up the career ladder for anything *that* unappealing." Jo bit a cracker. "What a disappointment you'd be to the old professor who raised you."

"Don't start on Dad. He's just too old to get mad at anymore."

"Okay. What's Commander Perfect's fatal flaw?"

"Fatal. Hah. That's just it." Jessica narrowed her eyes, thinking about how many times he'd referenced not coming home from work. "He seems to think he's going to die."

"We all are."

"But he's a risk-taker to the nth degree."

Jo chuckled. "Not if he doesn't want to fall in love with you, he's not."

Jessica looked at her. "I never thought about it that way."

She reached up to the table over her head and grabbed the small white plastic pregnancy test. Could she ever do this?

Was she a risk-taker? Was she up to the one challenge that she didn't feel smart or competent enough to tackle?

She moved the wine glass and absently rubbed her tummy. She'd never met anyone who made her think of such possibilities.

But at that moment, they seemed as infinite as space.

Chapter Seventeen

Deke swore under his breath as he whipped the bow tie open in frustration for the third time, then concentrated on looping an even knot. With a final tug, he stepped back to appraise his work. He was satisfied, but couldn't resist reaching into the collar to pull at the stiff fabric that choked him on the balmy December night.

He grabbed his keys in arrogant defiance, knowing full well that a limo driver lingered in his driveway, looking completely out of place leaning against a pearly stretch Lincoln Continental. Deke had all but barked at the poor kid when he'd arrived ten minutes ago with a stammering explanation that he'd gone to Jessica's house first, but she wasn't quite ready and had sent him down here. Deke glared at the clean-scrubbed driver and immediately disliked him for no rational reason.

He just didn't want to drive fifty miles to Orlando staring across the ridiculous expanse of a limousine with some goofy kid at the wheel trying to act like he wasn't listening or watching. After ten days, Deke wanted to be completely alone with Jessica.

"Tell you what." He put a friendly hand on the kid's shoulder. "You follow. I'm taking my own car."

"Uh, sure. You got it, sir." The driver hesitated for a moment and squinted at Deke. "Sir? Is she going with you or me?"

Deke grinned. "Damn straight she's going with me."

Driving the short distance to Jessica's house, Deke finally indulged in the anticipation that had been quietly fighting for a share of his mind over the past week and a half. He'd gotten very adept at ignoring the subtle pressure Jessica Marlowe put on his subconscious, spending nearly every waking moment at the Orbiter Processing Facility.

He'd studied every seal, tube, and wire he could get his hands on, reviewed the reports on the last mission, and quietly grilled Skip Bowker. In general, he put the engineers through hell trying to ensure that whatever caused the hydrogen leak on *Columbia* wouldn't happen again on *Endeavour*. The whole process had left little time for romantic reveries.

But he'd wake in the violet-gold half-light of dawn and walk out to the end of his dock with a cup of coffee to admire the heavenly reflection on the water every morning. Only then did he acknowledge that he missed her. Truly missed her. He'd wonder what she was doing at those same moments, imagining her sleeping in her home in cold and cloudy Boston, the now familiar stirring of desire shooting through him.

He wanted her so damn bad, he felt like a teenage boy.

With the exception of a few hours on Christmas spent with the Clarks, Deke had only allowed himself one free evening since she'd left. He used that to invite Caryn Camden for a quiet drink and to tell her that he wouldn't be calling anymore.

The news didn't seem to surprise her, since she let him off the hook with a sweet smile and only a shadow of sadness in her eyes. He couldn't enjoy the playful distraction she offered, not when his mind dwelled on a completely different woman. Regardless of what Jessica decided, he wanted to be free for the possibility.

He approached her front door, which had been left ajar, and gently pushed it in as he knocked.

"Hey, anybody I know in there or did she send down a pinch hitter from the majors?"

Familiar laughter greeted him, then a flash of something ice blue and shimmering squeezed the air from his chest.

"Whoa." He felt like an idiot, but it was all he could manage.

She literally took his breath away and all he could do was stare. Up and down. From the thick tussle of dark curls cascading out of some sparkly clip over bare shoulders, down to a slash of satin that clung to her breasts and waist in some kind of magical, miraculous way.

When he finally made his way back to her face, he caught the glint in her eyes as she reached over to touch his bow tie. "You clean up nice, too, Stockard."

"Maybe we should go in the limo after all." He stole another glance at the dress. And the cleavage she rarely showed in her business attire.

"What do you mean? It's here, isn't it?"

"Yes, but I wanted to drive. Just to have my own car. He can follow. But you look so...amazing."

She surprised him with an agreeable tilt of her head and a shrug. "That's no problem. But, once we get to the Universal party, you need to leave with Sydney Lynn in the limo. No one arrives at the red carpet in a Corvette. Not even you."

He watched her gather up a wrap thing that matched her dress and inhaled the sultry, smoky perfume that clung to her. She picked up a tiny handbag, a small leather notebook, and her cell phone, reminding him that she was going out for work, not play.

"I would like you to drive over with me, though." He held the front door open for her and couldn't resist running his knuckles over the tempting soft skin of her shoulder. "You know, so you can coach me on how to act and what to say."

She shot him a skeptical look, then a wry smile. "Just remember. Sydney Lynn's your date. That's the whole idea."

Everything about her glistened. Her eyes, the subtle evening makeup, even the lipstick that made her mouth downright appetizing.

He ached for a taste.

"I know you're on duty, sweetheart. I'll be good."

Jessica inhaled the leather of the Corvette and noticed how it mingled with Deke's clean, masculine scent. As much as she wanted to pretend this was *their* date, she flipped open her portfolio and began to review the typed agenda and press list.

She tried to concentrate on briefing Deke about what to expect but repeatedly lost her train of thought as he hit the accelerator, catapulting her into the seat with some baby-Gs, as he called the force that left her breathless and him amused.

"We've arranged some interviews with the media that will take place before you meet Syd—"

His hand left the gearshift and settled onto her thigh, a steady thumb circling the fabric. "Am I distracting you?" he asked.

"Yes."

"Good. You know I hate even talking about the media."

"Why are you doing this?"

"Because I missed you."

Turning to look out the window, Jessica let his comment sink in and destroy all her resolve.

He reached over and flipped the portfolio closed. "Stop working and talk to me. How was sunny New England?"

She sighed. "Not."

"And your boyfriend, Jo?"

She grinned at him. "Pregnant."

"Guess that sort of complicates things."

He had no idea. "It was the only bright spot in an otherwise dark week," she admitted. And even that bright spot only left her questioning her own choices regarding motherhood and marriage. And fantasizing about Deke.

"No snowboarding down Beacon Street?" he asked. "No fine dining at *Bahston* hot spots?"

She dropped her head back on the seat. "Your imagination is as far off as your accent. I spent the days at my office and the nights at my condo. That's my life."

She didn't want to tell him that her world had turned cold and unwelcoming in her absence. Even Rita seemed to believe the rumors that Jessica was on the outs. When Jessica had asked her to get her stacks of client supplies, files and stationery, Rita had returned with only NASA materials and the coy response that Carla had instructed her not to give Jessica anything for the other accounts.

She considered confiding her professional worries for a moment, but it all seemed so blissfully far away from the purring engine of the Corvette, her dreamy silk dress, and his relentless hand resting just above her knee. Forget Carla. Forget babies that would be born to other women. This moment was too nice.

"How 'bout you, Deke? Been busy?"

"Yep. Living at the OPF, taking things apart and trying to put them back together again."

"Any progress?"

He shrugged. "Some, but not enough."

"Will it launch on time?"

"Has to. No choice. We're doing everything possible. Skip Bowker, though..." He shook his head and sighed.

"What? What's the matter?"

"I just can't figure that guy. There're a lot of holes in his work, but I can't find any evidence of a mistake."

Jessica studied his profile. "Deke, would you go up on *Endeavour* if you were scheduled?"

His features grew tight and the fine vein in his neck became slightly visible. His response to what she considered a rhetorical question surprised her.

"It would never occur to me to question any assignment. That's what I'm trained to do." Then he turned to her. "Don't go there."

Hurt by the strength of his warning, she turned back to the window so he couldn't see the look on her face. She felt his hand on her leg, a gentle touch.

"I just meant I don't want to dwell on it tonight. You're too pretty to talk about shuttle launches." He shot a sidelong glance and smiled broadly. "Way, way too pretty."

"You better be prepared to dwell on it tonight. You're talking to reporters and it could come up."

"All true," he said. "But you *are* pretty."

She tried to smirk at him but couldn't find the heart in the face of his genuine compliments. She'd just have to stay away from the *Endeavour* subject. "So, what do you want to know about Sydney Lynn? Have you seen any of her movies?"

"Was she in the one with the three women plotting to kill their husbands? *Dance Lessons?*"

Jessica nodded and smiled, knowing what he'd say next.

"With the, shall we say, rather *memorable* outside shower scene?"

Of course. "The only thing any man liked about that movie."

"What's not to like?"

"You're being a good sport about this," she told him as they pulled into the lot at Universal. "And I know you're going to do really well."

He grinned at her. "Blondes are my specialty." At her surprised look, he added, "But not my preference."

The minute they arrived at the richly appointed ballroom on the studio lot, the entourage of Universal people took over and hustled Deke away. Jessica held back, wanting to let him get fully immersed in the experience but watching with fascination as he worked the crowd and charmed everyone in sight. What a remarkable and complicated man he'd turned out to be.

As her gaze stalked his every move, he turned and caught her staring from across the room. He winked, sending fireworks down to her toes.

Finally, the double doors of the ballroom opened, and Sydney Lynn Lancaster made a suitably grand entrance with her own entourage of hangers-on. She magnetically drew everyone's attention as an audible gasp rippled through the crowd. Signature platinum waves glistened like glass, cascading over a red, sequined dress that dropped backless to the very lowest possible point of her tailbone.

Deke greeted her with his most devilish, appealing smile. Sydney Lynn practically melted at the sight of him, never allowing more than six inches between her and her date. She slipped her arm into his and introduced him to everyone as "my commander" and acted as though they'd known each other since childhood. Intimately.

At the imposing entrance to the IMAX theater, the press and photographers filled the first several rows of many bleachers lining the red carpet. Jessica and Stuart worked together to find the most important reporters, give them fact sheets and press kits about Deke, and encourage the photographers to get a shot that every wire service in the world would pick up.

Just before eight, the deafening cheers signified the arrival of the big names. Standing behind the first few rows of camera crews from *E!* and *Entertainment Tonight*, Jessica whispered some instructions to the producers and on-air talent, wanting to be sure Deke got some interview time and that he wasn't lost next to Sydney Lynn.

As his limousine pulled up to a stop and the official greeter opened the door, Deke stepped out and the crowd responded. How did he know to do that perfect wave? He looked like he'd done this his whole damn life. He reached back into the limo and held out a hand to assist Sydney Lynn and the crowd exploded with love and the excitement of seeing her in the flesh.

Sydney gave them what they wanted. Her smile was as bright as the thousands of flashing cameras, her dress as daring and unforgettable as the roles she played. Jessica couldn't help but notice how her long red glove stayed wound around Deke's arm and that the movie star treated her date to almost as much attention as she gave the crowd.

He certainly didn't seem to mind, showering her with

admiring gazes and whispering in her ear, making her laugh as he slowly escorted her down the red carpet and through the screaming crowds. *What the hell was he saying to her?* Didn't matter. He was doing what he was supposed to do. He was just doing it really, really well.

As they reached the press section, the impromptu interviews along the red carpet started, and although Sydney was the focus, Jessica could see that Deke managed to get a few seconds here and there of airtime.

She stepped back into the crowd as he approached her section, not wanting to distract him. But as he stood close to Sydney Lynn, offering his undivided attention to the answer she was giving an excited young reporter from FOX News, his gaze moved up into the stands and he found her. A hint of a secret lifted his lips and an instant, lightning-like realization shook her to the bone.

I'm in love withhim.

☆

The rest of the event passed in a blur. Jessica managed to talk to enough reporters and photographers to be sure Deke got included in the coverage as more than just 'Sydney Lynn's date.'

She went through the motions of answering questions. She handed out press kits. But her whole being buzzed with awareness of new feelings. She'd have to face him and fight the longing to tell him. She'd have to be near him and resist holding him and loving him. Somehow, she'd have to resist the ache to make love to him.

She could barely breathe with all she couldn't do, but wanted to.

It was past eleven by the time the lengthy drama finished

and the stars had accepted their rounds of applause and the producers had all made their speeches. The last venue for celebration was a cavernous restaurant owned by the world-renowned chef, Dante Cardinelli. The wood and chrome two-story atrium of "Inferno" had been transformed into a play place for lovers of airplanes and combat. Deke and Sydney Lynn were strategically placed at a table in the center of the wide-open room with other stars.

From her vantage point across the room, Jessica watched him lean on one arm, close to Sydney's ear, whispering, making her laugh. The room echoed with the jazzy sounds of an orchestra that couldn't begin to drown out the party banter of the crowd. A reporter from the *New York Daily News* hollered above the din to get Jessica's attention and ask for an interview.

"You can try," Jessica answered with a shrug. "But I don't think she's doing any more interviews tonight."

"I don't want Sydney, ma'am. I want that fighter pilot astronaut guy." The young reporter looked over to the center table. "He's the great story. And I want a photo. Of him alone. One nobody else has."

Jessica couldn't resist the request. "Let me see what I can do. I have to get his attention."

Which wouldn't have been that hard about three hours ago, but she was beginning to doubt her ability to tear him away from the incredible Ms. Lancaster.

She worked her way through the room to his table, only to see him rise to take Sydney to the dance floor. *Jeez. You don't have to dance with her, too.*

Mesmerized, Jessica watched Deke put his arm on Sydney's bare back and guide her around, never taking his gaze off her, never pausing the easy conversation.

She wound her way back through the crush of tables and

partiers to find the reporter and tell him they were finished with interviews. She wanted to go home.

"I don't think it's going to happen," she told him.

He looked disappointed, but suddenly his face brightened. "Here he comes!"

Jessica turned and saw Deke making his way to her, loosening his bow tie. His direct gaze burned a hole in her as every cell came back to life at the fire in his eyes.

"Hey," he said as he approached. "Where've you been?"

Her pulse ratcheted higher as she tried to steady her breathing. "Working, Stockard."

Ignoring the reporter, he leaned down close to her ear. For a moment, she thought he was going to kiss her, but he just whispered, "She's boring."

"Oh, I can tell." She smiled and held his gaze far longer than necessary. "Will you do one more interview?Then I promise I'll leave you alone for the rest of the night."

"Don't make promises you can't keep." His sexy voice nearly did her in.

"One more interview." She tried to stay professional. "Then I'm going home with Stuart and Wendy."

"What? Why?"

"I'm done, Deke. You're not."

He put his arm around her shoulder and glanced across the room. "Come with me," he whispered.

As he guided her away, he turned to the reporter. "I need to speak with my publicist for a moment, then I'll do your interview. Excuse us."

He led her into the direction of a darkened hallway off the kitchen. In an alcove full of cartons and supplies and the overpowering scents of the kitchen, he stopped and put both arms around her.

"Deke? What's the—"

He kissed her hard on the mouth, crushing her lips and pulling her tightly against him. She had no thoughts except the raw response that shook her. Opening her mouth to him, she kissed him with the same fury. Their tongues connected, wet and warm and delicious.

When they finally parted, all she could do was attempt to regain her balance. And nearly failed.

"Don't go to sleep, sweetheart. I'll see you later."

Chapter Eighteen

This time, Jessica lit the candles and drew her bath expecting Deke's late-night visit. She mulled over the implications of his parting comment, certain that she understood what he was telling her. Although it killed her to take off the incredible gown she had found in Bloomingdale's last week in Boston, she wanted to bathe and relax and relive the extraordinary moments of the night. She wanted to prepare for him.

Tonight, she was breaking the rules. Good girl Jessica Marlowe, straight-A student and star employee would be smashing propriety and agency rules to bits. She'd go back to being an overachiever tomorrow and hide her sin from whomever she had to. But, tonight, she wanted to give her body and soul to the man she loved.

After luxuriating in a long and fragrant bubble bath, Jessica fluffed her hair and slipped on a thin cotton tank undershirt and a silky pair of men's boxers.

She waited on the patio deck, leaning against the wood railing. The half-moon illuminated the calm water of the Banana River while Jessica remembered the kiss and his secret smile. Lost in her daydream, she mustn't have heard his car, because the first sound to steal her attention was his voice from the side yard, steps away from the entrance to her patio.

"You didn't take that dress off, did you?"

She didn't turn, but kept her attention toward the moon. "I wanted to take a bath."

He hopped the railing and approached her from behind, leaning against her, trapping her with a hand on either side. "Too bad. I'm devastated." The breath of his whisper touched her cheek.

"Why?"

She felt him lift her hair and place a hot kiss on her neck, sending goose bumps dancing down her back.

"Because you've denied me the singular pleasure of figuring out how to take it off you." He moved his kisses down to her shoulders. "Now you've left me with nothing but..." He caressed the other shoulder. "...this ordinary little tee shirt, which poses no challenge at all."

His hands circled her waist, his fingertips almost touching each other. Slowly, he grazed her stomach and moved lazily up to her breasts. She heard his intake of breath as he realized she had nothing on underneath. His fingers brushed her nipples, hardening them, his teeth and mouth pressuring her neck.

Easily, leisurely, he turned her around. His hands slid up to her neck and he pulled her face even closer to him. Her gaze traveled down to his beautiful mouth and lower to the open collar of the shirt, long relieved of the bow tie he obviously hated.

She inhaled the musky scents of Dante Cardinelli's fusion cooking, mingled with a hint of Sydney Lynn's perfume. She liked taking him from another woman. She liked that he came to her. She loved it, in fact.

"I want you, Jessie." He closed in on her to take a gentle,

languishing kiss, wetting her mouth and teeth and lips. "Tell me yes, baby."

Tingling and sparking in her deepest center, Jessica responded by pressing herself against him and tightening her lock around his neck as he kissed her. He lifted her easily off the ground and brought her up to sit on the railing, the crotch of her thin, silky shorts rubbing slowly over his erection. He ran his hands along her thighs, down to her calves, wrapping her legs around his waist. With her seated on the rail, they were the same height, face-to-face and eye-to-eye.

He looked right into her eyes. "Are you sure? You have about ten seconds to change your mind."

Ageless words of love rose in her, but she only nodded, biting her lip to keep from saying something she shouldn't.

That's all it took for him. Like a dam had broken, his mouth seized hers, preventing her from thinking of anything but the anxious force of his demanding tongue. Cuddling her bottom, he effortlessly lifted her and turned toward the house, keeping her wrapped around him.

"Where are you taking me?"

"One guess."

She laughed and kissed his neck. "You're carrying me there?"

"I like to go fast...until it's time to go slow."

Kissing her all the way into her dimly lit bedroom, he finally let her fall softly on the bed and climbed on top of her without ever ending total body contact. With slow, deliberate ease, he pulled her tank top over her head. He dropped it on the floor as his hands roamed over her bare breasts.

"I can't believe how long I've wanted to do this." He lowered his head to place his mouth over one breast, then the other, sucking gently, sending an achy, torturous longing snaking through her. Her legs clung to his hips as his tongue flicked slowly around each of her nipples, making her want to scream and moan and hold his head tightly to the perfect spot that he'd found.

She started to unbutton his tuxedo shirt but fumbled with the French studs that replaced ordinary buttons.

"I'll do it," he said huskily.

He sat up, straddling her, and began to unfix each clip. With every move, his shirt opened more, offering her an unimpeded view of his chest, but he fumbled, too, with the tiny buttons.

"You've invaded my head, Jessie," he whispered as he popped off one stud in frustration. "I've wanted you for so long, I can't think straight anymore."

"Let me." She easily pulled him down to her side, then slid on top of him. Her silky boxers slid over his tuxedo pants, tormenting them both as she straddled him and leaned over to finish the buttons.

Her hair fell around his face while his fingers played with every forbidden thing he could finally touch. Sucking her nipples to hardened nubs, he tugged at the waistband of her boxer shorts and inched them over her backside. She took the buttons of his tuxedo pants between her fingers, a ragged breath of anticipation escaping her lips.

"Wait," he whispered and reached into the pocket. He pulled out a couple of foil packets and dropped them next to them on the bed.

"Always concerned about safety, my astronaut." She kissed his chin, then opened her mouth to bite it. "Thanks."

He didn't respond but placed her hands back on the button of his pants and helped her undress him. Then they tumbled again to find the place that felt just right for their aching bodies.

She touched him everywhere, inhaling the musky scent of

masculine sex emanating from every pore, licking the salty skin of his neck, his shoulders and his nipples. He responded to her fingertips like they were lit matches.

"I want to touch you," she rasped, her hands finally circling him. He squeezed his eyes shut and choked her name, gently lifting her hips toward him.

With quivering hands, she put the condom on him, loving the feel of him. Firm and completely male. She kissed his stomach and tasted his muscles and skin.

He gently tugged her up to him, reaching to touch the soft folds of her. "Now, Jessie. Now." He inched himself into her body and then plunged all the way inside, making her gasp.

They moved in instant, easy, ancient rhythm, kissing in celebration of their union and reveling in each sensation that drove them further and faster.

She lost every ounce of control. Dizzy, she clung to him, squeezed him further inside her.

"Take your time, baby," he whispered to her. "We have all night."

"I can't, Deke. I...can't." *I have no power over this.*

She heard her own breath with each aching push, and she felt his body taking her up and over a cliff that she couldn't stop racing toward. She looked at his face, dark with passion and lust and that just moved her further, to the point of being completely lost in him as her entire focus centered on the place where he penetrated her. She kissed him and bit his lip so hard she thought she tasted blood.

The shockingly intimate connection threw her over the brink and the pulsing ache exploded, shattering her body into a million pieces as she fell spiraling down the edge in a long, agonizingly wonderful release.

As her electrifying climax throbbed around him, he shuddered and grew harder and fuller inside her. He whispered her name, plunging inside her. Over and over. Jessie. Jessie. With each syllable he arched into her with raw urgency. As she rode the crest with him, he joined her climax, and holding her entire body as close and tightly as he possibly could, he spilled, just as uncontrolled, into her.

Neither one could possibly breathe a word, finally spent and satisfied.

The red digital numbers of Jessica's alarm clock read 3:35 a.m. by the time Deke guided her up to the pillows, and they climbed under the sheet, wrapping their bodies together and drifting in and out of sleep. He quietly got up to extinguish the candles throughout the house and close the sliding doors. Then he slipped back in her bed, loving the length of her taut, bare legs as they curled around his. Her hair fell on his shoulder, tickling him, as he tucked her comfortably under his arm.

"All right," she sighed. "You *are* good at everything."

He laughed softly and kissed her head, drinking in the clean smell of her shampoo. "Nah. But I get great PR."

Deke closed his eyes and enjoyed the images of her he'd captured during the evening. He pictured her moving like liquid mercury in that luminous dress through the crowds, in the bleachers, at the restaurant. She looked like an angel in his memory. And, now, this. Amazing. Just amazing.

He wanted to tell her but didn't know the right words. He wanted to reassure her and admire her and consume her again.

"Jess?" He ran his hands over her smooth, soft skin of her stomach.

"Yeah?"

"How old are you?"

She looked up suspiciously. "Twenty-nine."

"What's your middle name?" He inched one hand up to trail his finger over the sweet slope of her breast.

"Lynn. Like Sydney." Even half asleep, she made him smile.

"Where'd you go to college?"

"Boston College." She leaned up on one elbow. "Is this twenty questions, Stockard?"

He stroked her perfectly smooth flesh, the nipple hardening like magic under his thumb. He could do that to her. He could take her right to the edge of control and beyond. "I just want to know you. Completely. Don't you want to know that stuff about me?"

She kissed him on the closest piece of skin, which happened to be his shoulder. "I know it all, honey. I wrote your bio, remember? Although I didn't know your real name was Deacon."

He wanted to tell her every thought he had about her and far more about himself than what was written in his bio. He suddenly had a powerful desire to uncover the mystery of the woman he had just watched experience a rare loss of self-restraint.

Thinking of her exquisite expression at the moment he took her to climax, he felt himself grow hard again.

He let a strand of her hair play through his fingers for a moment, wondering if the erotic sensation would pass.

"Deke?"

"Hmmm?"

"Did you really think she was boring?"

He laughed and turned on his side so that their bodies lined up against each other, warm flesh touching top to bottom.

"She's no Jessica Marlowe." He had to kiss her again,

just one more time, a slow and deep expression of the emotion that was tugging at his heart, pulling him deep into dangerous and foreign territory.

The sun blazed high over the river and sneaked through the cracks of the plantation shutters before Jessica heard the shower and turned to the empty spot where Deke had been in her arms all morning. She ached for him already, stretching like a satisfied cat as she rose. She grabbed a short robe from a chair in the corner and slipped it on before she visited him in the bathroom.

The shower curtain was closed and the room was filled with steam and heat.

"Good morning, Commander," she said, just loud enough to be heard over the water.

He opened the curtain a crack and grinned, covered with water and magnificently naked. His wet arm reached out and went straight for the tie on her robe. "I was just thinking about you."

He grinned and tugged, opening the silk panels with one easy movement and making her squeal in surprise.

"Don't get modest now, sweetheart." He pushed the material off her shoulders and put his hands under her bare arms to lift her into the tub. "Come here."

The pounding shower soaked her while his soapy hands lathered her, stopping to concentrate on particularly appealing areas and taking her back to the sensual weakness she'd felt just a few hours ago. He covered her with slippery caresses that made her laugh and gasp until the water splashed in her mouth. Then they dripped back to the bed and depleted each other once again.

"I guess we need some nourishment to keep this up," Deke mused as they lay together. "Got anything?"

"Eggs. Cheese. Water. Chocolate."

"All the essentials. Take me to your kitchen."

Deke delivered two perfect omelets, complete with sautéed mushrooms and gooey Swiss cheese.

"Amazing what a stove can do in the proper hands," Jessica commented as she savored the taste and the expansive view of the river. The latter was made even more appealing by the man lounging comfortably across from her in a pair of sexy white Calvin Klein boxers and an oversized Dash Communications 10K tee shirt Jessica normally wore for running.

"It's too bad you didn't have shallots." He pointed his fork toward her, making her laugh. "Don't laugh. Shallots are serious business in an omelet."

"What meal is this, anyway?" She looked at her wrist for a watch that wasn't there. "Breakfast, lunch or dinner?"

"I have no idea. Looks like it's about three by the sun. Could be any of the above, I guess." He narrowed his eyes and shot her a sexy smile. "I don't really care. Do you?"

While Jessica put their dishes in the dishwasher, Deke sat on the floor of her living room, going through the few CDs she'd brought from Boston. Suddenly, the soft strains of an old Van Morrison song filled the tiny house, and she smiled at his perfect choice. Then his arms were around her, turning her to dance to"Tupelo Honey."

"I love this song," he said as he moved her in a small circle around the galley kitchen.

I love this man. She looked up and found his mouth and tasted the mushrooms and cheese with a bold and inviting kiss.

He sang the words of the love song to her, dancing and

guiding her a few feet into the living room where they dropped to the sofa. Slowly, he unbuttoned the silk pajama top she wore and eased his way down her tummy with a stream of delicate kisses. She sighed as he reached her panties, closing her eyes in anticipation of what his tongue would do to her.

Then she heard the knock at the door.

"Someone's here." Surprise cracked her voice.

"You have every right to ignore it. This is America."

She inched up the sofa. "Where's your car?"

"In the driveway." As her eyes widened in horror, he shook his head. "In *my* driveway. I'm a trained military professional, Jess."

The doorbell rang. "But who could be here?" she demanded.

He closed her top button. "You could always ask."

"Jess? You in there?"

Oh, shit. Stuart.

Chapter Nineteen

"Oh my God. I think he called before." Jessica sat up and pulled her panties back in place. "I—I didn't answer the phone."

Deke smiled and slipped her second button through its hole. "You were busy."

Another knock. She jumped from the sofa and stood frozen, staring at Deke. He started to laugh. "You want me to hide?"

For a moment, she considered it. Then shook her head and held up a finger to her lips. "Just be quiet," she whispered and he started to laugh again. "Please, Deke."

He nodded and reached up to tug at her top. "Don't forget the last two buttons."

She looked down at her half-undone top and underpants. Dear God. Stuart was here.

"Just a second, Stu," she called out. "I'll be right there." With another glare at Deke, she dashed to the bedroom, grabbed a pair of shorts, and pulled them on.

When she came back, Deke still sat on the sofa, watching her like she was performing in a sitcom. She slipped around the wall that blocked the living room from the doorway.

Opening the front door a crack, she feigned a yawn and a

sleepy wipe of her eyes. "Late night." She smiled guiltily. "What's up?"

Stuart frowned and glanced at his watch. "It's four thirty, Jess. You okay?"

She nodded and fake-yawned again. "Just tired. I decided to take a nap. Is something wrong?"

He glanced beyond her, obviously waiting for an invitation in. She leaned against the doorjamb and offered none.

"Well, I called earlier. Didn't you get my message?"

She shook her head.

"You haven't seen the *Times*?" He couldn't hide his surprise as he stuck a newspaper in her hand. "Have you been online? The AP photo has him front and center!"

She couldn't quite match the enthusiasm in his voice, but she tried. "Oh, that's great." She glanced at the picture of Deke and Sydney Lynn in front of her. "I, well, I actually haven't seen the coverage yet."

"I can bring the rest of it tonight," he offered.

"Tonight?" Jessica frowned at him.

"Did you make other plans?"

She had no idea. Her only plans included sex. A lot of it. "Ah, well…"

"You didn't forget tonight is the Colonel's New Year's Eve party, did you? I think you're expected to be there."

New Year's Eve. Of course. New year, new decade, new millennium.

New *man*.

Behind her, she heard that very man stir. Oh God, let him stay put. She inched the door closed. "I—I guess I'll try and drop by."

She saw him glance beyond her and her heart stopped. She was terrified that she would turn and see Deke in boxers and her tee shirt, grinning from ear to ear. Stuart had to have heard the same noise she did. She didn't dare look.

"By the way," Stuart said. "Nobody can find Deke. Jeff said he's called him all day, but no answer. Think he's still with Miss Hollywood?"

"Who knows?" She shrugged with enough nonchalance to beat Sydney for an Oscar. "They seemed to hit it off last night."

Stuart started to say something, but she held up the newspaper. "Sorry. I gotta go. I'll see you later, okay?"

He nodded and his gaze dropped a little. "Sure, Jess. See you tonight."

When she closed the door, she thought her legs would surely buckle under her. Only then did Deke come around the corner. They stared at each other.

"Did you forget about the party tonight?" he asked, amusement tugging the corners of his lips.

"I was preoccupied."

"You could be my date."

"I could not."

"Then we'll have to just throw knowing glances across the room. You don't just blow off the We Survived Y2K party at the Colonel's." He smiled and stepped closer to her and tugged the collar of her pajamas.

She rocked into him. "But we haven't survived it yet."

"Just how long do you think you can hide this?"

She shrugged. "As long as it lasts, Stockard."

He flipped the button open. "That could be a while."

They'd stayed together until the very last possible moment, when Deke left Jessica's house and promised to behave when he saw her at the party. Of course, after the Colonel greeted her at his door, the next person she saw was the one she'd spent the day making love to. As he promised, the sexy smile melted her from across the room.

"You finally got dressed." Stuart's comment made her jump.

"Sorry if I seemed a little out of it, Stuey. Rough night at the premiere."

He smiled and handed her a stack of newspaper clippings. "But the coverage is awesome. Good work."

"Has Deke seen these?" she asked casually.

"I don't think so. He just got here. And he sure ain't sayin' where he's been all day." Stuart flashed an evil grin.

He knew. She put the papers on an end table with her evening bag. "Let the poor man have some privacy. We've invaded his personal time enough."

"We sure have." Stuart laughed, leaving her to wonder just what the heck he knew or didn't.

She deliberately avoided the stare she felt from across the room and went through the living room to the patio. She wasn't cut out for subterfuge.

At the patio door, she accepted a glass of ice water from someone working a bar. Then the scent and feel that had become achingly familiar over the last twenty-four hours invaded her senses.

"You look good enough to eat," he whispered in her ear, almost skimming her hip with his hand. "A lady in black."

She turned and offered her most distant social smile. "Hello, Deke. How nice to see you." She took a sip of water.

One hand on the doorway, he leaned close to her ear. "Come home with me tonight. I want you again."

She swallowed the water carefully to keep from choking.

She tried to communicate fury with her eyes but knew he'd never believe her. "Please, don't."

"I'll behave," he assured her. "Just say yes. So I can count every minute until midnight."

"You will anyway," she said with a satisfied smile. "It's New Year's Eve."

He was never more than ten feet from her and Jessica wondered how many people noticed. When the entire party packed into the family room to watch the sights and sounds of Times Square just before the calendar changed to 2000, she wasn't surprised that he was right behind her, leaning against a bookshelf with his hands in his pockets.

The deafening din of conversation and laughter mixed with horns and noisemakers blended into a countdown chorus at ten seconds to twelve. Somewhere around five seconds, she felt powerful hands slide onto her waist. At two, he tugged her into him and she could feel every masculine inch of him against her back. As the bells rang and the hollers of celebration reached a crescendo, he turned her around and gathered her up in an embrace.

"Happy New Year, Jessie." Without giving her a chance to respond, Deke pulled her into a deep and sensual kiss that lasted long after most others had completed theirs. His lips parted, seeking her tongue, promising more and more. For one blissful instant, she simply didn't care who witnessed their mutual and public display. She didn't care what price tag was attached to this moment.

This kiss was worth whatever it cost.

☆〰

Deke never dreamed he'd find the study of toes—pink-tipped and appealing as they might be—more interesting

213

than the Bowl games. But they were. Along with every other inch of the enchantress who distracted him from his New Year's ritual of football marathons. They awoke at his house on New Year's Day as close as two bodies could be and managed to stay that way all afternoon. He'd normally hunker down with the games, but instead, he missed every play. For toes. And legs. And curves that didn't quit. And that incredible laugh each time he touched something new.

He tried to figure out what down it was—good God, what *quarter* it was—but then she'd picked up a copy of Jane's Encyclopedia of Aviation and started making fun of his light reading. He *had* to torture her for that.

When the phone rang, he cursed yet another interruption.

But he sprang to attention at the sound of Colonel Price.

"Happy New Year to you, sir," Deke greeted him.

Jessica immediately closed the massive tome and paled as she stared at him with wide eyes and pursed lips. The poor girl was stricken with guilt.

"We have a serious situation in Houston, Deke. I need your help."

"Anything. What's the problem?"

"Colin MacAffie is having some health problems. Some mental health problems that will preclude him from taking *Endeavour* up."

Deke clenched his jaw and felt his teeth press on each other. He had known Mac was on shaky ground when he was in Houston last week. He'd been flying erratically and acting damn near manic-depressive. He waited for the inevitable.

"You're going to command *Endeavour*, Deke. You're closest to the crew in training and you know that orbiter better than anyone."

Colonel Price may have thought this was a surprise, but Deke knew it had been coming. He just knew it.

"Of course. I can be in Houston tomorrow morning."

Jessica's frown deepened. That wasn't the look of a woman who didn't want to be abandoned. No, her expression was pure worry. Damn it, he hated that look.

The Colonel thanked him and then cleared his throat for another question. "I have to trust Bowker to find the cause of the hydrogen leak before you get that bird to fly. Can I?"

Deke closed his eyes. "I have to trust him, too."

"You can jump into the schedule in Houston. Every minute you're not in training, I want you to check on those inspections."

"You can count on it, sir."

"And, Deke," the Colonel added, "you can stop all the PR stuff now. Petrenko's all that matters now."

Deke swallowed his 'I told you so' and quietly agreed. When he hung up, he nearly smiled at the irony. *Be careful what you wish for.*

"What's the matter?" Jessica asked, still holding the book on her lap.

"I'm taking *Endeavour* up in February." He watched for the reaction. "Mac's been taken off the schedule. I'm next in line."

She just stared at him, her jaw dropping a little, her eyes widening a lot. "*Endeavour*? In February?"

He nodded and picked up the remote to silence the TV. She slowly leaned forward, understanding obviously starting to sink in.

"Why you? Don't you need to be here for the inspections? What about—"

His sarcastic smirk stopped her cold. "What about PR?"

215

"No, Deke." She threw the book on the table. "I'm not going to ask that."

"What about *us*?"

"Stop it!" She blazed at him. "You know what I'm going to ask. What about that hydrogen leak? Is it safe? Shouldn't you say no?"

He knew this would happen. The worry, the fear, the pleading not to do what he had to do. He should have listened to his gut. Instead he listened to his irrepressible male urges. And worse, his heart.

"I've always known this was a possibility," he said.

"You knew? You've never said anything about it."

He shot her a warning look. "I don't have the luxury of saying no, even if I wanted to. And by the way, I don't want to. I'm an astronaut and I'm in the military. It's a life of accepting assignments, whatever they are. That could mean spinning around in fighters on a carrier for fun or it could mean stupid PR interviews on TV or it could mean bumping my mission schedule up by three months. Doesn't matter. I do it."

He turned from her, determined to hide his emotions as he continued to tell her what had to be said. "That's why...that's why I don't..." He sighed, searching for the words. He could only be honest. It was the only way he knew. "That's why my life is what it is and why I live it alone. That way, if anything happens to me, I'm not leaving behind a miserable heartache."

She turned on her heel and walked into the bedroom. In a minute, he heard a zipper. Not the jeans kind. The satchel kind. Of course she'd go home now, guilty from breaking her company's code and pained by stepping all over his. He ran his hand through his hair and stared at the silent TV screen, a blur of beefy jocks playing ball in the snow. What a mess.

Jessica's fingers shook as she dropped her toothbrush into the overnight case. It was time to go home. Real home. Boston.

The sound of his sigh in the doorway sent a chill down her spine.

"What are you doing?"

"Packing." She zipped the bag like an exclamation point.

"I thought you might stay the night."

She shook her head and whipped a hair out of her face that clung to an eyelash. "You have a lot to do, a lot to think about. It's time for me to leave."

"I understand if you want to do that. It's not necessary."

She straightened and stared at her bag. "I don't want to be anyone's miserable heartache."

She looked up to see his reaction. If it hurt him, he didn't show it. His eyes softened and his arms fell to his sides as though he wanted to reach for her but didn't know if it would be welcome.

"I'm just trying to tell you that you can't ask me not to do things that I have to do. You don't have to leave, Jess."

"Yes, I do. I can't show up to work tomorrow in the same clothes I wore to Colonel Price's party. Although, half of those people probably expect it after that kiss." She yanked at a snap on the front of the bag.

"*I* don't care who knows we've—we've been together." She heard the hurt turning to anger in his voice. "*I'm* not ashamed of it."

She swallowed hard. Not ashamed? He couldn't even say the words 'made love.' "Deke, I have a job to do—a position to protect." A future somewhere else.

"So, you're just walking out? I've never known you to quit. I thought you were driven to succeed at everything."

"I am, Stockard. I'm not *quitting*. My job here is done. I've succeeded. You're going up on *Endeavour* and the whole world will be watching with bated breath." She raised an eyebrow and gave him a wry smile. "Those posters ought to sell like hotcakes now."

She picked up the shoulder strap of her bag and avoided his gaze, trying to navigate a route around him, but he blocked her.

"Please, Jessie," he said, gripping her arms. "Don't ruin this weekend. Just let me get to Houston and figure this whole thing out."

"I want to go home." She knew he couldn't argue with the finality in her voice.

He stepped aside so she could walk past him to the living room. "I'll drive you."

She shook her head and put her hand on the latch of the sliding doors. "No. I can walk the path."

He closed the space between them again, wrapping his arms around her. She hoped to God he couldn't feel her quivering. He didn't need to know how he got to her. To him, it was a weekend not to be ruined, a thing to *work out* when he got to Houston.

To her, it was love. She hadn't said it. But she'd thought it every time she looked at him. Every time he touched her. Every time she spiraled out of control with him inside her.

"I'll call you," he whispered.

Man's worst words. They should never have been invented.

"You do that, Deke."

She opened the door and stepped onto the gravel, determined not to turn to see if he stood watching her.

Chapter Twenty

Kennedy Space Center buzzed with the news. Jessica knew as soon as she arrived that the atmosphere had changed with the new command of *Endeavour*. She decided to go straight to Colonel Price and announce her intention to return to Boston but knew she'd have to get Stuart and Tony Palermo to agree. She didn't expect an argument.

She dialed the R&C offices in New York with a sense of purpose and dread.

"It's great news," Tony announced when he finally took her call. "It's fair to say your job just got easier, don't you think?"

"Easier? I don't think so. He's not going to do anything else. He's gone to Houston and will be virtually invisible for the next six weeks. No media. None. He won't do it."

She heard papers rustle as Tony sifted through his mail. "You don't need him, Jess. You just keep the machine going. Use the same pictures, recycle some interviews. You'll have him built up to hero status in no time."

"The Washington account team can build him up, Tony. I'm not needed here anymore and I'd like to get back to Boston." The farther away from the man who had to live alone, the better.

"No way, Jessica. You've got to stay. This is your baby. You need to be there straight through the launch."

He couldn't make her stay. She opened her mouth to argue, but Stuart stuck his head in her office. "Jessica, Colonel Price would like to see you immediately."

Tony's computer keyboard clicked in the background and she felt herself drop another notch on his priority list. She nodded to Stuart as a band of frustration squeezed her lungs.

"I really would rather not be held prisoner here, Tony." Too bad if her voice sounded strained. "My job is in Boston. And my life is there. Not here. I would like to come home."

She knew by the silence he'd stopped reading his email. Jessica Marlowe never argued with the boss.

"NASA will surely cut our budget to nothing if they feel they've lost on the investment they've made in this project. You won't have a job if you walk out on this assignment."

She considered slamming the phone in his ear, but spoke between clenched teeth. "Colonel Price wants to see me. I'll call you later."

She nearly mowed Stuart down as she stomped out of her office and waved him aside on her way to Headquarters. By the time she reached Colonel Price's office, she'd almost pulled herself together. She refused to let him see her as an emotional wreck.

"I hope you had a nice time on Saturday night," he said as she perched on the edge of a chair across from his desk.

Oh God. *He knew.*

"I did, Colonel. I haven't had a chance to call you and your wife and thank you for including me." She searched his face for a clue. Did he know what she'd been busy doing?

He picked up a gold fountain pen and slid it into a brass United States Air Force penholder at the edge of his desk.

"I take it you've heard about the change in *Endeavour's*

command." His dark eyes narrowed. Was he trying to gauge her response? Did he expect her to burst into tears at the possible loss of her lover? Just how many men in authority would jerk her around in one day?

"I have, and I realize that it will eliminate my role at the Cape."

He lifted his black eyebrows and something that looked distinctly like disappointment flashed in his eyes. "On the contrary, Jessica. We need you more than ever. I expect you to stay. For the launch." He glanced down at his desk and back to her. "And beyond, if appropriate."

Her head exploded with mixed reactions, control of her life disappearing faster than she could handle.

"What exactly would you have me do here, Colonel? Certainly Commander Stockard is foregoing a publicity campaign at this point."

He leaned forward on crossed arms. "He is, but we need good PR more than anything except flawless inspections on *Endeavour* and a safe ride up to the space station and back. Every newspaper and TV station in the country will cover this mission. Looking for a mistake, sniffing out a story." He shook his head as though he dreaded the onslaught. "Cosmonaut Petrenko will be front-page news, right alongside Commander Stockard. NASA has to come out on top on this launch. I trust you more than anyone else from Ross & Clayton right now. We need you here."

She bit her lip and held his gaze. If she stayed and the press coverage was negative, Carla would have her job in a New York minute. If she left, she'd be fired or at least left to rot in the basement of Emerging Technologies.

"Anyway," the Colonel said with a half-smile and a knowing gleam in his eyes, "I had the distinct impression you were beginning to fall in love with the space program."

Her stomach flipped. Was that a warning? Blackmail to get her to stay? Or did the old man have a soft heart for romance?

"I'll do whatever needs to be done, Colonel."

The good girl had returned.

It was nearly eleven o'clock when Deke slipped the key into Suite 510 and threw his bags on the sofa of the tiny apartment. Ironically, the furnished one-bedroom with a kitchenette and narrow balcony felt a little like home. He'd stayed there often enough to know all the staff that serviced the complex just outside of Johnson Space Center and had gotten used to getting the same suite every time he was in Houston.

Opening the undersized refrigerator door, he silently blessed his favorite chef, Mona, for the neatly wrapped Italian sub. She must have heard he was coming in tonight. He grabbed one of the ice-cold liters of bottled water and made a mental note to stop by on his way out tomorrow and give the sweet old girl a kiss.

He flipped on the TV to a cable sports wrap-up to get his mind off the day's events. Was it only yesterday he was lounging at home counting toes instead of touchdowns?

He tried to focus on the scores and not dwell on the enormous task ahead of him, but it was impossible.

His body and brain could easily handle the eighteen-hour days. It was his spirit that needed preparation...and the rest of the crew's as well. Even with Mac's problems, they had revered the former commander, and slipping into the other man's slot wasn't going to be easy for Deke.

The necessity of getting to the space station on time and

the frustration of being yanked from the satisfying affair he'd begun with Jessica made it even more aggravating. Even with the demands on him, he couldn't stop thinking about her.

He wanted to erase their last conversation. He wanted another chance. Just to talk to her. To hear her voice. He looked at the phone next to him on the end table, then to the clock. With the time difference, it was too late to call.

He kicked off his shoes, slumped back on the cushions and stared at the TV. But all he could see was the skeptical stares from his fellow crew members or the guilty fear on Skip Bowker's face during their final conversation at the OPF on Sunday night. And, of course, the look in Jessie's eyes when she said goodbye.

Aw, hell.

She answered on the first ring. A jolt of pleasure kicked him at the sound of her voice.

"I thought you might be asleep," he said huskily.

He heard her suck in a surprised breath. "Stockard. Why aren't you floating around in a pool somewhere practicing your weightless skills?"

"You know I like it when you're a smart-ass. It doesn't deter me at all."

"So few things do."

He smiled at the truth of it. The question that hung in the back of his mind tumbled out. "So, are you packed? Flight booked back to Beantown?"

He heard her sigh and imagined her slipping deeper under her comforter, her hair falling around her shoulders, her face scrubbed clean. "Not exactly."

The vague reply gave him hope. "What do you mean?"

"I've been, uh, convinced to stay for the launch. NASA needs PR support."

Hope melted into relief. She wasn't going home. Not yet, anyway.

"Don't worry," she insisted before he could talk. "They just want as many people as possible geared up to handle the international attention on this mission. No fluff. No spin for you. I'll leave you alone."

Don't do that, Jessie.

"To be honest," she continued, "I didn't plan on staying. I didn't expect all of this crisis control...or any of this..." She paused and he held his breath. "This other stuff."

"This other stuff being me, I take it?" He wanted to hear her talk about it. About them.

He heard her soft moan of admission. "Yeah. That'd be the stuff."

"I miss you already, honey." He had no real control over his words. He needed to say them.

"Don't do this."

"I need to. I need to talk to you. I can't be here, isolated and away from you. I want to call you and know I can talk to you." His gut twisted with the confession as he waited for her response.

All he heard was the gentle static of long distance. Then she spoke so softly, he hardly heard her. "I guess it can't hurt to talk to you."

He closed his eyes at the reprieve and realized the sound he heard was the beating of his own heart.

"So, how are they treating you at Johnson?"

He flicked the remote to turn off his TV. In the dim light of the apartment, he leaned back on the sofa, ready to unload his troubles. "Mac was God. I'm Poster Boy. Use your imagination."

She laughed softly.

"And we had another bitch of a landing today."

"Tell me about it."

She meant it. He knew that. She relieved all the pressure on his brain and, in the process, lightened his very soul. She listened and laughed and understood. He couldn't believe an hour had passed when she yawned and reminded him of the time difference.

"Sorry if I cut into your beauty sleep, Jess. But hell, you don't need it anyway."

"You're sweet. You can call and compliment me anytime." The sincerity in her voice touched him. "Now, get some rest, Stockard. You *do* need it."

"I know. But I needed this, too."

He needed *her*. She had no idea how much.

Jessica let the warmth of his goodbye soothe the ache that had been in her heart all day. It was no solution, one phone call in the night. Just a truce. Just a stopgap until...until what?

With her feet dangling off the bed, she stared into the darkness, replaying every word, every nuance of their conversation. Suddenly, she reached for the lamp and bathed the room in soft light. She slipped her bare feet onto the cool tile floor. Opening the top dresser drawer, she reached into the corner. There, among some lingerie, she found what she wanted.

She took out the neatly folded Navy-issue handkerchief she had intended to return to him. Holding it, she tiptoed back to her bed and turned off the light.

Then she unfolded the soft piece of cotton and smoothed it over her pillowcase, laying her cheek on it with a soft sigh. She only wanted to fall asleep with the man she loved.

Chapter Twenty-one

As the next two weeks passed, the focus of Jessica's life shifted entirely. During the day, she worked as any other employee of the Public Affairs staff, handling media requests and positioning the messages NASA delivered. At night, she waited for Deke's call and the hour of secret bliss it gave her.

All the interview requests for Deke were declined, with the one exception of Paul Zimmerman of *Newsweek*. Jessica quietly continued negotiations for a cover story. This would be the definitive NASA story. Not about Deke, but a chance to remind America that the men and women who risked their lives were true heroes—twenty-first-century pioneers who made a profound difference to humanity.

That was the feature story she wanted, but Paul continued to dig for dirt. A *Newsweek* cover on NASA would be a coup for her, but more importantly, a turning point for the space program.

Jessica confided her strategy to Tony Palermo the first time they spoke since the harsh conversation instructing her to stay at the Cape. She wanted to open communication with him again, hoping for some answers.

"It's a gamble, Jess," Tony warned her when she told him

about *Newsweek*. "Without Stockard as the centerpiece of that story, you have to keep the focus on NASA's successes and not safety issues or the danger that cosmonaut is in. We don't want another *Today*show debacle."

"We certainly don't," she agreed. If Carla Drake would stay out if it, things should be fine. But she didn't mention the other vice president's name. Moot point, she decided.

"On the other hand, if you pull it off, I suspect our budget for next year would more than double on the NASA account," Tony mused. She could count on Tony to get to the heart of what mattered to the agency. Profits.

She took a deep breath. "We need to talk about my role when I return."

"I've been carefully examining the management structure in Boston. I personally like the idea of you heading up ET, but I know you don't."

"No, I don't. It's not what I want to do."

"I understand. However, it makes sense to me." He paused, and she didn't dare interrupt but visualized the corner she was being backed into.

"I'm prepared to offer the position to you with a twenty percent salary increase."

Not such a dark corner. She wished the money mattered, but it didn't.

"What about my staff?"

"You can keep most of your staff, not everyone. I'm not sending you to Silicon Valley. And you know that's where this job ought to be."

So this was it. He offered a partial staff, a twenty percent increase, and a promise not to relocate her away from Boston. Take it or leave it. Damn, this wasn't fair.

She wanted the GM job so badly and deserved it so much

that she could scream. But what option did she have? Another agency? No, that's not what she wanted.

"I hear you. I'll do it." She kept all enthusiasm out of her voice. "But, please, don't announce it until I'm home."

"You got it, Jess. Keep up the good work down there."

Yeah, sure. It really made a difference. "You bet."

Jess pushed her chair back with the sudden and urgent desire to leave the stuffy little office. Without even taking her purse, she bolted into the hallway and headed for the lobby. She needed air. She needed to think.

Thrusting the glass doors open, she stepped outside and inhaled, gazing into the vivid azure of Florida's winter sky. Days like this occurred about five times a year in Boston and everyone took two-hour lunches or called in sick to celebrate and treasure the beauty. Here, perfect days were the norm.

Maybe it wasn't the worst place on earth.

Silently blessing her choice of flat loafers that morning, she walked the winding paths of the Space Center and before long she arrived at the entrance of the Visitors' Center. Most weekdays were quiet at that end of the complex, with a few school field trips and a smattering of international tourists. It seemed like a safe escape from the problems that plagued her.

Flashing the Kennedy Space Center employee badge that hung around her neck, she skipped the ticketing process and crossed the main entrance without the slightest idea of where she wanted to go. Slowly passing exhibits and gift shops, she stepped into the courtyard.

She followed the intended flow of the Center, wandering through the Rocket Garden, an expansive outdoor exhibit of giant fuel-burning cylinders that had thrust men and monkeys into space.

Lingering at the base of the towering rockets, she realized

that the more she learned about space, the more it amazed and inspired her. Astronauts were a magnificent breed of human beings. Hungry for knowledge, curious, and driven to push the boundaries of earth. It humbled her.

She found *Enterprise*, a retired orbiter, at the far end of the Visitors' Center. In about four weeks, Deke would get in a space ship exactly like it and trust technology to take him so far off this earth that he would not even feel the most fundamental pull of nature...gravity. Why?

Because the son of a bitch flies seventeen thousand miles an hour.

He'd lied to her. His reasons were far nobler than the appeal of speed and risk. He just didn't want to admit it.

Climbing the metal stairs that took tourists inside the cargo bay of *Enterprise*, she peered into the cockpit where the commander and pilot sat to fly the shuttle. Jessica stood directly behind the glass to study the gauges, switches, dials and controls that swam before her. *How did he know what to press?*

She leaned her forehead against the glass, feeling the distinct weight of embarrassment and shame. What difference did it make if she wasgeneralmanager or nothing? Her job seemed so insignificant, so frivolous in the face of his world-altering challenge.

She had no desire to rush back to work. Leaving the exhibit, she took the inclined path that led to the only area she hadn't yet seen at the Visitor's Center. For some reason, the drama of the Astronaut Memorial finally drew her in.

At the top of a slope, a black onyx monolith, nearly a hundred feet wide and tall, balanced on a slowly rotating platform that followed the sun. It reflected a mirror image of the sky in its glistening ebony surface. Carved into the stone were the names of the men and women who had died in their efforts to expand man's horizons, giving the appearance that they were floating forever. Each one forever destined to touch the sky.

The impact was heart stopping.

Taking a seat on the single bench in front of the Memorial, Jessica paused to appreciate the perfect and changing replication of the clouds against the sparkling surface. She read the twenty or so names, some so familiar, some she had never heard.

In one cluster were the seven astronauts of *Challenger*, now etched into her memory from the day she'd watched the accident repeatedly in her college dorm. The teacher, Christa McAuliffe. The teacher that America had fallen in love with. Gone.

To the right of the *Challenger* names, the astronauts of Apollo-1 who had become little more than a lesson in her grade-school education. Gus Grissom. Roger Chafee. Edward White. All colleagues of Deke's namesake, Deke Slayton. All gone.

She stared at the etched names. Others could, and would, be added. No stranger this time. No two-dimensional photograph in a history book. But a real and loved human being. He could be gone, too.

Tears burned her eyes. She gripped the edge of the bench as worry and love squeezed her heart. Daring, risk-taking, gravity-defying heroes. Isn't that what she came to this place to find? Well, she certainly had.

And in the process, she'd learned a lot about the definition of success. Giving your life for progress and mankind. That was success. Not a well-placed photo op.

She tried to swallow the lump in her throat but failed. It didn't matter. She surely wasn't the first person to sit on this bench and weep. Wiping her cheeks, Jessica knew that late tonight when Deke called her, she would tell him about her conversation with Tony. And she'd tell him that she found some comfort in the Rocket Garden and that a tour of a retired orbiter helped her put it all in perspective.

But, she would never, ever tell him of her visit to this sacred ground.

Deke turned the corporate jet into the clouds above Houston, activated the reverse thrust, then struggled with the difficult drag that simulated the dead-stick landing of the orbiter. It pulled and tortured his arm until he finally saw the runway and landed the trainer.

"That's it for now, *Endeavour*." The static words crackled in his headset. "Crew is to report to building thirty for a briefing."

Deke frowned at his pilot, Kurt Muir, when he heard the command. "Roger that, but we'd like another pass before we hit the remote manipulator," he told the training manager through his microphone. "And we have time for on-orbit procedures in the sim."

"Negative, Commander." The response was eerily definitive. "We got a situation change on the ISS. Director Casey has called a briefing."

Deke grabbed his shoulder harness and threw a knowing glance at Kurt. A situation change on the space station did not bode well. Wordlessly, the crew deplaned and jumped on the waiting golf carts that took them across Johnson Space Center to a meeting with the man in charge of the entire operation.

A black pit formed in his stomach when he saw the astronaut standing next to Casey. Janine Harmon. One of three heart surgeons in the astronaut corps. It could only mean one thing.

Without any introductions, Richard Casey confirmed his fears. "Micah Petrenko has had a pulmonary embolism. He's not responding to the anticoagulant."

No one said a word as they waited for more information.

"He is stable and not in shock," Casey said. "However, his chest pain is increasing and he's coughing blood. He needs surgery to insert a clot-trapping filter and to avoid a potentially fatal myocardial infarction."

A heart attack. Not something to have in zero gravity orbiting around the earth. Deke studied the surgeon, her expression unreadable.

"How much time does he have?" one of the crew asked.

"A week is pushing it, but it's the best we can do." Casey leaned back in his chair and put both hands on the table in front of him. "Obviously, we're changing the mission schedule. We need to launch as soon as possible with the addition of a surgeon on board." He glanced at Janine, who caught Deke's gaze with a terse smile and nodded.

"As you know, Janine Harmon has two missions on her bio, including a trip on *Endeavour* two years ago. She'll start emergency training with you today." Casey's tone left no doubt as to the finality of the decision.

"What's the launch schedule?" Deke asked.

"The shuttle is on the crawler as we speak, on its way to the pad," Casey told him. "You'll all leave for the Cape on Thursday morning. We're scoping the trajectory paths and weather radar and expect to launch Sunday at 5:45 a.m. That way you can dock with the ISS in less than eight hours. When Janine sees Micah, she'll make the decision to perform the surgery under zero gravity on the station or turn *Endeavour* around and bring him straight home."

Six days. They would launch in six days, eliminating the last month of inspections. Deke hoped like hell Skip Bowker and company had solved their problems. Otherwise, there would be eight dead astronauts and one really sick cosmonaut. But they had no choice. They *had* to go get him and *Endeavour* was all they had to fly.

On Thursday morning, Jessica and the Public Affairs staff huddled around a conference table, adding the finishing touches to the press release that would surprise the world. They debated the language, the timing, the quotes, leaving her no opportunity to dwell on the fact that the T-38s would be landing and Deke would be near her again within the hour.

He had so little time between now and Sunday morning. She doubted if they'd be able to see each other. He had made her promise to stay near her cell phone so he could at least talk to her before the launch.

"Jessica, you have a call on line two. Paul Zimmerman with *Newsweek*."

She looked up to meet Stuart's worried gaze.

"Could there be a leak?" he asked her. "Is it possible he already knows we're launching Sunday?"

She stood to go to her office. "We're about to find out."

Paul didn't mention the accelerated launch schedule when she greeted him, but jumped right into why he called.

"I've got another memo, Jessica. This one looks authentic and current. I've got to have a comment."

She dropped into her chair. "What does it say?"

"Do the phrases 'imminent disaster due to shoddy inspections' and 'drastic budget cuts' mean anything to you?"

The snide tone wasn't lost on her as she tried to absorb the words. "Who wrote it? Where did it come from?"

"It's anonymous. It's on NASA letterhead with the sender and recipient's name blanked out. But it looks official as hell."

"Who's your source?" she demanded.

"Get real, Jessica. I'm not going to reveal my source. I want a comment. I was on to this story two months ago and you put me off with hot air from that astronaut. If this bomb can't be defused, it becomes a feature to run next week, before Endeavour launches."

She bit her lip. "Then you'll be too late, Paul. Endeavour's going up on Sunday morning. There's a change in the situation on the InternationalSpace Station and the shuttle is taking medical supplies and a heart surgeon up to Micah Petrenko."

He muttered a curse. "You've got to get me Colonel Price on this. I need an official comment for the online story I'm going to do."

There had to be some give and take. "Send me a fax of the memo and I'll get him for you."

In less than fifteen minutes, Jessica stood in the Colonel's waiting room in anticipation of an interview with *Newsweek*. She looked at the copy of the memo again, the words swimming in front of her. Would they really risk the lives of eight astronauts for one cosmonaut? Everything she knew about NASA said no.

She stared at the oil painting of the shuttle, the achingly beautiful juxtaposition of a mountain of technology silhouetted against the peaceful sky. Below it, the words she'd read on her first day here. *Failure is not an option.*

Not with the man she loved in the cockpit of that shuttle.

But then, someone probably loved Micah, too.

When she handed Colonel Price the fax she'd just received from *Newsweek*, his gaze moved immediately to the upper left-hand corner and then scanned the contents. "Get him on the phone."

Jessica hit the speaker button and dialed Paul Zimmerman's number, now etched into her memory. He picked up on the first ring.

Colonel Price leaned forward on his chair, eyes blazing like a stallion ready to charge. "I'm looking at your memo. Whoever is sending you mail is using stationery that hasn't been in use at any NASA facility for over two years."

Jessica bit back her surprised gasp and looked at the paper in front of the Colonel. Of course. She hadn't even noticed the outdated, stylized NASA logo in the upper corner. It was subtly different from the contemporary design currently used. Still, she was sure she'd seen this one recently. Somewhere.

"Really?" That was all Paul Zimmerman could manage for a moment. "Where could a person get their hands on it?"

"Every piece of stationery that NASA used to have at any facility has been shredded, recycled and turned into cardboard boxes by now. We're efficient like that. Whoever had access to this paper didn't get it from a supply cabinet at NASA."

"However," the reporter said thoughtfully, "someone could have it in their drawer, left over from two years ago."

"But that, Mr. Zimmerman, is exactly my point." Colonel Price looked at Jessica. "A renegade. A disgruntled ex-employee. But NASA did not issue this in any official capacity. The memo is a fraud."

"I see your point," Zimmerman agreed. "But the content of it is what I'm interested in. Is there any truth to it?"

Colonel Price stared at Jessica just long enough to send alarm snaking down her spine. "None at all."

Why couldn't she believe him?

"That's our official position," the Colonel continued. "If you use this memo in any story, please be certain to note that it is anonymous and printed on stationery that is no longer in use by anyone in any official capacity. And let your source know that, too. He or she might want to update their letterhead files."

As they hung up, Jessica looked questioningly at the Colonel and the memo. "Who do you think wrote this?" she asked.

The Colonel straightened the white sheet on his desk. She couldn't read his expression as he studied it. Finally, he looked at her.

"I have my suspicions but no evidence."

He wasn't going to say and she knew it. "Why? Why would someone do this?"

"Possibly to stop the launch. Possibly to sabotage our image. Possibly to force us to do a better job at inspections."

She didn't like the last option. Before she could respond, a distant rumble vibrated the glass in the picture window with a view of Launch Pad 39B. They both looked in the direction of the shuttle and listened to the whine of a jet engine as it landed.

"The T-38s," Colonel Price said. "The crew's arrived from Houston."

Jessica felt the blood drain from her head.

Colonel Price grabbed the memo, crunched it in his hand with one swift squeeze and dropped it into a wastebasket under his desk. "This belongs in here. It's garbage."

Another T-38 engine screamed before it shut down to sudden silence. Deke was here. And in seventy-two hours he'd be on top of that launch pad, poised to explode into space on the power of sixty tons of ignited liquid hydrogen.

She gave a warning look to the man ultimately responsible for Deke's life or death. "It better be garbage, Colonel."

Chapter Twenty-Two

The final preparations and medical checks dragged throughout the day. Deke submitted himself to each test, but by four o'clock he was snapping and unsnapping his flight suit for each exam with obvious impatience. He had someone he needed to see. Someone he desperately needed to talk to before he got on that shuttle.

Skip Bowker.

They finally released him from medical and he sat through three more briefings on the status of landing sites. They wouldn't be landing anywhere until his questions were answered. As the last briefing ended, he left the room with a muttered excuse and headed to the OPF.

But he was too late. With no shuttle in the sling, the engineers had gone home and Skip's office was as dark and empty as the rest. Deke knew he shouldn't leave the Cape and knew he was under a loose quarantine and expected to check into crew quarters within the hour. But he had to go with his hunch. He had to have one more conversation with Bowker.

He stood at Bowker's messy desk and closed his eyes to think. Without his car, he had no way to get to the house in Satellite Beach where Bowker lived. He grabbed Skip's phone and dialed a number he knew by heart.

"I need you, sweetheart," he said as she answered her cell phone. "Meet me outside the OPF, right now, with your car. And don't tell a soul I called you. Hurry."

In minutes, Jessica pulled into the parking lot and stopped in front of the wall where he stood. He jumped into the passenger side, smelling her clean, flowery scent even before his eyes adjusted to the dark and he saw her. The impact of her slammed at his solar plexus like a two-by-four. Good God, he'd missed her.

He took her face in both hands and leaned across the console, kissing her hard. When they parted, her dark gaze searched his face for answers.

He grinned. "Hi, honey. I'm home."

"Stockard." She pulled back and put the car in park. "What's this all about?"

He put his hand on the steering wheel. "As much as I'd love to sit here and make out with you, we can't. I need you to take me to Satellite Beach. I want to talk to Skip Bowker."

Without questioning him, she threw the car back into drive. "Let's go."

They didn't say much on the way down A1A, but her sidelong glances nearly steamed the windows. He admired her driving skill as she adroitly passed slower cars like rocks in a stream, as though she sensed his urgency. In the dark, he watched her skirt ride up her thighs every time she hit the gas. To her credit, she didn't push him. But he owed her an explanation.

"I won't bore you with the technical details, Jess, but over the last week, I had a chance to see some blueprints of shuttle upgrades they're discussing at Johnson. It made me realize something I'd overlooked all along. It might have caused the hydrogen leak. I just need Skip to confirm that he fixed it."

"What is it?"

He closed his eyes, visualizing the paperwork he'd seen. "There are pins—tiny plugs that can be found near the coolant tubes of the engine. One of them could have ruptured a tube and caused the hydrogen leak."

"What about the wiring? I saw a memo today that said faulty wiring caused a short circuit on Columbia."

He peered at her. "What memo?"

"Another one of those anonymous things to *Newsweek*. Colonel Price pointed out to the reporter that it was printed on stationery that was long out of date."

As Jessica recounted the interview Price had done earlier that day, a sickening feeling deepened in Deke's gut.

She looked at him as she finished the story with a frown. "Colonel Price thinks one possibility is someone who wants to force NASA to do a better job on inspections," she said. "Maybe someone who works for Skip?"

He shook his head and pointed to the right turn on Ocean Boulevard after they passed Patrick Air Force Base. Maybe Skip himself. Not that he was that cunning. "I don't know. But Skip can help us shed some light on this."

He found the side street from memory.

"I think it's one of these little bungalows," he said, peering into the night. "I was here once, years ago. After Skip's wife died."

"I didn't know he lost his wife." She tapped the brakes at a stop sign. "How sad."

"Yeah, he's never been the same since. Once the Apollo program ended and they shipped him from Houston to the Cape, I don't think he ever got excited about space again. When his wife passed away, he sort of rolled up into himself."

"Couldn't you just call him and ask him about the plug or pin?"

"I want to see his face. I want to read him." He saw the dilapidated Toyota in a driveway. "Here it is."

She pulled in behind the Toyota, her headlights reflecting on the picture window in the front of the house. They got out of the car and studied the bungalow, unlit and unwelcoming. He took her hand before they stepped off the gravel driveway onto the walk.

"You can wait in the car, Jess. This'll just take a minute."

She rubbed her arms and shook her head. "Doesn't look like he's home. But if he is, I want to hear what he has to say. I want to read him, too."

An explosion cracked in the night and they both jerked at the sound. The unmistakable echo of a gunshot.

"What the hell—" Deke grabbed her shoulders and pushed her toward the car. "Get in. Just get in and don't move. Don't even think about it."

He sprinted up the walk and flung open the screen door, bile rising in his throat. He knew the single gunshot hadn't been directed toward them. He knew who'd taken the bullet.

He shook the knob furiously, then slammed his booted foot into the wood. It sprang open and the acrid smell of gun smoke assaulted him.

"Bowker!" he yelled into the silence. "Bowker!"

He fumbled at the light switch on the wall, flipping two that did nothing, then a third. The room brightened as a floor lamp came on, shedding a soft golden glow over the shabby furniture. Instinct made him turn to the darkened dining room.

Skip lay slumped over the table, the blood from his mouth dripping into a wet pool around his head, a gun still in his hand.

It didn't take long for NASA officials to outnumber police, Deke noticed as he leaned against the refrigerator of Skip's dingy kitchen. When Colonel Price showed up, Deke nearly choked.

Mostly, Deke was relieved he'd convinced Jessica to go home with Stuart, one of the first people they called. And that hadn't been easy. She'd wanted to stay. She'd clung to him, shaking, until the police had arrived and the first few NASA higher-ups. But he had to get her out of there before they brought the body out.

She only agreed when he promised, gave her his Boy Scout, Navy, and astronaut word of honor that he would come to her house when this was finished. He knew he'd keep that promise. And not just to take her car home. He had to hold her one more time before he went back to the Cape. Before he went on that launch pad.

Colonel Price looked up from the kitchen table, grief etched on his weathered face. "I had no idea he had so much hate in him," Price said, referring to the suicide note they'd been discussing. "He was a hero. The heart and soul of Apollo."

"The space race with the Russians never ended for him," Deke mused. "There was nothing more irksome to him than a joint Russia-US space program."

"From that note, I take it he knew what caused the leak but kept it to himself, thinking we'd delay the launch." Colonel Price stood. "I don't think we can take the chance of launching *Endeavour*. Skip will win this one. Petrenko will probably die."

A hot fury shot through Deke. "Colonel, we've had

enough redundant inspections and enough extremely intelligent people—with no axes to grind—check every other aspect of the shuttle. He says it right there." Deke pointed to the note. "It's a plug. I know what he means."

"We have to get the shuttle down from the pad for a complete re-inspection."

Deke shook his head. "A man is dying. Let me get out there with the best engineers in tow. We can still get into the main engines with the shuttle on the pad. I just need to see the coolant tubes and check every single pin. We can fix that problem."

Colonel Price narrowed his gaze. "I don't think so, Deke. It might not just be the hydrogen leak that Skip mentions in this letter. We don't know for sure about anything else. What if he knew something about the wiring and kept that to himself? Another short circuit that knocks out a computer and maybe its backup? We can't be sure that won't happen again."

"I can handle a manual landing, if necessary, and that would be the worst that faulty wiring would cause."

Colonel Price looked warily at him. "No one's ever attempted a manual landing under those conditions."

"We've practiced it for weeks. I can do it in my sleep. We have to at least look at the plugs. We have to make a good-faith effort to try and get Petrenko."

Colonel Price's gaze shifted to the dining room, where police and CSI were still taking pictures and collecting evidence of what no one doubted was a suicide. "Go out with a team at daybreak and look at the mains. Then we'll decide."

Deke knew that was no small victory. "Thank you, sir."

"Now get back to crew quarters. They've grilled you enough here."

Deke nodded. "I will, sir. I have one quick stop before I go."

The Colonel started to disagree, then closed his mouth. "Yes, I imagine you do."

Driving Jess's car, Deke visualized the coolant tubes, ruptured by a pin he'd started to suspect could loosen from the vibrations of the launch. If it hit a tube at exactly the right spot, the internal pressure could cause the leak. So there'd be no break in the tube before the launch. Bowker knew it and figured they'd never launch with the hydrogen leak unsolved.

Could it be fixed? They had to try. They could not let that man die knowing they hadn't tried everything to save him.

He took a deep breath to clear his head, but it only filled his senses with the floral scent that lingered in her car. He recognized the soap from the time he'd taken a shower at Jessie's house. Lavender or some equally feminine thing. It hit him harder than if she'd been there to touch. He pressed the accelerator, longing to get to her. She waited like a refuge, a safe harbor. He grew hard at the thought of burying himself in her, his stomach twisting with desire and anticipation.

His throat closed at the sight of her standing in her doorway. She still wore the short skirt she'd had on for work, her blouse untucked and loose. She looked a little terrified, but as he approached, the worried look on her face dissolved into a smile.

"I really didn't think you'd come." She stepped onto the patio to greet him.

Silently, he folded her into his arms, inhaling the fragrance in real-time, feeling her silky hair against his mouth. He could die on Sunday, but he'd never felt more alive than at that moment. Nothing else mattered.

"What happened?" she asked quietly. "What did the note say?"

"He wanted to delay the launch and he thought he could do it by not revealing the cause of the leak. He didn't want the Commies to win."

Jessica took a step back, her mouth opening. "*Commies?* The Russians? They haven't been Commies for a while."

He ran his fingers through her thick hair, wanting to forget Skip and his ancient prejudices, wanting to get lost in the woman in his arms instead. "He's an old Apollo guy, Jess. You know how competitive we were with Russia then. He was taking it out on Petrenko. Remember, he's the nephew of a diplomat. An ex-Communist-turned-democrat diplomat."

"So, why did he kill himself?"

"If *Endeavour* blows, he'd have the blood of the crew on his hands. No longer a legend. A villain."

She paled at the words and he felt her fingertips tense on his shoulders. "What will happen to Petrenko?"

"We're going to try and fix the shuttle and go get him."

"*Try?*"

He closed his eyes so he didn't have to see the look in hers. He didn't want to go there. He wanted to forget Skip Bowker and Micah Petrenko. He wanted her to make it go away. An incredible need to hold her, kiss her...love her...rocked him.

"Not now, Jessie. Please." He buried his face in her hair, then searched for her mouth. She welcomed his kiss, and he eased her back into the house, her tongue igniting him. With one hand, he reached back and slammed the door closed behind them; with the other he explored her body, reacquainting himself with every lovely inch.

The feel of her sent gallons of blood to the lower half of

his body, shaking him withintensity. Skip's bloody face flashed in his mind, and he squeezed his eyes closed, eliminating anything but the feel and smell and taste of this woman he needed so much.

"Come inside," she murmured, moving toward the living room. "Talk to me."

"No." His fingers seized the buttons of her blouse, fumbling, then tearing. "We've talked for three goddamn weeks. I need you. Now."

He reached down to the hem of her skirt, tugging it up, running his hands along the silky skin of her thigh. He pulled the material over her hips and cupped the satiny front of her underpants in his hand.

She cried out, a startled and eager sound, giving in immediately. She pressed her warm, wet mound into his palm and let out a sexy moan as she slid down the entryway wall. He followed her, one of his hands popping buttons, the other finding his way into her hot flesh. She moaned in response, her fingers dug into his scalp, and she pulled him harder against her.

Kneeling on the floor, he dropped his mouth on the curve of her breast, unhooking the front of her bra. He suckled a hardened nipple, pulling the peak between his teeth, wanting to taste her, to absolutely consume her.

"Here, on the floor?" she asked in husky, unsteady voice.

"Here." He licked the dark circle, his tongue rounding the pebbled nub. "Now." His fingers probed the moist flesh between her legs.

He couldn't stop. His craving for her shut down every rational thought but the sensations that spiraled through him. Words choked him and he crushed her mouth with a kiss, unable to speak. They fell back on the hard tile floor. Her fingers tugged at the zipper of his flight suit. She yanked it off his shoulders with as much force as he felt driving him. He sat up to free himself from the suit.

Reality set in. "I don't have a—"

She yanked him down toward her. "I don't care. You've been through every medical check known to man."

"What if you—"

She covered his mouth with hers. "Just don't stop. *Don't stop.*" She nipped at his lips and pressed against him, igniting him into granite-like hardness. "Go back to here. And now." She reached down and circled his flesh with her hands. "Right here. Right now."

He pulled the crotch of her silk panties aside. He couldn't wait for them to come off. They murmured in each other's ears, erotic pleas, senseless commands—all drowned out by the blood rushing through his brain.

Her bare legs clamped around him and he thrust inside her, as deep as he could go, to touch the very core of her.

She cried out and he pulled back, muttering an apology. She shook her head and grabbed his backside, pulling him into her again and again and again until he felt her flesh quiver and heard her whine and gasp in response.

He braced himself over her, his hands flat on the cool tile floor. With each arch of her body, the pleasure shot through him as she clutched him with her arms, her teeth, her feminine flesh. She vibrated with an orgasm, calling his name, biting his neck, and he lifted her to his chest, blinded by the need and desire and, finally, a dizzying, satisfying burst of pleasure as he exploded over and over inside of her.

He couldn't speak, couldn't move. Aftershocks shook her, squeezing his flesh and leaving them both gasping for air. She'd taken over his soul. This woman who touched him so completely. This woman who had changed everything that ever mattered to him. This brilliant, beautiful, relentless woman whom he loved.

"Deke." Her breath warmed his cheek and he lifted his head to look into her eyes. *Don't say it, Jessie. Please, don't say it before I get on that shuttle.*

But he knew he couldn't stop her. He could read her certainty in her eyes. Nothing could stop Jessica once she made up her mind. "Deke, I love you."

He dropped his head into her hair and choked back the lump in his throat. How had he gotten to this place he swore he would never, ever be?

Chapter Twenty-Three

Deke scraped the concrete of the launch pad with the steel tip of his work boot, studying Scott Hayes's expression as the engineer glided back to the ground in the bucket of a cherry picker. Of the men who'd ventured into the main engines of the orbiter that morning, this one's opinion mattered the most.

"What do you think?" Deke asked the engineer.

Scott didn't answer as he climbed out of the harness that held him.

"It was the plug," he finally said when he reached the ground.

"How'd we miss that?" another engineer asked.

Deke walked over to the blueprints and computer readouts they'd spread at a work area. Not everyone missed it. *Someone* saw it. Someone who was willing to lose his reputation as a space legend for revenge against an ancient enemy. He erased the image of Skip Bowker from his brain. He had more important problems to solve.

"It released during launch and ruptured the coolant tube," Deke said to the group. "There's got to be a simple solution."

Only six engineers, including Deke, had taken the lift into the mains. But more than a dozen people had an opinion on what could be done. The more conservative voted for no launch. Deke remained firmly on the other side.

"That pin has no critical function," he argued as they pored over the computer readout. "It doesn't even exist on*Atlantis* or *Discovery*. It's a holdout from an old design and it makes no sense that it's part of *Endeavour*."

The debate continued, but he could feel most of them starting to agree with him.

"We could widen the combustion chamber," someone suggested. "That would reduce the pressure and the temperature."

"It would also require taking the orbiter off the pad," Scott commented. "A long, long delay."

"What about a shield?" Deke asked as he tapped the blueprint in front of him. "Can't we protect the nozzle from a flying pin or even secure the plug into place so it can't come loose?"

Scott leaned forward and peered at the readout. "A couple of months ago I suggested that we fashion a safety wire around the plugs for a completely different reason. But it would keep the same thing from happening again."

One of the engineers holding a PLIC logbook looked up. "I never heard about that."

Scott shook his head with a rueful smile. "You know what they say about NASA. Great engineers…"

"Lousy communicators." One of them finished for him.

Deke knew what was lousy. And it wasn't communications. But Skip was dead and they had to fix this problem.

"Do you think it could be done with the shuttle still on the pad?" Deke asked Scott.

"Oh, yeah." Scott nodded and peered at the blueprint. "We can do it."

"Come on." Deke didn't want to debate another minute. "Let's brief Rourke and Price. We need their blessing. Then we can get the right people out here to fix it."

They met John Rourke, the mission director, in the waiting room of Colonel Price's office, and the three of them went in together. Deke immediately saw the sorrow that darkened the Colonel's eyes, noticing the man looked all of his fifty-five years that day. Skip Bowker had been a lifelong friend of the Colonel's and the previous evening's events couldn't have been easy on him.

With Skip's death, Scott Hayes had become the de facto head of Safety and Logistics. Deke let him take the lead in explaining their findings to the Colonel and Rourke.

Scott sketched his solution on a yellow pad, making it look remarkably simple. Maybe too simple. Deke studied the Colonel's expression for a clue.

"This is not the way NASA likes to work," Rourke said before the Colonel spoke. "It smells of Apollo-13 and jury-rigged fixes. We've come a long way since then."

"We don't have a choice," Colonel Price announced, silencing the debate. "I just received word that Micah had a cerebral embolism and has symptoms of a TIA. That's a transient ischemic attack, also known as a mini-stroke."

He stood and turned toward his window. No one spoke.

"The Russian government is clamoring for us to get up there to get him. They're in bad shape, having only the *Soyuz* for an escape and knowing that would certainly kill him. His uncle is in Washington meeting with the president."

Deke stared at the yellow diagram that Scott had just completed. They could be ninety-nine percent sure. But never one hundred. Not in this business.

The Colonel turned from his window view and looked at Deke. "Be ready to launch at 5:47 a.m. on Sunday. You'll take a skeleton crew that can get us up and back. A pilot, the surgeon, and two mission-critical specialists. Just enough to get that man home alive. Safety-wire the plug and start the countdown."

"Yes, sir," Deke agreed.

He closed his eyes for a moment as they left Colonel Price's office, realizing that somehow he'd become an ambulance driver and it could damn well cost him his life. When he opened his eyes, he saw Jessica in the waiting room.

The look on Deke's face told Jessica all she needed to know.

The launch was a go.

But she asked anyway, praying for a different answer, "What's the verdict?"

He put his hand on the shoulder of one of the engineers she recognized from the OPF.

"I'll meet you at S&L in ten minutes, Scott," he said. Then he took a step closer to her and whispered, "Let's talk outside."

She followed him through the lobby doors to the side of the building where round concrete tables were used for outdoor lunches and open-air meetings. Today the tables were empty except for a few mourning doves picking at crumbs.

Deke leaned against the edge of one of the tables. The adrenaline that had started pumping at the sight of him the night before surged again, threatening Jessica's stability. She wanted him to pull her close, to kiss her. Instead, he put his hands in the pockets of his flight suit and clenched a muscle in his jaw.

"We're launching with a skeleton crew on Sunday morning," he finally said.

"Why a skeleton crew?"

"The mission objectives have been realigned."

She crossed her arms and glared at him. "Don't give me NASA-speak."

"We're only going up for one reason, Jess. To get Petrenko. He's worse. Another embolism caused a mini-stroke. We're taking as few people as necessary."

The truth hit her. "Fewer lives to risk."

He narrowed his eyes. "Correct."

"But yours is one of them."

"Correct."

Brick by brick, he was erecting a wall, but she was determined to tear it down. "Why are you acting this way?" she demanded, taking a position directly in front of him. "What changed since I drove you home last night?"

He stared at her, a frightening darkness in his expression. "Everything changed. And nothing."

"What does that mean?"

"It means that this wasn't supposed to happen, Jess."

"What wasn't? This launch?"

He closed his eyes. "You're being naïve again."

"Then enlighten me. *What* wasn't supposed to happen?"

"This, Jessica." He pointed his finger from himself to her and back again. "This was supposed to be for fun and pleasure."

The words stabbed her. "It's not?"

"You know damn well what I mean. It's turned into a lot more than I expected."

"And just exactly what did it turn into?" She wanted to hear him say it. She needed to know.

He shook his head as though he were amazed.

"Somehow, it turned into a full-blown walk down the aisle, sweetheart."

She bit back a laugh, a weird giddiness electrifying her sleep-deprived body.

"I swore I would never put anyone through that kind of torture." His quiet statement erased the temptation to laugh.

She crossed her arms, a nervous smile threatening. "That might not be the torture you seem to think it would be."

But he didn't smile back. "It would be if you watch that shuttle explode into thin air on Sunday morning. It would be when we're doing an emergency landing in South Africa and the gear doesn't come down because of a computer glitch. It would be torture for both of us."

Slowly, she took a step back and stared at him as a painful realization hit with as much force as his casual reference to a walk down the aisle.

"You know, Deke, you are *not* the risk-taker you think you are. You may not be scared to die, but you are terrified to live. You've built this wall around yourself that protects you from the one thing that could hurt you *or* help you. Love. And, worst of all, you've done it with hypocritical nobility, telling yourself that you only want to protect someone. But the someone you want to protect is *you*."

He started to shake his head.

"No—" She held up her hand to stop his denial. "You're so sure that you might not 'come home from work,' as you say. Let me ask you a question. What is it you want to come home to, Deke? An empty house? A lonely sailboat? The encyclopedia of aviation?"

"Stop it," he said, taking her hands and pulling her closer, his navy eyes flashing. "I want to come home to the same kind of security my parents had. The same loving home that you envied so much when you were there. But I can't,

Jessica. I chose a different life. I can't guarantee any reunions and I just don't think that's fair to you."

He held both her hands up to his face, near his lips, and she could feel his breath on her fingers.

He searched her eyes, her face, a question in his expression. "So when did you decide you'd be willing to leave your glamorous job in Boston to live in the flats of Florida with an astronaut?"

"When I fell in love with one."

Then she held her breath. Waiting for the response she needed to hear. *Tell me, Deke. Tell me you love me.*

He pulled her to him and kissed her hard on the mouth— a frustrated, angry, hungry kiss. When their lips parted, he kept his eyes closed, but she watched his forehead crease. "I have to go fix that damn shuttle," he whispered, his face still close to hers. "I won't see you again until...will you be here when I land?"

Disappointment punched her. *He couldn't say it. He didn't love her.*

"Ahem." At the sound of the obvious intrusion, she spun around. "I've been looking all over for you, Jess."

Sunglasses hid his expression, but she recognized the admonition in Bill Dugan's voice.

Jessica jerked away from Deke and immediately regretted it. Damn Bill Dugan. What the hell was someone from Ross & Clayton doing here and why did he show up at the most critical moment of her life?

Deke must have read it as a cue, because he stepped two feet away from her. "I've got to go, Jess."

He started walking toward the parking lot. She fought the

urge to scream and run after him and kick Bill in the shins on the way. She was sick of hiding her feelings for this man.

Bill adjusted his sunglasses as he approached her and Deke disappeared around the building.

"What are you doing here?" she demanded.

"What *you* are doing here is a far more interesting question," he said with a sneer. "Pretty cozy with a client, Jess."

The adrenaline in her veins changed to hot lava and threatened to spew at him in the form of frustrated, angry words. "I was having a private conversation," she said through clenched teeth.

"Then you should have had it in private," he shot back. "Not on a pavilion in full view of NASA Headquarters and Colonel Price."

Damn, he was right.

"Are you here for the launch?" she asked, trying to control the temper that still bubbled at the sight of him.

"Among other things, yes. I started hearing some rumors and thought I might come down and check things out. Evidently they were true."

"Yes," she let the hiss stay in her voice. "They *are* true."

"Bad form, Jess." Bill put his hands in his pockets. "I hope it's not serious."

Based on the conversation she just had? Hard to say. A breeze took a pass at Jessica's hair, a strand flipping over her face and, she hoped, covering her pained expression. "Why?"

"Tony told me that you're anxious to get home. I agreed to step into this assignment and relieve you."

A wave of resentment crashed inside her as she crossed her arms for stability and stared at him. "*What?*"

"You told Tony weeks ago you wanted to leave. When I

heard the, uh, rumors about your situation here, I told him that was probably the best thing for the agency. He agreed."

"Colonel Price has requested that I stay for the launch and I intend to accommodate that request." She started to walk by Bill, clinging to her composure. "I'll call Tony right now."

"I wouldn't do that if I were you," he warned. "He's pretty ticked about the hanky-panky with your client. Push him any further and you're liable to be job hunting."

She spun on her heel and slapped her hand on a concrete table, the birds scattering and her flesh stinging. "No! I will stay here for the launch and finish what I started. I have a commitment to NASA and this may come as a shock to you, but I care about this launch and these...people."

"That much was obvious."

"All of these people," she said, gesturing around her. "What I don't care about is you or Tony or the rules and regulations of Ross & Clayton."

"Then you don't care about your job."

"Not that one. I care about this one." She pointed a finger toward the launch pad in the distance. "That's all that matters to me now."

She ignored Bill's stunned expression and began to walk toward the press facility.

She had to call *Newsweek*. She had to help with the media. It was all she knew how to do and she had to do her part to make this mission a success. Not her original mission. The *real* mission.

Only then would she leave. When she got home, she might have to figure out how to live without Deke Stockard, but she'd do it knowing she did everything possible for them to succeed.

Chapter Twenty-Four

Arriving at the press viewing area two hours before lift-off, Jessica paused to drink in the sight of the brilliantly lit shuttle atop a gentle cloud of steam, poised for its venture into space. Only three miles away, she stood at the closest point any non-essential person could be to a launch. She could clearly see the outline of the external fuel tank, the rocket boosters coupled tightly with the orbiter itself and the complex, towering mass of metal that was the connecting gantry. It was breathtaking and awe-inspiring. And terrifying.

She knew Deke and the four other astronauts had already been dusted and dressed in the brilliant orange protective gear, crossed the catwalk, and buckled in to monitor the computer and video screens.

The sky, although still black and starry, was clear with an air temperature of an unusually warm sixty-two degrees. Since all the landing sites had good weather, the only possibilities for a delay were the innumerable technical and computer difficulties that so many launches encountered. The launch window was short, just under eight minutes, and they couldn't miss it. A rescheduled flight wasn't an option on this mission.

The loudspeakers played the audio feed from Launch and Mission Control communicating with the shuttle. Periodically, the muffled, microphoned voice of the man she loved broke through the static as he responded in terse monotone to instructions from the launch manager.

She hadn't heard his voice for two days. Since Friday morning, when they talked on the pavilion, he had been immersed in non-stop, last-minute training.

Each time she heard him on the speaker, her heart constricted and she gazed toward the sight of the illuminated launch pad. There he was, ready to take off, ready to save someone's life. She quaked inside.

She thought of Valerie and Jack Stockard in the VIP viewing area on top of the Launch Control Center. They were the only other people here who could love Deke as much as she did, who could care as deeply.

By four thirty that morning, her nerves frayed and ready to snap, Jessica sipped a warm cup of tea and stepped away from the hordes of reporters.

A moment later, Stuart stood next to her. He put his arm around her and the brotherly gesture nearly brought her to tears. "I know you well enough by now to try and help you."

She looked at her friend, not sure what he meant, but happy to have the gentle touch after the biting attacks of the media she'd spent the past forty-eight hours trying to defuse. "I'm fine, really."

"We're swimming with Public Affairs staff, Jess. You don't have to be here."

"Where else on earth would I be?"

"With the families. With the spouses and loved ones of the crew." He squeezed her a little tighter. "Where you belong."

She studied the warm twinkle in his eyes. "I guess I haven't done a very good job of hiding my feelings, have I?"

"Pretty tough to hide the fireworks when the two of you are in the same room." He laughed softly. "Go be with the families, Jess."

The possibility was so appealing she nearly cried. "Could I really do that, Stuart?"

"With that badge, you can go anywhere." He gave her a little nudge. "It's a two-minute drive. I'll take you."

Without thinking, she put both arms around him. "Stuey, you are the best. Let me get my purse...and cell phone, of course."

Jessica had toured the Launch Control Center and knew exactly where the Stockards would be. Most of the VIP spectators were gathered on the main floor, a large, glass-walled room that faced the launch pad on one side and the dozens of computers, technicians, and video screens that formed the Launch Control Center on the other. Everyone waited for the instruction to move to the second floor, where they would sit in rooftop bleachers for an unobstructed view of the launch.

Entering the main area where families and VIP guests mingled and chatted, Jessica showed her badge to the guard and quickly scanned the room. As soon as she caught the bright blue eyes of Valerie Stockard, the older woman's face broke into a smile and they rushed to each other.

"Jessica! I was so worried we wouldn't get to see you!" Valerie kissed her cheek, erasing any remaining doubts she had about watching the launch with Deke's parents.

Jessica held both of Valerie's hands and saw the strain on her face. "Are you all right?"

"Wait till you become a mother, dear. From the first bike ride with no training wheels, it's hell."

The comment struck a bittersweet chord that squeezed her throat. If only she could find out.

Jack appeared at Valerie's arm, beaming with pride and offering a bear hug to Jessica.

"Can you stay here with us or do you have to be with the media, dear?" Valerie asked.

"I can't take another minute of them, quite frankly. I'd love to watch the launch from here. With you, if you don't mind." It felt so right, so completely perfect to be with them. Far from the reporters, far from the job. Here, with family.

"We'd be delighted," Jack responded with a heartfelt smile.

At T-minus nine minutes, at the start of a built-in ten-minute hold on the countdown, the VIP guests were guided upstairs to the outdoor viewing area. Once on the viewing deck, the families naturally grouped together. Alongside Jack, Valerie pulled Jessica next to her as they took seats on the bleachers. The simple act touched Jessica and she wished she could tell this dear woman how much her kindness meant on that nerve-racking morning.

The Florida sky remained suspended somewhere between nighttime and dawn, painted in a dramatic smoky violet that left both the stars and a few puffy clouds strangely visible at the same time. In the distance, Jessica saw the curved sliver of the moon hung low, a reminder of the glorious days when families gathered here to watch their loved ones take off for a walk on that orb.

The countdown continued at T-minus eight minutes and fifty-nine seconds and a hush fell over the viewing area. The loudest sound came from the single speaker, crackling with static and the staccato conversation between the crew and Mission Control and the periodic announcement of the countdown status.

Every time they heard Deke's voice, Jessica saw Jack Stockard's jaw clench, a familiar muscle tensing in his handsome face.

At T-minus seven minutes and thirty seconds, the catwalk was pulled away from the orbiter and Mission Control instructed the ground crew to begin their exodus from the gantry. That was it. Just the five brave souls inside *Endeavour* remained on the launch pad, a small team of courageous rescuers, determined to risk their lives to save Micah Petrenko's.

At T-minus four minutes, the flight crew was ordered to close the airtight visors on their helmets.

"Roger that. We're sealed up."

"That's it," Jack whispered. "He won't say another word till he's in orbit." Then he smiled at the two women next to him. "Relax. He can fly anything."

The sound of Deke's final words to her rang in her ears. *Will you be here when I land?*

At T-minus forty-five seconds, a massive cloud of steam mushroomed around the engines of the shuttle.

"What causes that steam again, Jack?" Valerie asked.

"Three hundred thousand gallons of water. Less noise, less damage to the shuttle."

At T-minus twenty-five seconds, Mission Control announced that the main engine firing sequence was turned over to the onboard computers. Valerie reached for Jessica's hand and squeezed it, looking first to her husband and then to Jessica. Her eyes were filled with tears, and a mixture of pride and fear froze the features on her face.

At T-minus ten seconds the crowd began to chant, and for

a moment, Jessica remembered the feeling of Deke's arms around her as they counted down to the New Year together.

Nine...eight...seven...

Oh, my love, be safe.

At T-minus six seconds, the main engines fired. An explosion of brilliant orange flames spewed forth, a blinding and intense inferno of color nearly as big as the launch pad itself, filling the air with a pungent, acrid smell and assaulting the senses of every onlooker. Jessica instinctively squeezed her eyes closed to protect them from the fiery brilliance. Tears splashed on her cheeks.

Four...three...two...

A rumbling eruption and a second billowing cloud mixed with flames exploded and sent earth-shattering thunder across the flat land of Kennedy Space Center. The Launch Control Center trembled with the force of the rolling explosion, shaking the bleachers and rattling Jessica to her bones. Propelled by the fire and fuel, the giant rockets gradually and deliberately lifted from the ground.

Jessica wiped at the tears streaming down her face with one hand and held Valerie's in a death grip with the other. *Deke, please get up there. Darling, please, I love you so much. Please, please be safe.* Her heart hammered in her chest, her breath suspended as she waited in terror and anticipation and utter amazement.

In less than three seconds—an eternity—*Endeavour* cleared the tower of Launch Pad 39B. With a glorious plume of flames and smoke, it rose higher toward the heavens, then rolled on its back to continue its journey. Jessica's eyes stayed fixed on the flame in the sky and she finally exhaled as the solid rocket boosters dropped silently into the air. Still the shuttle continued at the top of a mile-long white contrail that cut through the morning sky.

Farther and farther he went until there was no more than a millimeter of flame, then the external fuel tank dropped and the main engines were the only light visible to earth. It was his last stroke of color in the dawn-tinted sky, a final farewell before Deke took over the flight deck, masterfully and flawlessly guiding his ship into the blackness of outer space.

Jessica dropped her head on Valerie's shoulder and fought back a sob. She felt Jack Stockard's arms come around both of them as they formed a tiny circle of three.

Valerie wiped her face and laughed a little. "Now all he's got to do is fly through outer space, attach a thousand-ton spacecraft to a moving target, and rescue a dying man."

"That's not all, Val," Jack added with a wry smile. "He has to land the son of a bitch that's held together with bubble gum and tape."

Jessica looked from one to the other with her own unsteady smile. "He can do it."

She had to believe it. She just had to.

☆〰

Adrenaline still coursed through Jessica's veins an hour after *Endeavour* launched. After a short celebration with the Stockards, Jessica decided to return to the Press Facility and continue the revelry with her hard-working friends.

Along the path that joined the two buildings, she stopped to peer at the silhouette of Pad 39B outlined against the rising sun. Silent now, and empty, the pad was a wildlife preserve tucked into the coast of Florida that for one brief moment every few months was shattered and shaken apart by the impact of technology. A smile tugged at her lips and Jessica realized that the beauty around her had been there all along. It just took a while to see it.

The last few hours had overshadowed all of her fears about her future—or lack of one—with Deke. Today was not the day to wallow in self-pity. It was a day to thank God and the brilliant engineers of NASA, including the late Skip Bowker, that *Endeavour* was safely in its orbit around the earth. Yes, Deke had to get Micah and get home. But step one was over.

She stared at the sky, cornflower blue now and broken only by enormous powder puffs of white clouds. Without knowing it, she moaned out loud, an unstoppable response to the emotion that seized her heart. Never, in all her years of striving toward goal after goal, had she felt such a magnificent sense of accomplishment. It made her want to dance to her office and throw her arms around all the people she knew shared that sense of achievement.

Once in the building, the joy faded at the sight of Bill Dugan sitting behind her desk, on her phone, scowling. He hung up when she walked in.

"What's the matter?" she asked.

He pushed the chair away from the desk and blew out a dramatic breath. "What's not? I just got off the phone with Zimmerman."

Anger zipped through her. "What are you doing talking to *Newsweek*, Bill? That's my story."

"Now don't get your panties in a bunch." He smiled and leaned back in her chair. "More influence on him can only help. Let's get our launch report out to the team."

A slow, steady throb in her temples replaced euphoria. Ignoring the discomfort, she came around the desk and tapped him on the shoulder to get him out of her chair. "I'll email everyone. Let me sit down and get online."

"Not necessary. I've already drafted something on your computer while you were still over with the, uh, families.

Let's print it out and fax it to Tony's house. It's Sunday morning. He won't look at his email today."

She didn't even know Tony's home fax number, but she didn't feel like fighting him now. "Sure. Go ahead and a print a hard copy."

He looked at the printer at the edge of her desk. "Got any R&C letterhead? This'll go to Price and I always like the client to see the agency logo on everything. Makes us look like we're all over the account."

"Jeez." She shook her head as she opened the supply cabinet. "I had no idea you were such a political animal, Bill."

"And I had no idea you were so friendly with your client's parents."

The unmistakable inference in his tone grabbed her.

"They live in New York," she said calmly as she lifted a box of file folders to get to the stationery. "I had the opportunity to meet them when Deke did the *Today*show."

"And by the way, I don't recall you asking to leave the media facility to go to the Control Center for the launch."

Her fingers curled around a sheaf of R&C stationery that she'd brought back from Boston. "I had no idea I needed a hall pass from you before I left a facility."

He looked up sharply from the keyboard. "Easy, Jess. You're on shaky ground."

She grabbed the ream of stationery with every intention of slamming fifty pages or so on the desk to accompany a defensive comeback. But she froze instead, riveted to what she saw underneath it.

With a little gasp of horror, she dropped the whole stack of paper in her hand, and sheets ruffled to the ground around her.

Stark blue letters on a white background. The imprint of NASA. The old, outdated, supposed-to-be-shredded letterhead that the anonymous memos had been written on.

"Oh my God. Look what's in here." She lifted a piece gingerly and turned to Bill, nearly afraid to talk. "The old NASA stationery."

He nearly leaped around the desk and took it from her. Then his pale blue eyes flashed in accusation. "Where did this come from?"

"I...I don't know." She looked back in the closet at the box it had been in and suddenly, she had the answer. The sickening, pathetic, ugly answer. No one at NASA had sent those memos. "It came from the Boston office of R&C." She remembered her secretary preparing the box for her, nervously mentioning that Carla Drake had instructed her not to include any other client information. "Rita packed up supplies for me when I was up at Christmas."

"Jessica," he said quietly. "What have you done?"

"What have *I* done?" She gaped at him. "You think I sent fake memos? Please. But it would certainly help someone trying to get my job to make me look guilty. Or just sabotage the whole NASA campaign and make me look inept."

"What are you saying?"

"Carla Drake. Evidently, she's the most political of all of us. Only she didn't bother to check that the Boston supply of client stationery was out of date." Jessica shook her head and stared at the paper. "Is she so hell-bent on ruining my career that she'd risk the account and the agency's reputation? It's outrageous."

Bill looked hard at Jessica. "Unless you can prove she did something like that, Jessica, I doubt anyone would believe you. The stationery's in your office."

"She let the cosmonaut story break without warning me," Jessica insisted, picking up the receiver of her phone. "She's behind this somehow. I'm going to call Tony."

Bill's hand clamped on her wrist. "Don't do that, Jess."

"Why not?" Jessica tried to yank her hand free.

"Because she's Tony's golden goddess right now and you don't stand a chance of accusing her without proof. You'd look like a fool. And maybe a guilty one."

She would have laughed in his face if his expression hadn't been so sincere. "You can't be serious. I'm the one with the least to gain by this. I've lost almost everything I've ever worked for over the last three months."

"If this gets out, the agency will lose the account."

She dropped the phone in the cradle. "Is that what you're worried about? This is a felony, for God's sake. Someone tampered with government property. Someone could have cost Micah Petrenko his life if they'd scrubbed a launch based on the content of those memos."

He turned away and picked up the jacket he'd thrown over her guest chair. "I've got a meeting with Colonel Price. I'll handle this, Jessica. You'll get nowhere accusing Carla Drake. You may end up in more hot water than you're already in."

He left her standing with the R&C stationery around her feet like a pile of freshly fallen snow.

Chapter Twenty-Five

At seven o'clock that evening, Jessica finally left Kennedy Space Center for her home on Sea Park Road. Bill had never come back to her office and she'd spent most of the day watching the shuttle feed in Stuart's office and marveling at the perfect docking with the space station. Step two completed. *Was there nothing Deke Stockard couldn't do?*

She hadn't called Tony, knowing Bill was right and she needed more evidence. Nor had she taken the issue to Colonel Price. Instead, Jessica called Jo and suggested an unorthodox plan. Jo, bless her adventurous soul, agreed to it immediately.

After changing into sweat pants and tee shirt, Jessica absently sliced a tomato for a salad and imagined Jo and her husband, Bobby, going in for their covert operation.

On the TV, the local NASA channel that ran the shuttle feed played softly in the background: the shuttle camera only transmitted a frozen shot of Earth, presumably from a window of the orbiter. Stuart had told her that image could stay on for hours until the crew moved the camera. It seemed crazy, but as long as that camera was running, she knew Deke and the crew were alive. The link to him made her feel better.

269

When her phone rang, she dropped the knife and seized the kitchen extension.

"We're in," Jo whispered before Jessica could say hello. "Thank God I married a computer geek, huh?"

"Is anyone around?" Jessica imagined the empty R&C offices on a Sunday night.

"Believe it or not, a few ambitious account executives who want to grow up and be you. But I oh-so-coolly explained that my husband had a consulting job to upgrade some computers. They bought it."

"Good thinking. I'm just certain that hacking into Carla's computer will prove she sent the emails to *Newsweek*."

"Don't be so sure." Jo warned. "I already looked through the client letterhead. The NASA stationery here is all the new logo."

"Maybe she took a stash and hid it in her office," Jessica suggested. "She would never risk asking Rita to get her NASA stationery."

"Maybe. I'll look. Bobby hasn't found anything yet. I'll call you back."

Jessica hung up and glanced at the TV, her heart jumping. The screen had gone black. With a gasp, she grabbed the remote to turn up the sound, but a pounding on her door stopped her.

Still holding the remote, she peeked around the entryway wall and peered through the glass panels. Bill Dugan offered an apologetic half-smile. She had no idea he even knew where she lived.

"I'm sorry we never got to finish our conversation," he said as she opened the door and he stepped in. "Can we talk now?"

"Not if you're going to keep defending Carla Drake and reproaching me," she said sharply. "I need help, not condemnation right now."

With an easy hand on her shoulder, he guided her back into the living room. "You're right. I was too harsh this morning. Anyway, I've had a long talk with Price and I want to present an idea to you."

He sat on the sofa and Jessica looked at the TV screen. Still black. What was going on up there? And why didn't Jo call back?

"What is it?" she asked, hoping her tone adequately conveyed her impatience.

"I want you to hear me out. Before you say a word, just listen to me."

She stole another look at the darkened TV screen and stayed standing. "Okay. Shoot."

"Except for the work you've been doing, Colonel Price is not thrilled with the agency."

His words caught her attention and she ignored the NASA feed for the first time in hours. "What do you mean?"

"There's a lot going on behind the scenes you don't know about," he said vaguely.

She had no time for games. "Be specific."

"Well, they're happy with the Stockard campaign, but overall, R&C is expensive and our results haven't always been what they're looking for."

A tingle of understanding started to spread as she let him continue.

"They're considering a new agency. I've proposed to Price that I open my own shop. NASA would be my first account. At their current budget level, it's a healthy start. And you must have figured out by now that they like your work, Jess." He adjusted his glasses and looked up at her. "Come and work for me. Pick your title. We could grow the business together and you could continue to work on this account and any others we get."

She knew she smelled treason. He hadn't come down here because of rumors. He'd finally figured out that Colonel Price valued her over him. And that didn't fit in with his plans.

"Did you tell the Colonel about the stationery in my office?"

He shook his head. "Not yet. But it ought to seal the deal for us. I think your idea of pinning it on Carla is a good one."

Jessica reared back, surprised. "My idea of pinning it on her? I want to find out the truth."

The phone rang and she grabbed the cordless on the coffee table before he could react.

"Carla's clean," Jo whispered and Jessica's heart dropped. "The emails haven't come from a server in Boston."

"Oh." She couldn't hide the disappointment in her voice.

"But we might have found the culprit."

Jessica waited, silently, staring at Bill.

"The server is in Washington, D.C., Jess. The one that's used by R&C Washington."

Jessica swallowed hard, a slow, icy drip of realization sliding through her veins.

Of course…Bill.

She'd been looking at the real political animal all along. It wasn't Carla Drake who wanted the agency to flounder. It was the man who planned to steal the NASA account. The man who knew enough about the program to write an eloquent memo…maybe even fueled by information he was getting from Skip Bowker. A man who certainly knew how to seed a story with *Newsweek*…and was in her office with enough time to plant some of the old stationery in her cabinet, just in case someone from her company had to take the blame.

"Really? That's very interesting. I better go now. Bill Dugan's here."

She disconnected, then set the cordless phone on the table, preparing her accusation. "When's the last time you updated your client stationery files, Bill?"

He slowly rose from the sofa and they stood eye-to-eye. "Who was that?"

"An employee of mine. The one who just found the server that was used to send the emails to *Newsweek*."

He narrowed his eyes. "You can't prove anything that way."

"No. But you're opening your own agency, Bill, and stealing a big account. Your motivation to make R&C look bad is pretty strong. Did you put the extra stationery in my office while I was out of the office so you could pin the memos on me? Or was that just dumb luck?"

He took a step toward her and she jerked away.

"Where did you get all the information?" she demanded. "Did Skip Bowker leak all that to you? So you'd be his puppet with your media contacts? So you'd leak the story about the cosmonaut and the inspection problems?"

He just narrowed his eyes, a thin sheen of sweat forming above his lip. "You're crazy, Jess."

She shook her head. "No. No, I'm not. You've been sabotaging me all along. To make R&C look bad so you can have the account. And now that you know they like me, you want to use me—"

He lunged at her across the coffee table and she jumped back. Stunned that he would try to hurt her, she froze. "Get out of here. You're dead in the water, Dugan. Your list of transgressions is a mile long, starting with tampering with government property."

His face paled. "Don't be a fool, Jessica. I've run the

NASA account for years. No one would believe I'd do anything to hurt the business."

She pointed to the door. "Get the hell out of here."

The TV flashed to a white screen and crackled. They both turned at the same time.

NASA Coverage Discontinued, a simple banner read.

She glared back at Bill. "Go!" she screamed, her focus dragged to the TV and what this could possibly mean. Grabbing the remote, she stabbed in the number of an all-news channel and looked back at Bill, realizing he'd stepped into the kitchen.

"What are you doing?" She used the remote to point to the front door. "Get out of my house."

His eyes darkened, but he held up one hand in surrender. "I'll leave the back way," he said, and she saw him step toward the sliding door to the patio.

"We have word from Johnson Space Center's Mission Control that a problem on the space shuttle *Endeavour* has resulted in the loss of one of its onboard computers." The newscaster yanked her attention and she spun back to the TV.

"Oh my God," she covered her mouth in horror and stared at the screen, aware of the sound of the sliding door opening, grateful that Bill had left. She'd deal with his lunacy later.

The image switched to a familiar network reporter she'd spoken to many times in the last few months. She punched the volume, desperate for information.

"NASA has not released official word, but the open feed to the shuttle has been closed off to the public and only Mission Control in Houston is in touch with Commander Stockard and his crew at this time." Her heart froze at the mention of his name. She upped the volume again, as if making it louder could change the news.

"We've been given no word on the status of the

cosmonaut Micah Petrenko, only that he has exited the Space Station and is under medical surveillance on board *Endeavour*. NASA has reported that the space shuttle had begun its firing sequence to undock and return to Earth when one of the onboard computers failed."

Jessica's throat closed in terror, a white heat suffocating her as the reporter continued, "A landing with only redundant systems functioning is considered an emergency and is unprecedented in well over one hundred shuttle missions. The only other option, should the redundant computer fail, is an in-flight crew escape system that has never been tested except in simulated training exercises."

It would be torture for both of us.

Yes, Deke, it might be. A moan escaped her lips and her legs threatened to buckle as she listened to the reporter close his story.

"It remains to be seen if Commander Stockard will opt to bailout by parachute at thirty thousand feet tonight or early tomorrow morning." Bailout by—

The hand clamped on her mouth, making her stumble backward as Bill jerked her other arm behind her. She gasped for air, but only sucked the skin of his hand and he twisted the other arm harder.

"You will not screw this up for me," he growled in her ear. Then she saw the glint in the hand that covered her mouth. Blindingly close, she could make out the serrated edges of her knife, still wet with tomato juice.

Jessica started to scream, but Bill's hand strangled her into a mumble.

"Shut up!"

She closed her eyes, blood rushing through her head, barely hearing the phone ringing on the table. He tugged her arm up at a painful angle.

"Poor Jessica," he whispered and slowly started backing her out of the room. "Her career shot to hell. Her promotion lost. Her boyfriend in trouble—maybe dying—in space. She must have *snapped*."

He cracked her arm in time with the word and her shoulder exploded in agony as he dragged her toward the kitchen.

"I'll be the one to find your body," he said quietly, a bit of glee in his voice like he was in a brainstorming session and the ideas were just *flowing*. "You'll be in the river. I'll help them piece together exactly what happened."

As he forced her from the living room toward the darkened patio, the last thing she saw on the TV screen was a still shot of Deke Stockard standing next to his T-38, a look of amused annoyance captured by the photographer.

☆

To Deke's left, Janine Harmon floated up from the middeck, a worried look in her eyes.

He shook his head to indicate he couldn't talk to her as he listened to Mission Control read the coordinates on the orbital maneuvering system.

"Roger that, Houston," he responded. "Your OMS coordinates match our redundant system. Ready to fire."

Deke glanced down at her, then back to one of the nine displays he'd been studying. "We're still on one backup computer system, Doctor." The backup had lasted long enough to get them undocked and headed back to earth.

An instruction from Houston crackled in his headset.

"Roger, Houston." Deke reached forward and set his finger on one of twenty-eight switches on the panel to his right. He knew the correct one by feel.

276

"Fire thrusters on," he said. "Fire on five, four, three, two, one." He pressed a button and the orbiter jerked to the left, its steel frame creaking.

"OMS and thrusters positioned, Houston," Kurt Muir reported from the seat on Deke's right.

Momentarily relieved, Deke leaned back from the stick and looked at Janine. "How is he?"

"Bad. Way worse than we were led to believe. He's not responding to the anticoagulant. How long until we land?"

"We're not far from the reentry orbit headed to Kennedy and should touch down in less than two hours." He turned to his co-pilot, now struggling with the new computer readings. "If the redundant computer holds out. If it doesn't, we land manually or we abort and bailout."

Janine floated higher, her eyes wide. "I've trained on the new escape system. It's a bear. I'm not sure Micah would survive it."

Deke resisted the urge to say what he and Kurt both knew. None of them would likely survive it.

"If we abort," Deke told them, "we'll go into autopilot glide, then depressurize the cabin to equalize outside pressure and jettison the hatch." He swallowed hard at the thought. "Starting with you and Micah, we'll each hook up the parachute harness to the escape pole and jump out. Remember to use the pole for the trajectory to take us below the left wing."

"At what altitude?" Janine asked softly.

"Thirty thousand feet."

She paled. "He'll never make that jump, Commander."

Deke knew she was right. Petrenko looked closer to death than they'd expected. Deke had met him a few years ago and remembered the vital young Russian with sparkling green eyes and nearly platinum hair. His eyes had no light in them now; his skin was as pale as his blond locks.

"We have forty minutes to make a decision and watch this computer. God willing, we'll land with it. If not, we can land the old-fashioned way. On a wing and a prayer."

The three of them shared a look.

"But just in case we decide to abort, suit up now and get everyone in jumping gear," he instructed.

Silently, Janine floated back down to her patient and Deke and Kurt rose to help each other into the orange pressure suits.

After he was suited, Deke returned to the cockpit and listened to Kurt quietly discussing his calculations of trajectory paths and readings with Houston. Deke peered into the blackness of space soaring past him. He closed his eyes to the stars and let his imagination go where he longed to be.

Jessie. He could see her face and hair, hear her infectious laugh, inhale her flowery scent. The will to survive nearly jolted him.

He didn't want to die without holding her again. He didn't want to die without telling her he loved her. He didn't want to live...without her.

The screech of an alarm broke his reverie. "Auxiliary power unit one is failing, Commander," Kurt announced. "Wing flap and landing gear moving to aux power two."

Good God, they blew a fuel cell in an auxiliary unit. "Remove the panel and override it," Deke barked to Kurt, then into his headset, "Houston, we're moving wing flap and landing gear to aux power two."

Forget the wing. Now they'd have to land on just a prayer.

Chapter Twenty-Six

Bill kept a hand clamped on Jessica's mouth and twisted her arm so viciously that flashes sparked behind her eyes, the only light on an otherwise pitch-black evening.

"Don't make me stab you, Jess," he warned. "Get in the water and give up. You are about to kill yourself."

He was a madman. He had no plan. He was insane and would panic any minute.

She could outsmart him. All she needed was...a creative idea.

He jerked her head toward the sky, but from memory of the dozens of mornings she'd jogged this path, she knew exactly where she was. Past the queen palm that she used for leg stretches. She automatically lifted her foot, knowing a rock jutted out on the path. Bill stumbled over it and cursed.

Oh, yes. Her advantage. She knew every inch of this path, even in the dark. Many mornings she'd run before sunrise, to clear her brain and work her body. Every time she made it past the stand of oaks at the half-mile point, she'd start counting the steps until she reached Deke's dock.

Deke's dock. If she could escape Bill, she could lose him and hide on the boat. Maybe even sail it away.

Her property ended in a mass of mangrove and pepper trees, a jungle of roots and branches that blocked direct access to the river. He'll never get through it, she thought.

"One word," he warned as his grip over her mouth loosened. "One word and this knife goes straight through your back. I'll weigh you down so you'll rot at the bottom of that river and they'll never find you."

He let go of her mouth and she gasped for air. He twisted her arm with his left hand. With the knife, he whacked at a mangrove branch. Leaves fluttered and he tightened his grip on her and swore in frustration. They took a step into the roots and she felt the cold water lap against her bare feet.

The knife thwacked another branch and Bill pushed her farther into the water, now lapping at her knees. They were trapped in the mangroves and he took another angry swing at a branch, then another. In his determination, she felt the grip on her arm loosen. Ever so slightly. One more swing and he almost let go of her.

As the blade sliced a branch, she tore her arm out of his grip and took off, stones and roots stabbing at her bare feet, the wind whistling in her ears the minute she found her footing and started to move.

"God damn you!" he called with a flutter of leaves and a grunt. She hoped he tripped and got caught on the roots, but didn't turn to see. With every stride, she stretched her legs farther, willing herself to get to the boat before her enemy caught up with her.

She reached the dock, stealing a look down the path as she struggled with the latch of the wooden gate. She heard a twig snap in the distance, but couldn't see Bill. She had to take the chance, praying it was dark enough to sneak to the end of the Deke's dock. The latch slid and Jessica stepped on the wooden boards, hoping they didn't give her away and remembering to lock the gate behind her so he wouldn't notice it open when he reached the dock.

The sailboat seemed miles away, though she guessed the long river dock to be only seventy or eighty feet. Her bare feet hardly touched the planks as she bolted to the *Tailwind*.

She slipped onto the deck of the boat and dropped flat on her stomach, gasping for air and shaking. Her arm still hurt where Bill had twisted it and the look in his eyes burned in her memory. She heard a pelican splash. The mast rigging clanged as her weight swayed the boat. She silently swore and managed to calm her breathing.

She tried to listen over the thumping beat of her heart. Had he seen her?

She heard nothing. She stayed absolutely still, her face and body smashed against the fiberglass bottom of the boat, the brackish smell of river water and fish permeating her nostrils.

She inched her face around to breathe, expecting to see Bill jump at her any second. Instead, she saw a brilliant, glimmering star in the sky. Somewhere, limping along in his spacecraft, was the man she loved and needed as much as the very air that she breathed. How she longed for him to save her. But first, he had to save himself.

She had to stay alive. She had to be there when Deke landed that shuttle. She squeezed the cushion and stared at a single star in the night sky. They needed to stay alive. Both of them. They had so much to live for.

That was her mantra as she waited. So much to live for. Deke and Jessica. Love. Family. Children. Home. A life filled with the exhilaration that comes with knowing you are doing something that really matters. Together. Jessica and Deke. She would not, could not, live without him. She had to convince him they were meant to be together. They were both wrong about what they thought they wanted. They wanted each other. She would convince him.

They had so much to live for. They had each other.

☆

The flight director spoke calmly to Deke. "We're not recommending the bailout, Commander. But the final decision is yours."

"Roger, Houston. We're talking about it."

Deke looked back at his crew. Two mission specialists, one pilot, and a doctor. On the middeck below, one very sick cosmonaut. All suited in matching pressure suits and prepared to do what he decided. He held all of their lives in his hands.

And his own.

"You can bring this thing in on manual even if we lose that computer." Kurt finally said to him. They all knew that had never been done before, except in a sim. And, whoa, that had been ugly.

But he had no choice. Petrenko would surely die in a bailout.

"We're going to attempt a landing, with or without the computer." Deke said to all of them. "I don't think we have a shot at surviving a bailout and it'll kill Micah."

They nodded and silently moved to their various positions. No one questioned the decision.

Before Deke announced his plans to Houston, he imagined what he could say to Jessica. What he *would* say. Because, damn it all, he was going to land this bird and finding her would be the first thing he did when his feet hit Mother Earth.

"Houston, go ahead and get your media circus on runway

thirty-three." He smiled. She'd get *that* message. She'd be there. "We're coming in."

How long had she been hiding, Jessica wondered. Twenty minutes? An hour? She hadn't moved, hadn't dared give Bill any clue that she had hidden in the boat. Her fingers burned where she clutched the cushion. Slowly, she relaxed them and tried to inch the vinyl pillow to a different spot under her head. As she did, something under it clunked.

She bit her lip and froze at the sound. Then, in the moonlight, metal flashed. A key. On a floatation device. He'd hidden a key. She could motor away to safety! *Bless you, Deke Stockard.* He'd saved her after all.

Did she dare start the engine? In the dark, she felt under the helm for the ignition she remembered seeing when she'd been in the boat with Deke.

The lines. She had to untie the boat from the pilings of the dock. Slowly, she lifted her head like a periscope and peered over the edge of the boat toward the darkened pathway, looking for a flash of the white shirt Bill wore. Farther down, much closer to her house, she thought she saw something move in the shadows. Did he actually think she'd return while he was there, or was he just waiting for her to give away her hiding place?

She climbed out onto the dock, her quivering fingers seizing the ropes that Deke had, of course, tightened securely. She untwisted the knot, feeling the rope slide free. The stern line was tighter and sweat dripped between her shoulder blades as she struggled with it. Her nail bent backward and she gasped, then heard the creak of the gate.

The rope released and she grabbed the side of the boat

and fell back toward the helm. There was a pedal and a throttle and she remembered Deke had used both to motor them around.

Holding her breath, she felt along the side near the helm for the rubber ring of the ignition. Damn, she'd been so busy watching Deke that she hadn't paid any attention to what he'd done to start the motor. She found the circular opening and slipped the key in.

The footsteps sounded closer. Slamming her foot onto the pedal and moving the throttle stick at the same time, the diesel engine started with a cough, then died.

Oh God. She twisted the key again and stole a look at the dock. He'd found her. He was jogging toward her, the knife blade reflecting the meager moonlight.

The engine turned over and she put all her weight on the floor pedal and screeched the throttle. The boat moved away from the dock. Slowly, inching, not nearly fast enough.

She heard Bill grunt as he leaped from the dock and grabbed hold of the side of the boat.

She threw the throttle down harder and the engine sputtered as it gathered strength. She willed the boat to move.

She turned to see Bill hanging on and she reached over and banged his hands against the fiberglass as he struggled to gain a hold.

"Get off, you bastard!" she screamed and pounded as the *Tailwind* inched farther into the river.

She slammed his fingers and tried to bend them up, but he pulled his body up to a half stand and was about to fling himself into the boat when Jessica lifted her right leg and kicked him as hard as she could.

With a gasp, he fell into the river and the knife flew into the air, splashing at the same instant he did. The boat picked up a little speed and each second it took her farther into the channel and away from Bill, who was sputtering and flailing toward the boat.

Into the black night she motored, breathing only when she was sure he couldn't catch her. She had no idea where she was headed, but she had to figure out how to get out of the water and up to Kennedy. If *Endeavour* really had started its journey home, she had to be there when he landed.

About a mile from Deke's dock, she picked up the handset of the radio and started pressing buttons; a reassuring static told her it worked. Of course it worked. Everything worked. This was *Deke's* boat. She dropped her head back and stared up at the star. Somewhere up there, she had a guardian angel. Now who was looking out for him?

Deke glanced at Kurt as they harnessed themselves in and did a verbal situation status check with the rest of the crew. Everyone was ready.

"Start deorbit burn in five seconds," he instructed Kurt.

The pilot executed the deorbit burn sequence easily. The orbiter jerked in response and Deke could see the protective tiles on the nose in front of him beginning to glow.

Deke guided the stick to the proper nose-first attitude as they braced to hit the atmosphere. His gaze moved from screen to screen, every cell in his body concentrating on the sequence of events. The blackness of space began to lighten, shock waves of air rolled and exploded as the spacecraft vibrated and groaned.

"Deorbit burn complete, Houston," Deke reported.

"Roger, *Endeavour*. You can start your S turns, Commander."

Outside the window of the cockpit, the skin of the shuttle now burned bright red with the heat of reentry. With more effort, Deke pulled the stick and the orbiter shuddered through the first of a series of wide curves that would lower the speed. The pressure dropped, his flight suit weighing down on him, his visor vibrating on his helmet. He peered at each computer screen, willing them to function.

"Houston, our altitude is seventy-five thousand feet." He kept his voice steady regardless of the violent shaking of the orbiter. "We're descending at one six three per second. We are one hundred and forty-five nautical miles from Kennedy. Over."

"Roger, Endeavour. Ground track and nav are go."

Deke took the stick and held it as steady as he could.

Another alarm screamed. "The rudder readout is dead," Kurt shouted over the racket. "We lost the computer."

For the first time, Deke knew his chances of getting home were next to nothing. *You can never be a hundred percent sure.*

Chapter Twenty-Seven

Jessica could see the lights of the Coast Guard ship coming toward her. God bless the radio. She'd finally reached someone and help was bouncing in her direction over the waves of the Banana River.

The Coast Guard speedboat zipped next to the *Tailwind* and an official-looking young man climbed onto her little ship.

"Did you radio for help, ma'am?" he asked.

"Yes, please. Can someone please take this boat and get it docked somewhere safe and get me to the Cape? It's an emergency. I have to get to the space center immediately." She heard the alarm in her own voice.

"Don't you want to stay with your boat, ma'am? Then someone could probably get you up to Kennedy."

"No, no. Have you heard anything about the shuttle?" she demanded, ignoring his suggestion. "Are they okay?"

The man looked at her questioningly. "They were having some trouble a few hours ago. Haven't heard the double sonic boom. You always hear that right before it lands safely."

"Please," she grabbed his arm and didn't care if she looked like a lunatic. "I need to get to the landing facility. My...my...my future husband is on that shuttle."

He must have a soft spot for lunatics. They helped her transfer into the speedboat and cut through the waves toward a Coast Guard station. A captain hustled her into a waiting van with a driver and kindly let her use a cell phone during the half-hour trip up to the Cape.

Before she could get any information on *Endeavour*, she knew she had to get someone after Bill Dugan. She'd alerted the Coast Guard and they promised to get the police to search the area around her house. She managed to reach Tony at home. This time, he didn't defend the culprit. In fact, he admitted that he had no idea Bill had even gone to the Cape.

"Now, Jessica, about your job in Emerging—"

"I'm quitting, Tony."

Stone silence met the announcement she hadn't even realized she was going to make until the words were out. And, damn, they sounded good.

"Is this about Carla? Because I'm having second thoughts about her as GM and I think you'd be perfect for the job. The folks at Dash have uncovered some, let's just call it, 'creative' accounting issues and—"

"I don't care about Carla, Tony. She's your problem. And I don't really want to be general manager."

"What are you going to do?"

Stay with Deke. Marry him. Have babies and laughter and love for the rest of her life. "I'm thinking about working in Public Affairs at the Cape," she said. "I think Stuey will hire me."

"Stuey?"

The van driver turned on the radio and she heard the only word that mattered to her.

Endeavour.

"I gotta go, Tony."

They'd reached the guard gate at the runway field. But her heart suddenly dropped again when the driver turned and asked for her ID.

"An *ID*?" She gasped. "I don't even have shoes, for crying out loud."

"Ma'am, we can't let you anywhere near the landing site without proper ID."

From memory, she dialed Stuart's cell phone.

When he answered, she thought life itself had just been given back to her.

"Stuart, where are they? What's happening?"

"They're coming in with no computer on a manual land." Stuart's usually calm voice had an eerie tone of panic in it. "You better get out here."

"Please, Stu. I don't have my ID. I'm at the south guard gate at the landing facility."

"Put the guard on the phone."

☆

Deke refused to let imminent death cloud his thinking. He could do this. He had to do this. "Go to backup avionics," he ordered.

"Backup is black."

"Well, that's a problem," Deke said through teeth clenched so tight he could draw blood. "'Cause we're inverted."

"*Endeavour*, we see you on energy approaching KSC. You are approaching at zero seven zero niner. Fifty-five thousand feet. You need another deorbit burn to get into position for landing."

Son of a bitch, he *knew* that. Sweat droplets trickled across his cheeks as Deke reached for the rudder adjustment and ordered the burn to start. He squeezed his eyes shut to visualize the right position. From the sim, he should know it. He *should* know it.

"Get ready to roll," he hollered to Kurt and the crew. He felt the orbiter respond, spinning and careening through the sky.

"Hold steady at zero seven zero, *Endeavour*," Mission Control announced to them. "You are in position for landing."

Deke didn't dare exhale over the small victory. "We must have blown some fuel cells or shorted again," he said to Kurt as they stared at another blank screen.

They had, thank God, prepared for this. Only it was in the sim. And they damn near missed the landing.

Deke felt the steady beat of his heart and the vein in his neck that always pulsed under stress. He gently moved the stick to the left, then brought the ship back up a bit.

"Good glide, Endeavour. We can see you on approach. You are at thirty-thousand feet."

If they were going to bail, they would have to do it now. Right now. Then the ship would crash into the ocean and they would fall to their probable deaths.

He wondered, is Jess watching somewhere? Is she watching the NASA feed and listening to him calmly making life-and-death decisions? If she was, then he could tell her now, over the microphone, what he should have told her before he left. That life without her isn't life. He wanted to be tied to her, connected to her, married to her forever and ever. He loved her completely.

"*Endeavour*, you're on glide slope and centerline. Right where you want to be, Commander."

"Roger, Houston." Deke pulled gently at the stick, tugging at it to get the attitude of the nose right. *Easy, easy.* He waited to hear the landing gear drop.

"Drop the landing gear, *now*, Captain," he ordered.

"I'm working on it, Commander."

Deke stole a look to his right. Kurt struggled with the manual controls.

"We're starting manual lock of landing gear, Houston," he said in his mouthpiece. As if committing to it could get it to work.

"Damn it all," Kurt muttered.

Deke could feel the gravity pull every muscle in his body, the pressure on his chest like an anvil. He held the stick with all his strength and tried to find the land below him, despite the fact that his eyeballs vibrated in their sockets.

"Come on, man," he demanded. "We're too far gone to bail now."

They burst through a cloud and the brilliant lights of Runway 33 appeared like a pinpoint beacon in the distance. He had to get home to her. He *had* to.

"You are at two hundred feet, *Endeavour*."

He heard Kurt exhale. "Got it."

The shuttle rocked with the force of the landing gear dropping into place. Kennedy loomed closer. Deke pushed down on the stick.

I'm coming home, sweetheart.

"I can't go any farther, ma'am," the van driver said apologetically. "I'm afraid you have to walk to the runway from here."

She nodded. As if she cared at this point. "Thank you. You've been—" The air suddenly shook with a shotgun bang and another immediately following, jerking Jessica back against the seat. *Endeavour exploded. He's dead.* "What was that?"

The driver smiled a little. "Just the sonic boom, ma'am. Shuttle broke the sound barrier. Should be here in a few minutes."

She didn't care that heads turned from the dark skies to stare at the wild woman in sweat pants and bare feet running toward the landing site.

Hot tears welled up and threatened to blind her.

Then she stopped. From the night sky she saw the lights, eerily silent as the magnificent machine glided in.

With perfect precision, the landing gear touched down and a parachute plumed behind it. The crowd, still a half-mile hike from where she stood, roared to a deafening crescendo.

Jessica heard her own shouts of joy,scraping her throat raw as she yelled with everyone else. Euphoria melted over her as she stared at the orbiter. She was part of it now. Space was in her blood, her heart. She cared about it and loved it. *It mattered.*

And so did the fact that she loved Deke Stockard with every fiber of her being.

He heard the cheers of the crowd through the headset.

"Main landing gear touchdown, Houston and...nosegear touchdown." Deke grinned at Kurt. "*Endeavour* is home."

"Roger that, Commander Stockard. Congratulations to the crew of *Endeavour*."

Deke barely heard the last comment as a spontaneous shout came from the crew around him.

"Send the stretcher for Micah first," he instructed. "We'll be right behind him."

He closed his eyes for a moment and dropped his head

back, realizing he was still smiling. Well, of course. He was officially the happiest man on earth. As they waited for the shuttle to cool and allowed the effects of gravity to drag on their bodies, Deke had no thoughts of the debriefing and medical examination he was about to go through.

None of it mattered to him. All he wanted to do was find Jessica. In the middle of the media tent, no doubt, her beautiful hair blowing and her sexy smile blinding him. He had to get to her. First. Had to tell her. He loved her.

Finally the hatch opened and medics climbed in and gently transferred Micah to the stretcher. After they left, Deke and his crew wobbled down the stairs to place their feet back on Earth.

He couldn't discern the powerful pull of gravity from the sensation tugging his heart. He scanned the gathered crowd as he shook hands with the VIPs that waited to greet the returning heroes. He found the pack of press people and he peered beyond them. *Where is she?*

He looked into the group of Cape employees and engineers, some faces familiar and all smiling, waving, and applauding. He waved back and his skilled pilot's eyes scoped the crowd. *Where is she?*

They moved to the area where families waited and again, his heart filled with hope. He saw his parents and waved, then looked around and behind them. *Where the hell is she?*

Someone was telling him where to go. Someone was saying he had to get to the medical examining room for a post-flight check. No, he wanted to scream. He had something he had to do first.

Then he saw a flash of mahogany. Beyond the press booth, toward the end of the runway, running. Her dark hair flying, her eyes wide. Was she barefoot? Was he dreaming? Was it some strange aftereffect of the landing? No. No.

Jessie. He knew he couldn't keep the grin off his face and sensed that the crowd was following his gaze.

Jessica ignored the faces turned toward her and scanned the crowd, her heart knocking against her ribs, her feet scraping concrete.

Her gaze moved beyond the dozens of TV cameras, which, for the first time ever, she didn't notice or count. She searched the crowds, beyond the ropes, to where the VIP greeters stood. Had they gone? Had he gone in for a medical yet?

Then she saw him. A big carrot-colored arm waving at her. Calling to her. He was *calling* to her?

"Jessie!" The crowd parted to let him through. Beautiful, wonderful Deke Stockard in a blinding-orange flight suit.

She arrived under the awning precisely as he did, driven by a force she didn't know could propel her. They stopped just short of one another, her breath coming in quick, hot spurts.

"You made it," she whispered between panted breaths.

"You doubted I would?" His smile was sly, teasing. But his navy eyes were not.

"Never sure in your line of work, Stockard." Something was crushing her chest. Not lack of oxygen. It was love. Blissful, suffocating love.

His gaze dropped down to her bare feet, returning to her face with a concerned expression. "Are you okay?"

She nodded, taking one step toward him. "I am now."

Without warning, the orange arms were around her, lifting her in the air.

"Sweetheart, I'm home." He buried his face in her hair, his lips on her ears. "And I hope you are, too."

She searched his face as he brought her back to the ground. Did her feet even touch?

"Of course I am." She pulled back enough to see him, to touch his face, his lips, his hair. "You saved my life. You didn't know it, but you saved my life."

"Then we're even." He touched her face. "Because you just saved mine."

"What are you talking about?"

"I figured it all out, Jessie. My life is incomplete and insignificant and unbearable unless you're in it." He ran a finger along her chin and tilted her face up to his.

She laughed. "I could have told you that, Stockard." The love was crushing her again. A good, delicious, solid crush.

"I needed to figure it out myself."

"What else did you figure out?" She pulled at him, wanting him closer, wanting to savor each exquisite word as the beauty of the moment washed over her.

"That I'm going to come home from work every night, no matter what I do. And I want to come home to you." He cupped her chin in his hand and stared at her. "This is life, Jess. This is love." He kissed her softly, just a touch, then pulled back. "I love you. With all my heart. I want to be with you forever. Please. Please, marry me. Please stay with me for the rest of your life."

His words washed over her like sunshine. Warm and comforting, brilliant and blinding. "Yes, I will marry you." The words caught in her throat and choked her. She wanted to say them over and over.

His slow and deliberate kiss tasted sweet and salty from the tears that wet her cheeks. Could she really spend the rest of her life this happy? She would burst, just completely come undone, from the joy of being Deke Stockard's wife.

And then she heard it. The whirring, the clicking, the flip of the notebooks.

"Oh my—" She broke the kiss and looked around at the pack of reporters staring at them, recording their every word, documenting the scene. "Deke—I didn't do this. You have to believe me, I—"

His laughter started deep in his throat, sexy and completely genuine. "You really expect me to believe that, spin doctor?"

"I do."

"Oh, I like those words. Say them again."

"I do."

"Tell it to the minister, sweetheart. Just like that. Because I love you, Jessica Marlowe."

In one smooth movement, he picked her up and spun her around. Then he shot an irrepressible grin straight into the lens of the minicam riveted on them.

"I *love* her. I'm going to marry her. Did you guys get that?"

Epilogue

"**A**tlantis is home. Its journey complete. A moment to be savored."

Mission Control's announcement echoed through the press booth, where Deke stood ready to go live, his gaze on the viewing window and not the camera in front of him. The drag chute flapped behind the shuttle as the crew brought her to a halt, a signal that he'd be on-air in less than thirty seconds.

But the cheers and shouts of the crowd inside drowned out the news director's voice in his earpiece as the normally under-control facility overlooking Runway 33 rocked with the party atmosphere of a perfect landing…one last and final time.

The cameraman popped his head to the side to holler over the noise at Deke. "The AD says wait until it quiets down in here."

Deke nodded, pressing his earpiece to pick up additional instructions, grateful for the extra time. Not that he couldn't ad-lib or battle the emotions that gripped his chest when he watched Commander Ferguson silently cruise *Atlantis* through a plasma of heated air. He'd been the CNN Space Correspondent for six years now and had been bringing in the shuttles since flights resumed in 2005, after the tragic loss of *Columbia*.

But today was too bittersweet for even the most seasoned soul in the NASA family to stay dry-eyed.

After thirty years, a hundred and thirty-five missions, and countless hours in orbit, the era of space-shuttle travel had come to an end.

And, so, Deke thought, had an era of his life. But then, a new one had begun thirteen days ago. He inched around the camera to eye the crowd, most of them still focused on the runway in the distance, but one face turned toward him and their eyes locked.

"She asleep?" Deke mouthed.

Jessie nodded, laughing at the irony only the two of them fully appreciated.

"We'll go back to Deke in the booth in three minutes," the news director announced in Deke's ear. "We're staying with the shuttle to pick up Commander Ferguson's comments to the crew."

Three minutes was a lifetime in television, certainly enough time for Deke to unhook his earpiece and return to his wife and their newborn baby.

"Hey." He put his arm around Jessie. "We have three minutes."

Her eyes glistened, bright against the shadow of sleeplessness. "So you want to see your girl."

He grinned and placed a soft kiss on her hair. "Both of them. How's she doing?"

"She slept through the twin sonic booms and that last

cheer," Jessie said. "Why can't she sleep through the night?"

Stuart Rosen approached, his eyes crinkled in hearty laughter. "She's not even two weeks old, Jess. You expect perfection already?"

"We have perfection," Deke said, reaching to take the baby from Jessica, still in awe at just how light a seven-pound baby girl really was. "Skye is perfect."

"Her timing is," Stuart said. "Arriving on launch day and taking her first outing to the most historic landing in our history."

"We waited twelve years for this miracle, Stu," Deke said. "And her first act was to prove she isn't going to follow our schedule."

Jess and Deke shared a look, the memory of the morning she'd gone into labor two weeks early still fresh. He stroked the little blue NASA cap that warmed Skye's head, grateful he'd been able to get an ambulance in time for Skye to arrive safely in a hospital. Barely in time.

Jess laughed. "That's for sure. She's sound asleep all day and wide awake at night. But..." She took the baby's tiny fingers. "So worth the minor disruption."

"Deke, change in schedule." The cameraman called over. "You're going live in ten seconds!"

"Oh, I'll take her," Jess offered, holding out her hands.

"No time," he said, already heading back to the reporter's stand in front of the NASA emblem. "She can come with me."

"Deke, you can't take her on camera!"

He threw a grin over his shoulder at his wife. "Mom's been running Kennedy Space Center public affairs for a decade and Dad's been on TV since he retired from the astronaut corp. Skye Stockard is right where she belongs."

Still holding the baby secure in one arm, he snapped in his earpiece and picked up the count.

Three, two, one...

The camera light turned red and Deke blasted a smile he'd been wearing for quite a few years.

"That was Commander Chris Ferguson giving congratulations to his crew on a successful mission and safe landing of *Atlantis*, the fifty-fourth such landing at Kennedy Space Center in the long and impressive history of the space shuttle program. Here at Kennedy, there are a lot of tears, a lot of memories, and..." He glanced down at the baby. "Some are oblivious to the historic moment."

He paused, his gaze shifting for one millisecond from the camera lens to the woman who stood next to it, getting that sweet jolt the sight of Jessica Marlowe Stockard always gave him.

"I can tell you there's an air of both bliss and sadness up here in the press booth." He lowered his voice in a way that warned viewers he'd be getting personal. That wasn't unusual; Deke had been sharing the "astronaut's view" of the space program with his audience for years, and the personal approach had not only made him a popular correspondent, it had done a huge service by elevating public opinion of the program.

Not enough to keep the federal funding of the next generation of shuttles...but enough to help raise the capital for a private fleet. And that, like the baby in his arms, made for a very exciting future.

"As you may know, I've been involved in this program in one capacity or another for nearly fifteen years. I had the honor of commanding four separate missions, played a role in the safety program, and have been privileged to bring the space story to CNN's viewers for six years. I even..." He grinned and winked at Jess. "...got to be a NASA spokesperson for a brief time and have to say that was the most, uh, unforgettable chapter of my career."

A dozen or so friends joined Jess by the camera, friends who were more like family after all the years they'd worked together. He skimmed the crowd, smiled at Jeff Clark, and nodded to a few others before returning his gaze to the camera.

"The era of space travel by shuttle has ended," he said softly. "And I admit that deeply saddens me and the thousands of Kennedy Space Center workers who are here today to celebrate three decades of amazing success."

He hesitated briefly, swallowed the lump in his throat, then lifted his beautiful baby daughter just enough to make her shudder with a sleepy sigh.

"But if anyone out there thinks this is the end of space exploration, then let me assure you, it is not. Woven into the fabric of our country is the need to stretch our boundaries, our knowledge, our capabilities, and our world. Our children will want to be astronauts, engineers, scientists, and..." He glanced at Skye. "Pilots. And they will be. The end of the space shuttle program is not the end of our story. In fact, thanks to the foundation of success laid by every person at NASA for the past half a century, today is just the beginning."

The room exploded in applause, just loud enough for Skye to open her eyes, blink in surprise, and look straight up at her daddy.

"You want to be an astronaut, honey?" he whispered, lifting her closer. "I can help you with that."

She opened her mouth and wailed, almost drowning out his signoff and toss to Atlanta, and earning a burst of applause from the crowd. And that just made her cry louder.

Jessie was next to him in an instant, taking the baby with a certainty that already impressed and amazed him. They'd given up trying for a baby several years ago, content with their busy careers and happy married life. Until the total jaw-dropper of a surprise nine months ago.

"Nice speech, Commander," Jess whispered, up on her tiptoes to give him a kiss. "I couldn't have written better sound bites than that."

"Came from the heart, as you know."

"It made me think of the day I met you." She lifted Skye gently, which quelled the crying for a brief moment.

"When you plastered my face on a screen in Headquarters and announced I'd be your poster boy?"

"No." She leaned her head on his shoulder. "When you marched down those auditorium steps and made a speech about astronauts and explorers and what NASA is all about. Do you remember?"

"I remember your cleavage."

She elbowed him. "I'm serious."

"I remember the day, sweetheart. I remember how I hated your idea and jumped down your throat and tried to get you to back down." He laughed softly, stroking Skye's cheek. "Don't even think about getting Mom to back down, kiddo."

"You reminded me of that just now. That man who believes so much in his mission that you can see the fire in his eyes." She smiled up at him. "Let's give that passion to Skye. Let's teach her to grab hold of space, reach for the stars, and shoot for the moon. Promise we'll do that for her?"

Skye sucked in a breath and launched into high C, so loudly that Deke had to lean closer and put his mouth near Jessie's ear. "Count me in, spin doctor."

Love a romance set in Florida? Kick off your shoes and head on over to Barefoot Bay, Roxanne St. Claire's popular romance series! Every book in the Barefoot Bay series stands alone, but they are all set on the shores of a sun-drenched island resort off the Gulf Coast of Florida. Find them all at www.roxannestclaire.com.

Books Set in Barefoot Bay

The Barefoot Bay Billionaires
Secrets on the Sand
Seduction on the Sand
Scandal on the Sand

The Barefoot Bay Brides
Barefoot in White
Barefoot in Lace
Barefoot in Pearls

Barefoot Bay Undercover
Barefoot Bound *(prequel novella)*
Barefoot With a Bodyguard
Barefoot With a Stranger
Barefoot With a Bad Boy

About the Author

Roxanne St. Claire is a *New York Times* and *USA Today* bestselling author of nearly forty novels of suspense and romance, including several popular series (*The Bullet Catchers*, *The Guardian Angelinos*, and *Barefoot Bay*) and multiple stand-alone books. Her entire backlist, including excerpts and buy links, can be found at www.roxannestclaire.com.

In addition to being a six-time nominee and one-time winner of the prestigious Romance Writers of America RITA Award, Roxanne's novels have won the National Reader's Choice Award for best romantic suspense three times, and the Borders Top Pick in Romance, as well as the Daphne du Maurier Award, the HOLT Medallion, the Maggie, Booksellers Best, Book Buyers Best, the Award of Excellence, and many others. Her books have been translated into dozens of languages and are routinely included as a Doubleday/Rhapsody Book Club Selection of the Month.

Roxanne lives in Florida with her family (and dogs!), and can be reached via her website, www.roxannestclaire.com or on her Facebook Reader page, www.facebook.com/roxannestclaire and on Twitter at www.twitter.com/roxannestclaire.